UNIVERSAL MAN

A novel in three volumes

Part One
Graceful
Runner

Meredith Eugene Hunt

Chaotic Terrain Press
Asheville

Chaotic Terrain Press
62 Wolf Road
Asheville, North Carolina 28805
www.chaoticterrain.com

This is a work of fiction.
The story begins on September 8, 2012.

Cover art is *Linguistic Site*, by Grace Carol Bomer. Protected by U.S. and international copyright laws. Used with permission. Soli Deo Gloria Studio, www.carolbomer.com

ISBN   978-0-9845111-0-5

Printed in the United States of America
1 3 5 7 9 10 8 6 4 2

For Gene

Prologue

Dr. Sterne dismissed the early Monday gathering of Chinook Assembly directors and stepped outside of the sunlit, wood-paneled room to his car. Just then, his mobile telephone rang. Sterne glared at the phone for a moment, turned his eyes skyward as if he prayed, and pressed the talk key.

"Good morning, General," he said.

As the deep voice on the other end spoke, Dr. Sterne's face grew pale.

"Can you take them down?" Sterne asked.

Sterne listened and said, "I understand. How much time— That little? Well then, carry on, sir; good luck and God bless you. I need to prepare . . . Thank you." Sterne disconnected, and immediately pushed two telephone keys. "Miss Oliver, this is Dr. Sterne— Yes, good morning. Miss Oliver, I won't be able to see my Portland patients this afternoon. Something urgent. I'm sorry. I suggest that you ask Dr. Morrison to fill in for me."

Sterne again paused and this time interrupted the voice with, "I know he's not on call, he'll manage. Thank you, Miss Oliver."

He checked his watch, jumped into the car, and sped up the hill away from the Chinook Assembly portion of the Mollicoat Estate toward his family property. As he approached the Bluff House, his phone rang again. He looked at the incoming number, and to himself said, "The radar."

"Yes," he said crisply. "Thank you, I already know. Please alert everyone here at the Estate. I will see Mrs. Sterne. There's nothing we can do but be ready for the end."

Sterne parked the car and jogged to the house. Miriam Sterne was in the kitchen preparing for a luncheon and she looked up when her husband entered. When she saw his face, her expression of surprise turned into one of fear. "What is it?" she asked.

"B-2 bombers will arrive soon."

Mrs. Sterne gazed across the room at nothing. Then she said, "We always knew this was possible. But I never guessed the Government would be so desperate. How soon? Is there time to get away?"

Dr. Sterne shook his head and glanced to the clock on the wall. "Two minutes, or less. Is there anyone in the house?"

"No family members."

"Let's go on the deck."

They walked outside and found the housekeeper and a gardener already there looking into the sky toward a small, dark spot. The gardener peered through binoculars. The housekeeper was speaking into her telephone. Dr. Sterne shook the gardener's hand and Mrs. Sterne gave the housekeeper a hug, and then Dr. and Mrs. embraced each other. Mrs. Sterne's knees buckled and Dr. Sterne held her more tightly.

"Any regrets?" He asked her softly.

"No, except that our daughter Mindy is lost."

"Yes. The other children should be fine," he said. "They'll do fine."

They heard the soft roar of an airplane approaching high up from the north.

"I love you, Miriam."

"And I love you. Let's pray, OK?"

"One second—something I must do first." He punched numbers into his phone and then held the phone with his thumb on the send key. "OK."

At that moment, as the plane was nearly overhead, Dr. Sterne noticed two elongated specks had broken off and seemed to be growing larger. The Sternes had enough time to embrace once more and say, "Lord have mercy" and "Jesus take me."

UNIVERSAL MAN/Graceful Runner

I am lying in bed in the early morning. It's in a narrow basement apartment. Everything is tidy and comfortable. I have such a feeling of contentment and acceptedness that I never felt before. While I am still on the bed, a beautiful girl is leaving through the apartment door. She is my wife and loves me intensely, except I don't know who she is. The girl says goodbye. The scene shifts without meaning. I have been busy. Work, I think; and I am alone. Suddenly, I remember the girl who had been in the apartment, but she has been gone for months. How can I have forgotten her? She has moved across the country for an inexplicable reason. My heart aches and I sob with grief. How can I ever find her again?
    -from the dream journal of Stan Timmons.

Chapter One
They Will Be Sisters

Bursting from the woods, the horse and rider vaulted the bole of a fallen, moss-covered, hardwood tree, and as a single entity, they sped toward the middle of the wide, green field. The bay mare, muscular and built low to the ground, slowed to a jolting trot and then to a swerving walk. Its head pulled left, right, and back left. It was the far-flung daughter of cavalry chargers and wanted to race, or return to the barn, or to go anywhere as long as it was fast. The rider, also a daughter of warriors, sat straight and gripped hard with her knees. Holding the reins tight, her face muscles rigid, she was determined that they should ride forward in a mannerly fashion. The horse possessed an advantage, however; its rider rode bareback, which required negotiation, or an iron will for the rider. Making this horse walk was difficult, unless it was exhausted.

The rider called her mount to perform a slow canter, and at last they began circling the circumference of the unfenced field. The rider's thick, blonde braid bounced on her back as they followed the grassy track. She relaxed as she watched the mountains rimming the horizon; the field sat on a rounded knoll and commanded a fair view. To the west she could see the beginning of the coastal range. Beyond its evergreen ridges lay the Pacific Ocean—a powerful generator for this region's weather. Far to the north, east, and southeast stood snow-topped volcanoes, the older ones carved and shaped. The mountain to the north, barely noticeable in the ambient September haze, was a restless cone with its head lopped off.

The Saturday afternoon was a coolish beauty. Languid clouds pastured in the blue fields above. For this girl in green, heavy silk pants and a cream-colored blouse, riding came naturally, she having been near horses all of her twenty years. While she rode, she closed her eyes and allowed her mind to be as calm as a person drifting into sleep, yet she was as alert as one listening for sounds at night. After completing the loop, the girl relinquished her stillness and tried walking the horse again—and then suddenly she gave up, instead cantering half way around once more, still hoping to tire the horse to make it more manageable.

As the pair reached a point in the field opposite the path where they had entered, first one, then another, and then a packed line of human runners emerged from the woods at the corner behind them. The runners—members of the women's cross-country team from one of Portland's universities—approached the girl and horse. After a moment's reflection, the rider guessed how they came to be on her family's property. Not wanting to interfere, she pulled the horse away to the inside of the track.

Once in the open field, the runners accelerated. As the first of them passed, the horse became jumpy. More runners ran by. Suddenly the horse began hopping, and bucked. Rather than pulling her leg over the horse's back and landing on both feet, the rider embraced the animal's neck, then bounced, jolted loose, and came down hard on the ground, bottom first, as the horse took off toward the receding runners. Stunned, the girl helplessly watched. The horse was racing the runners! One by one, it passed them like a thundering streak, and some runners turned with startled looks and open mouths. One girl screamed; a few runners laughed and whooped, throwing up their arms; some dove into the tall grass on the field's edge; some crossed up their legs, stumbled and fell. The horse tossed its head as it galloped by. The reins flew behind in the air and lashed its body. As the horse rounded the first corner, it stepped on the reins—this jerked its head down, but it kept plunging forward in a wild, pounding gallop.

The rider rose up from the turf. She was stiff and dizzy, and she winced at a sharp pain inside her chest. Mishaps like this had occurred before. Last weekend the horse bucked her off into a stony creek.

She watched the horse's progress around the circuit and knew she could not catch up by following, so she ran and walked straight across the middle of the field, hoping to reach the other side before the horse did.

The horse had passed the mossy hardwood log by a hundred yards. A runner was leading the mare back to the unhorsed rider, walking on the correct side and holding the reins with firm control. The horse was lathered. It breathed heavily, and its eyes smoldered. The spirited dance never once left its step. The runner had short black locks and dark soft-sculpted features.

"Thank you. Thanks so much!" the rider cried out as she neared the runner.

"She's a fine animal, but you need a saddle!" the runner said with a British-like accent.

"I know," the rider said. "But where's the sport?"

"I see what you mean."

The rider took the reins. "I'm Mindy Sterne."

"Hi, my name is Beth."

"Hi!" Mindy patted the horse on its shoulder. "This crazy steed is Melody."

"Hi, Melody."

"Sorry about the scare," Mindy said, "I hope no one got hurt."

"Don't worry. It was exciting. How are *you*? You smashed the ground hard."

"I'm . . . OK," Mindy said, twisting her torso from side to side to stretch. "Dad taught us to fall, but I wasn't ready. I thought I could stay on, otherwise I would have dismounted."

"Do you ride much?"

"On the weekends, like today, but when we stay here in the summer, we ride every day. I use a saddle then because, you know . . . sweat. We ride English, which is nice because the saddle is small. I only ride bareback when the weather is cool."

Beth nodded and said, "Uh huh. Is this your place?"

"Yes, but we actually live in Vancouver. Dad's a physician there and in Portland. This is our family retreat. The stable is just behind these trees and we have a paddock and a pasture that runs down to the highway. Up on the hill we have a log house." Mindy had pointed into the woods and behind her to show the directions. "Where are you from?"

"Portland, and I was born there, but our family lived in New Zealand for a few years. We moved back this summer."

"Oh, I thought New Zealand, and you picked up a little Kiwi music—an accent, I mean."

"Yeah, and you know how? My two brothers and I began imitating it at home for fun and it got into my head. Now I can't stop."

The girls laughed.

"But you should see my Maori act!" Beth strutted a few steps, jerked her arms and barked a few fierce words, bugged her eyes showing the whites, and rolled her tongue out to her chin. Both girls laughed loudly and Melody shied away a step. Mindy held the horse's head.

"Oops, sorry," Beth said.

"That's OK. You must be a horseman," Mindy said. "How did you catch her? She's not easy to corral when she gets worked up."

Beth reached into a tiny hip pack and held up a crumpled wrapper. "I'm a chocolate addict."

"Ohhhh," Mindy said, and they laughed again.

"But also we rode in New Zealand. Your hair is so pretty. I should let mine grow."

Beth turned to look behind her. Another runner had called from the far edge of the field and waved her to come.

"Hey, you know," Beth said to Mindy, "I have to leave. They're holding up the college van for me."

"I hope I didn't keep you."

"No, it's hunky-dory. They've been cooling down. They'll not have been waiting long." Beth turned to leave.

"Ride with me sometime?" Mindy called. "We have tack and five horses at the stable."

"Sure," Beth said, skipping backwards toward the van. "Ring me up. I'm in the student directory. It's Telford, Elisabeth Telford."

Because Melody kept tossing her head, Mindy walked the horse to the stables. She hung up the bridle, opened up a new bale of hay, pitched a section of it into the horse's feed box, and broke up the rest of the bale and fed the other horses. She brushed Melody and then ambled up the hill toward the spreading, one-story house where the family often stayed in the summers and on weekends. She walked amidst dense trees underlaid with ferns and mosses up the wide path through what had once been the heart of the Mollicoat Estate.

All the surrounding land had once been part of vast holdings by a Northwestern newspaper and timber mogul of the late 1800's and early 1900's. On this western section of the property, a dozen buildings once stood, made from sawn lumber and logs from the estate. All but three of these older buildings had been torn down.

Dr. Sterne purchased the Mollicoat Estate before Mindy had been born, and transformed it into a conference center called the Chinook Assembly. The Assembly buildings, designed in a traditional, open Finnish style, were clustered lower in elevation further to the east on the estate. The Chinook Assembly operated as a non-profit educational institution, focusing on constitutional theory and international law. Speakers and guests came from around the world. The Assembly also delved into ethnic and cultural issues. Outside groups regularly rented its spaces for conferences and retreats, and the groups hired the Assembly kitchen to supply meals in the spacious dining hall. Dr. Sterne no longer officially sat on the Board of Directors, although he frequently entertained conference guests at the Bluff House, so named, because it stood over a rock cliff overlooking the Tualatin Valley. This weekend, Sterne had collected a small group of such guests, and they were meeting when Mindy entered the house.

Once inside the utility room door, she removed her muddy shoes and tiptoed sockfooted to the front room. No one was there, but she heard voices on the outside porch, or balcony, where the guests had gathered for refreshments and to enjoy the spectacular view from the top of the rock face. As Mindy extended her hand to the screen door, she heard a distressed voice say, "This mustn't happen!"

Mindy pushed the door open. The guests stood politely while she introduced herself and shook hands with everyone. One guest whom she knew, Bennett Uchida, a widower in his mid-thirties, gave Mindy a warm greeting despite his usual reserve, and held her hand a second longer than the rest. She responded with firm, friendly politeness. He was a close friend of Sterne's—a Portland doctor whose Japanese born wife had died a few months ago, leaving him with two young children. His loss left him lonely, and Mindy was aware that he already

13

considered her a potential new wife and mother for the children. After the introductions, Mindy helped herself to a glass of water. She leaned against a wall and gazed out over the Oregon farmland stretching toward the coastal range. She had picked June strawberries in those fields not many years before.

Something, however, seemed amiss on the balcony—something that disturbed her thoughts. While chatter had been in full voice prior to her arrival, no one was talking now. She glanced around; each person seemed occupied with an inner meditation. A second later, as if he intended to dispel the awkwardness, a man with a white beard asked Mindy how her horseback ride was. She answered briefly, realizing that she had interrupted a confidential conversation. Silence dropped down again. A crow cawed in the distance. Two people in a corner murmured. Mindy waited a short time, scarcely sufficient for courtesy, and excused herself to change from her riding clothes and clean up. Afterwards, being aware that dinner was still a ways off, she made herself comfortable on the bed in her room. She opened a schoolbook. A clock ticked sedately from her bedside table. Fresh cool air flowed through the open window. She pulled a knitted wool blanket over her legs and promptly fell asleep.

None of the conferees stayed for dinner.

Mindy bounced up to the dining hall table refreshed from her nap, feeling no evidence of injury from her fall. She deftly filled water glasses, weaving in and out between the cook, Mrs. Hagensen, and Mrs. Sterne, both of whom bustled to and fro between the kitchen and the dining area. Mrs. Hagensen had worked for the Sterne family for as long as the children remembered. She was a local woman who had never been to the Sterne home in the city. Dr. Sterne justified hiring household help by saying at least once a year, "We come to the estate to recreate, and so, work should only be a pleasure, especially for Mrs. Sterne."

Mrs. Miriam Sterne, whose maiden name had been Becker, came from a wealthy family in New York State. She had married Dr. Eberhardt Sterne while she was still an undergraduate, and bore children in rapid succession—one pregnancy being a set of twin girls. Mindy and the other children had inherited their father's blondeness rather than their mother's darker color.

All preparations for dinner complete, Dr. Sterne gave the final call to come to the table. The younger children stormed in noisily, but by the time they sat down, they were quiet. The older two boys, Anselm and Bernard, were not home yet, having gone on a daylong rock climbing excursion, and they were late in returning. There was an extra boy present visiting for the weekend, and Mrs. Hagensen joined the family for the blessing, as was customary. Afterwards she would tidy up the kitchen and then take dinners home to her waiting family.

Dr. Sterne said, "Let's pray," and everyone hushed. "We thank you for the gifts our family enjoys, and we ask that each person be given strength and maturity to best use the blessings and talents that you, our Creator, bestow upon us."

The meal had as the main dish a spicy spaghetti—a favorite of the two youngest children, Luther and Mallory—and they twirled noodles on their forks and chewed happily. The customary analytical conversation was absent for the present. Out of a sense of duty, and to share an amusing story, Mindy told about the riding incident with Melody. The younger children all laughed when she described her fall and the runners panicking and diving into the bushes.

Dr. Sterne smiled, but did not laugh. "I've given permission for the University to use the estate as their home cross-country course, and they wanted to practice. There's to be an invitational meet here next weekend—it's a near perfect location and the Assembly said the teams could use its showers. The race traditionally is held at Cadonau Park, but last Saturday someone was murdered there again. City police revoked the University's race permit, for safety reasons."

So, Mindy thought, *the team was forced to flee one danger only to be subjected to another—a runaway horse.*

Sterne continued gently to Mindy, "I received a call from the coach while you were napping. She was upset."

Mindy now felt a sudden pang of guilt. She should have predicted that Melody would behave this way.

"I'm sorry, Dad," she said, "but I didn't know the team would be running there this afternoon, and I did take Melody to the side," she added in self-defense.

"That's true," Sterne answered, "and yet perhaps you could have dismounted when you saw the team coming or when Melody started jumping around. You could have held the reins."

"You're right, Dad; I am sorry."

"Well, don't worry. I'm not. The coach exaggerated the danger, no doubt." Sterne smiled, paused, and winked to her privately. "But you learned something and so let's just leave it there, OK? Unless you wanted to say something else?"

"You should have seen her run, Dad. She's a great horse."

Mindy began telling about the runner she met, the one who caught Melody, but the twins, Isadore and Chryseis, who were now 12 years old, started an argument with the boys about who got to ride Melody tomorrow after church. Dr. Sterne settled it by saying that the girls could ride Melody and the boys could take turns on the other horses.

"Dad, why the awkwardness when I came onto the deck this afternoon?" Mindy asked. "It was embarrassing."

"I'm sorry about their misplaced delicacy," Sterne said. "It must have seemed rude. We had been discussing gruesome hunting tales, and the other men were reluctant to talk about this in the presence of a young woman."

As Mindy expected, the boys then clamored for the story, but Mrs. Sterne tried to hush them. To herself, Mindy recalled the many times her dad had begun a story during dinner about a surgery he had performed that day and how Mom always shushed him. He was so accustomed to blood and gore that it didn't occur to him that others were not desensitized.

Dr. Sterne laughed and tried to divert the boys, but they persisted. "Well, maybe I'll tell you the whole story someday, but what happened in essence was this: the hunters attempted to capture the beast alive and he fought back and gored two hunters; one of them died later. It was a mess."

"That's enough, Abe," Mrs. Sterne said.

"Did they dart him, Dad?" asked one of the girls. "Why didn't they tranquilize him?"

16

"They shot him with a dart gun, but, you see, they were in a hurry and didn't wait long enough for the drug to take effect."

"Why not?"

"Because they were poaching and feared the game warden would discover and arrest them."

"Why were the hunters poaching?"

Dr. Sterne stared at his plate and glowered as he considered what to say. "It's an unusual story, and I'm sorry I can't give you specific facts because of the legal issues, but I will say this: the creature the hunters caught was from an endangered species. A certain tribe in that region planned to exterminate the species, because it preyed on another smaller species, one that the tribe prized because of their religious beliefs. The government in this rather backward country had neither the will nor the laws to protect predators or the prey. By capturing the dangerous creature alive and relocating him, the hunters accomplished two goals: they saved his life and helped protect the prey species. That's why the hunters believed it necessary to break the laws of this country."

Mindy seemed not to be listening, but the children, more fascinated than before, could hardly restrain their questions, and they fired them all at once: "Was it a water buffalo, Dad? Was it a lion? Did the hunters finally get the animal? Did they put him into a zoo? What was the endangered species? Were the poachers from Green Peace? Was this in Africa or the Amazon? Did you sew up the hunters, Dad? Were their guts hanging out?"

Dr. Sterne laughed again, and Mrs. Sterne's voice rose over the babble, her face angry. "I said, that's *enough!*" Mindy had seen her mother get this way before. Mrs. Sterne hated to see creatures suffer.

"Your mother is right. When you children are older you may need to discuss such matters in gruesome detail. Then if you wish, you can attend Assembly conferences. They often feature experts on how to deal with laws when they conflict with what we know is right."

The conversation moved on to a wide-ranging discussion about animal behavior, and Mindy excused herself from the table, cleared away her dishes and went to her room. After her initial question, she had said nothing. She had heard such exchanges her whole life, and in this case she did not believe her father's story. What the exact truth was about the interrupted discussion on the deck with the guests, she could not guess, but it wasn't about poaching.

Anselm and Bernard arrived at the Bluff House near 9:00 p.m. from their climbing exploration of some basalt cracks they had found. While they ate at the dining room table, Mindy joined them to hear their account of the day. The younger boys and their friend assembled animals and architectural works from colorful plastic building pieces on the carpet of the front room, while the twins played the piano together. Dr. and Mrs. Sterne sat around a Scrabble board.

On Sunday after early church in the valley and a cold sandwich dinner prepared by Mrs. Hagensen the evening before, some members of the Sterne family fished in the bass pond on the neighboring property, some slept, and some played chess. Part of the day they read, and part of it they rode horses. They kept no schedule. In the evening, Dr. Sterne cooked clam chowder made with fried onions, bacon, and potatoes, and they put on films of his travel in India when he was a bachelor. Mindy retired to her room before the films were over—she had seen them before. Later on, while taking a break from studying, she called Beth and arranged to ride together on the following Saturday, after the cross-country meet.

The next morning the Sterne family returned to their house in Vancouver. Mindy drove her VW bug directly to school in Portland and returned home to Vancouver after classes.

During the week she hoped to run into Beth again at school. On Thursday, walking across campus—a sea of forested emerald with islands and continents of grey stone and concrete, Mindy passed by the main cafeteria. A crowd had gathered around two students who were debating. She recognized one of them as, possibly, a student government leader. She thought he was named something about "rocks" and "shank." He was good looking, Mindy thought, but certainly not her type. He wore makeup, and there was something wrong about his face, perhaps from its muscles not being able to relax. She did not know the other student. He was not as tall as Mindy and was solidly built—a tad overweight—and he wore glasses. His neck seemed short, which gave him a stooped appearance. The Shank character was baiting him about the existence of God, and the other fellow gave succinct, logical answers. Students in the crowd listened intently, but occasionally one would yell an ironic comment to the protagonists.

Being in a hurry to eat and get to class, Mindy did not give much attention to the dialogue, but asked a student with a reddish beard about Beth. He did not know her, so Mindy described her to him.

He nodded and said, "Hmm. She was there." He was pointing up to the top of a pole at the cafeteria entrance, part of the building's structure. "She climbed up for a view of the dispute, then she left."

Mindy looked around a minute more. At last giving up the search, she sat at a nearby bench out of hearing of the debate, and ate her bag lunch.

On Friday she called Beth's parents' home—where Beth had said she expected to stay for the night—to confirm that she was coming for a ride and lunch tomorrow. A man whom Mindy supposed was Beth's father said that she was not in. He acted suspicious of Mindy by asking, "And *how* do you know Bethy?" but he painstakingly took the message and said he would pass it along. Over the telephone, Mindy could hear an outlandish drumming noise playing in the background.

UNIVERSAL MAN/Graceful Runner

It rains all night. I am a small boy in bed. We are living in my grandparents' old house down by the river. I look out the window and see below that the slough waters are muddy and rising fast. I call to my parents because I think that the water will flood the house. They are not paying attention and do not take me seriously, but I persist. Finally, they look from my bedroom window, and the water is rushing and foaming to fill a large new trough of the slough. I beg for someone to take baby Sarah and leave. My dad says there isn't any danger, and I yell how will they feel when the water starts pouring through the house and washes away the baby to be drowned? Changing his mind about the peril, Dad takes baby Sarah and drives our new van away. My mom and I stay behind to save what we can in the house. The water climbs the steps, and I feel it pushing up under the carpets. We run around putting furniture on the beds, thinking another foot or so might make a difference. The water keeps rising in the house, soaking it all. I wake up scared.

-from the dream journal of Stan Timmons

Chapter Two
Race at the Mollicoat Estate

On Saturday morning Beth felt nauseous during the drive from Portland to the cross-country meet at the Sterne place. Her mother had pushed a large breakfast on her, and Beth had given in to the maternal demand while her father played pool in the billiard room as the television blared cartoons from the corner. Beth did not think he had slept all night. At least when he smoked cigarettes he did not contaminate the house, but went outside on the patio, pacing up and down, left hand in his pocket, sucking in tar, chemicals, and gases with every breath. The ritual included flinging the butt into the overgrown landscape before marching inside.

When Beth had walked out the front door of her parents' house to her grey Toyota, her father emerged and tried to pat her on the fanny. Familiar with this obscene farewell, she anticipated his move and skipped ahead of the paw. He swung uselessly, lost his balance and fell, but caught himself from tumbling down the steps by grabbing the wrought-iron handrail. Holding on, he yelled to Beth: "Don't let those bastards get you! Keep your feet in a bucket!" This, to Beth's embarrassment, had been loud enough for neighbors in their up-scale community of older homes to hear, if windows happened to be open.

"Pop, you're *sick*!" Beth had hissed back over the top of her car, her eyes narrowed. But the next instant she felt a pang of tenderness when he ignored her diagnosis and waved over his head while he clutched the railing.

She called to him, "Pop, get some exercise today. Go for a long walk! Do some yard work!"

He waved again, repeated, "Don't let those bastards get you!" and struggled to get his feet under him.

She had jumped into the car, slammed the door, and driven away fast.

21

Beth wished she had not attended her father's birthday party the evening before. Some party. There were just the three of them—her parents and her. Even if her two brothers had lived nearby, they would not have come. And then, since she was staying for dinner, her mother had insisted over the phone earlier, "Why don't you bring your things and leave from here in the morning for your run?" Now Beth felt like throwing up, as memories played in her head like a sour song.

Dr. Telford was sick in the head—sick in his soul, which is why he had to quit the Foreign Service. Pop had been brilliant with his command of languages and interest in people, cultures, and botany; but "his luminance diminished," as Beth's mom said to her bridge friends. The healthy, happy man who would stop and strike up a conversation with anyone, the man she faintly remembered from her early childhood, was dead. Taking his place was this pale, perverted, and sometimes charming maniac—a fiendish clone of her real father.

Grandma Telford's suicide soon after her grandfather's death from cancer marked her father's breaking point. Pop had flown from New Zealand to Portland alone to attend to funeral business and the settling of his parents' estate. Two weeks later he came back changed. Beth believed that the deaths themselves were not enough to explain his transformation. She suspected some hideous secret. She also could never shake off the feeling that she herself was to blame.

Not long after Pop returned, she had gotten pregnant by her martial arts teacher. She never told her father, but she and her mom slipped away one morning to the abortion facility. Her mother had not agonized about this decision. Because she had been raised Roman Catholic, but had not practiced the faith for years, her mother had enough shame to wish to avoid the public exposure her daughter's unwed pregnancy might bring, but not enough inculcation of the Church's teaching to heed abortion's moral dimension. Beth remembered feeling ill on that morning trip. She did not remember much about her abortion, except that the nausea ended abruptly afterwards.

After her father's collapse, he was sent home with the family on a permanent medical leave, which translated into early retirement.

This morning of the race Beth felt sick—nauseous—as she drove along, with the undigested egg waffle and mushy frozen strawberries, topped with whipped cream and syrup, residing inertly in her stomach. While she did not mind eating eggs or milk products because animals did not die to produce them, she opposed the cruel treatment of animals in modern agriculture. She thought about the poor prisoners, the egg-laying chickens in huge barns, kept squashed and overcrowded in tiny cages, unable to flap their wings, their feathers worn off from desperate, useless ducking and peering for a way to escape to sunshine and grass. Beth just wished she could show a stronger will in dealing with her mother.

Beth rolled down the windows, flooding the car with a chilly breeze.

She was leaving behind the heavy traffic and exhaust-laden air of the metro area. A two-lane highway at last drew her through meadows and farms, and traced along a small river. She came to signs and arrows that led her to the guard station at the Chinook Assembly entrance. The gate was open, and the man on duty in the station motioned for her to pass through. Beth looked in her rear-view mirror and noticed that he had stepped out and was examining the back of her car, and then he wrote on his clipboard.

She followed more signs up the curvy, paved driveway that ran through the forest and past side roads. A deer and two spotted fawns browsed in the open. Unlike the previous week, Beth was unimpressed with the expansive green, grassy margins along the road, the lamp poles, each hung with a Chinook Assembly banner, and the neat rockwork of retaining walls, because she did not know if she would survive without losing her breakfast. Things seemed to be building to a climax. She neared the field where the race was to begin. Following an attendant's signals, she stowed the car at the field's edge, then staggered around to the passenger side, next to the trees, keeping one hand on the car and the other on her belly. She lowered herself into a sitting position and leaned over on one elbow; her mouth began to water. All of a sudden she felt herself losing control, and then she violently spewed up all the waffle, strawberries, whipped cream, and coffee onto the ground behind her front tire.

23

Stomach muscles ached from the exertion. She sat there a few minutes, eyes closed and nose dripping, breathing through her mouth, and then she got back into her car on the passenger side. She felt better now and cleaned her face with a damp hand wipe.

A man stepped from the trees behind her to her open window. Startled, Beth reflexively yelled and flung her arm up into a defensive position.

The man stepped back and said, "Excuse me for scaring you, Miss. Are you OK?"

She nodded. "I'll be all right now, thanks," and then she noticed "Security" in tan letters on the dark, mud-colored shirt and ball-cap he wore.

The fellow apologized again and walked away.

She drank from a bottle of a sport drink, nibbled a chocolate bar, wished she had eaten a bagel or two and a banana and drunk a glass of soy milk for breakfast, and hoped that she would be fit enough for the race.

The morning dew had soaked the grass of the field, which had been cut on the first of the week and baled on Friday, the day before. The round, fragrant bales remained scattered on the field like grazing bison. Roaming the pasture were handfuls of students from the colleges represented at the meet, some of the students being young men who came to score points with the girls.

Beth knew one of the men partly by sight and mostly by reputation—Talus Schenk, whom she had last seen earlier in the week debating the plain guy with glasses. Schenk seemed to be everywhere Beth went, popping around the campus shrubbery with a grin, and offering a sexual remark. Around him stood a knot of mostly male students. Schenk's voice boomed while he and two other students fought with mock swords they had made from stems of tall weeds. It appeared to be a friendly bout, until Schenk suddenly kicked his opponent hard in the rear end. The fellow laughed, but quit the fight and walked away. Beth watched a blonde braided girl—it was Mindy—advance toward Schenk, and it was clear by her animated movements that she was warning him to behave or she would have him thrown off the property. Schenk flipped an obscene gesture, and Mindy walked closer and slugged him in the face. Beth opened her mouth in amazement. When the smarting Schenk loomed to retaliate, security men emerged from the crowd and made a beeline for Mindy. Noticing them, Schenk backed off.

Beth checked in with the coach and warmed up alone, trotting back and forth on a sunny place in the field where the dew had evaporated. She saw Mindy now standing with people who must be her family members, all of them blonde, slender, and tall. Mindy waved when she saw Beth looking. Beth then joined the team for stretches.

In a few minutes the squads formed up in one group and the starting gun exploded. The course began with a half lap around the field. Beth aimed to be in the middle front of the pack. In the initial exertion she felt extremely ill again. Her body rebelled against the brisk pace, but her mind ordered her body to continue.

Beth monitored the positions of her teammates. The runners entered the woods and wound along the soft paths to a gravel road that turned right and up a hill. One of her teammates, quick in sprints but not durable in distance, passed her, saying, "Don't fall behind, gal."

A flash of anger surged through Beth from heart to feet. She kicked ahead of the other girl. "I might not place, but Sarah won't beat me."

The little push brought her body to the pace that her will demanded, and she soon felt strong as she climbed the longest hill of the course. Beth was good on uphill. She passed several runners from other teams as she neared the ridgeline and turned left off the road. Moving on a narrower trail and stretching her steps over fallen logs in the course, she noticed through the tree trunks the bright, vertical sections of the view to the west. The trail was on a slight decline now, and here Beth put on speed and passed another runner. Next, she came to a graded downhill section along the side of another field. There weren't enough switchbacks here, and the trail was too steep. This was hard, and her knees strained. Now it was her turn to be passed by a runner who slammed her feet onto the ground with every step. *"How can she punish herself like that?"* Beth thought and brushed the tickling drops of sweat from her nose.

She rounded the bottom of the hill. Turning left, the course paralleled the highway for a short distance. She had to stop a few seconds and jump in place while a runner ahead of her sashayed through a v-gate in a fence. They entered a wooded area overgrown with blackberry hedges where dried horse manure littered the trail. She could see barns across a creek. This section of the course was well marked, but complex. The course picked through a maze of paths and looped back upon itself where it climbed and descended a series of killer humps. Here in the winding curves and contours, Beth began to feel weak. She realized that losing her breakfast meant she probably did not have enough fuel for her muscles. She began to be angry with her mother, and this acidic bitterness weakened Beth further. Pain began stabbing her in the side.

All the teams had been given an opportunity to review maps and walk the course in advance, but with fatigue creeping up, some lead runners missed the turn for the loop and were sent back by judges, and the best of the leaders, a girl from another school, mistakenly ran the loop twice. Once she realized this, she quit in frustrated tears. Beth ran the loop fast, encouraged by the disorder. She pushed hard, ignoring the pain. When she emerged from the woods into the field where the race began and would end, she found only four runners ahead of her.

The moment after she cleared the tree line, she heard a noisy cheer rise from the circle of Sternes who stood a little apart from the finish. One child's voice rose above the others. As Beth forced her screaming body to press to its utmost, she felt a swell in her throat. She smothered it, but she knew it had been a sob of sorrow and joy. In all her life, she had never received a loving cheer like that—her parents never attended her sports events—and except for Mindy, these people were complete strangers. The sob surged again, and there was another cheer, "Go Beth!" from a shrieking chorus—surely Mindy's younger brothers and sisters. Beth's sudden joy released the tension she carried with her every day. No longer fighting an unknown, internal opponent, she found strength she had never experienced before. A few seconds before, the stitch in her side had been unbearable. Now she flew along the same path of the Sternes' horse, Melody, once it had been freed from its rider last weekend. Beth ran effortlessly and faster than she had ever run before after going that much distance. She scarcely noticed passing one runner, and another. She now rounded the final turn and saw the finish line ahead, and the Sterne kids were going wild. She could hear a man's voice shouting her name, too. The children jumped up and down and screamed her name over and over. Beth had only two runners ahead of her now, and she closed on them. She was right behind the second in line. Beth knew she must now add pain on top of this euphoria and push faster. This she did for a few seconds and edged past a runner just at the finish line. The Sternes redoubled their cheering.

Beth had placed second, behind a runner from another team. It was her best-ever race performance and she had set a new school record in the women's 6K cross-country run. She felt awkward and too sweaty to recover near the Sternes, so she trotted away from the crowd and paced around the field, breathing.

In a minute or two, Mindy walked over to meet her, and gave her a hug. "You ran so well, I had no idea. We prayed for you," she said.

Beth did not tell Mindy how she had felt when she ran into the field—first horrible, then incredibly happy. Nor did she mention how she resented someone "praying" for her. Mindy introduced Beth around the circle of Sterne family members. Dr. Sterne shook hands stiffly, saying nothing, and then he seemed to stand aloof. *Was it really his baritone voice I heard, or was it Talus Schenk's?* she thought.

During the award ceremony she watched Schenk at the back of the crowd closely attending Beth's teammate, Sarah. Schenk never looked Beth's way, and Sarah and Schenk left together in his snazzy Subaru.

The crowd thinned. Mindy and Beth talked about sports as they walked up the winding road to the Bluff House. After Beth showered and changed, Mindy and Mrs. Hagensen fed her a homemade Danish roll. While they waited for Mrs. Hagensen to make sandwiches that they could eat later, Beth admired the view of the valley from the porch. Beth had asked for a vegetarian sandwich, which Mrs. Hagensen was happy to make.

Mrs. Sterne was hurrying past the porch and stopped. "Oh, you must be Beth Telford, I've heard marvelous things about you. Sorry, I missed the race. I heard that you won."

Beth laughed. "Only second place. Soccer is my real sport."

"Isn't this the soccer season?" Mrs. Sterne looked to Mindy.

"Beth told me she returned to the States too late to attend the early practices. She played midfielder at her secondary school in Wellington and was a top scorer."

"I switched with the forwards a bit," Beth said. "We left New Zealand in a hurry for, um, for personal reasons. I wanted to stay and go to university there, but my mom wouldn't hear of it. The soccer coach—in Portland—was sympathetic and said I could practice with the team, and after he saw me play, he tried to bend his eligibility rule and put me on the roster, as a starter. It caused a ruckus and he had to retract."

"That's a shame," Mrs. Sterne said. "You must have felt let down."

"But," Beth said brightly, drawing out the word, "the coach promised me a scholarship next year if I remain a strong player. There's not much in the way of amateur soccer leagues going on right now. So, during the weekdays I usually practice with the soccer team, and I run cross country meets on the weekends. I'm just an alternate."

"And cross country provides the conditioning for the game you love."

"Yes."

"That's commendable. I'm very glad to meet you, Beth," Mrs. Sterne said, taking her hand, "and you're welcome to ride or visit any time."

"Thank you."

After Mrs. Sterne left the porch Beth said, "Your mom looks so young."

"She works hard to stay in shape."

The two girls strolled back down the hill toward the horse barn and they could hear noise of the younger Sterne children playing war games in the woods. Beth was intrigued by an abandoned log mansion, a derelict behemoth, and Mindy promised they could come back later and explore. As a deposit on the pledge, they left their lunches and Beth's bag near a stone pillar beside the mansion's front steps.

Once at the barn they opted for saddles. Neither wanted to ride Melody today. As the girls rode away from the stables, the mare whinnied in anger. Mindy's plan was to give Beth a tour of the whole property. Beth first got a glimpse of the Chinook conference center's main buildings. At one point they crossed the highway near a small paved airstrip and took a fast gallop along the side where there was grass. From the east end of the landing strip, paths led into neighboring property with open pasture, and beyond that there was a state park. They did not enter the park, but dismounted beside a pond to water the horses. From the far bank, bullfrogs harrumphed their final territorial songs of the season. When the horses approached the water, a frog barked once, then scampered across the surface for several yards, grunting with each stride.

"This part isn't our property, but my brothers come down here to fish for bass and frogs," Mindy said while she hunted for a flat stone to skip. "The owners don't mind."

"Ugh, how cruel," Beth said, shuddering.

"We don't hurt the frogs," Mindy said, mildly defensive. "The boys use a rubber plug and we turn the frogs loose. They hold out a stick and dangle the plug in front of a frog's nose. He turns and leaps at the plug, and if he gets it into his mouth, he is lifted out of the water over the grass above the bank. The older frogs are wise to it now and seldom try for the plugs. And if they do bite down, most of the time they spit it out and drop back into the water. The hard part is sneaking up close enough without alarming them. It takes patience."

"But the poor frogs!" Beth said throwing her arms down. "Shouldn't you just leave them alone? We don't have a right to torment them for our pleasure!"

Mindy paused while considering Beth's outburst. She skipped a rock across the water. "I agree," Mindy said softly, hoping to avoid an ugly argument.

After a few silent seconds, Beth seemed to calm down and said, "Pop used to take me and my brothers fishing. Once—I must have been seven years old—I wandered down a stream. I came to a pool and caught a fish, but I didn't know how to bring it in. When Pop came to find me, he looked into the water and said, 'Boy, it's a big one,' and it was. He squatted down and took the line to bring it into his net, but the hook came out. There was the fish below us in the stream. Pop didn't say a word. All of a sudden he jumped in with both feet and grabbed the fish. He scrambled up the bank with the fish clutched in his fingernails and water sloshing in his shoes . . . We were happy in those days."

The girls remounted and rode along in silence back across the highway. The great log mansion presently came into view through the trees.

Before they could eat, they had to return the horses to the stables to unsaddle, brush, and feed them, and this they did with the efficiency of experience. The walk back to the log mansion was not long. They recovered their lunches, and as they mounted the front stone steps, Beth exclaimed her awe over the massive structure. The solid wood door opened on its iron hinges without difficulty and they stepped inside. Beth stared, turning slowly and looking up and around. The room they stood in was a dusky cavern. Most of the wooden surfaces were lined with bark. The front room's ceiling was two stories high and, midway up, an inside balcony ran around the room on three sides. For handrails, small trees had been fashioned and installed by means of clever joinery. The girls passed through the rooms, and while no furniture remained, there was evidence of former luxury: a cast iron bathtub, an ornate mirror frame, brass locks on the windows. There were fireplaces in the larger rooms, even on the upper floors, and separate outside balconies. The girls walked onto a balcony looking north.

"See, through the trees there," Mindy said, "The dark building near the edge of the field?"

"I noticed it earlier," Beth said.

"It's called the Ebenezer. It was a family residence years ago; then it was used for indoor recreation. There's a bowling alley, billiard rooms, and a bar. There's a dance floor and the level below has a swimming pool. The building is sound, and it's full of hardwood trim and stonework, cathedral ceilings in several rooms, and a library full of dusty books. We used to wander around there when we were little and play hide and seek. It's got secret rooms and passages. I'd like to show you someday. The house is in disrepair—some of the plumbing and electrical wires are bad—and it's only used for storage. Dad wants to fix it up someday, when there's money. I've always dreamed of living there."

"Why name it Ebenezer?"

"It's what the Mollicoats called it. I suppose there's a story."

"What's the story of this whole place?"

"That I do know. Let's wait until we eat."

They continued exploring the third level of the mansion and soon came to another set of steps leading directly up to the ceiling, which was covered with thick knobby bark. Mindy reached and with both hands pulled hard on a rope. A crack opened in the ceiling as the trap door lifted. Mindy pulled again and a metal box smartly clacked as the rope locked into place. She tied the end of the rope to a spar and they walked up single file onto the fourth floor.

"Let's eat here," Mindy said as she walked onto a balcony. She grabbed the handrail and shook. When the rail gave no sign of weakness, the girls sat on the floor next to it and opened their lunches, which, by this late in the day, would make an early supper or a tea of sorts. The view looked over the tops of the understory trees, and the air gently waved leaves that were translucent in the sunlight. In an hour or so the sun would dip behind the ridge. Beth dangled her legs from the balcony and looked to the west. Mindy followed her example. Mindy paused a moment and bowed her head with her eyes closed before she began eating.

After the first bites of the meal staved off her hunger, Mindy said, "You asked about the Mollicoat Estate."

"Yeah. What was it about?"

"Well, it was the home of Herman Mollicoat. He and some other men—probably better known men—pooled their resources to build a papermill along the Columbia River to supply the *Oregonian* with newsprint.

"You've got huge trees here."

"A section of it has never been logged," Mindy said. "Timber buyers approach my Dad all the time, but he rebuffs them all.

He says there are always vulgar people who will destroy beauty for profit."

"No doubt. What about this massive house?"

"Obviously it fell into decay a long time ago, but for a while it was the party gem of Portland's fashionable elite. Portland was about an hour's drive away back then."

"I can picture the parties here." Beth seemed to be listening for the music.

"I can too. Some people would fly in from around the Northwest for the gala weekends."

"Hmmm," Beth said.

The girls finished eating in silence.

This particular silence was as immense as the house. The leaves whispered in the treetops. The sun shone in from the west. Shadows of leaves danced and frolicked in the light on the wall behind the girls. Solitary insects buzzed by. That was all.

Mindy began thinking about something that had crossed her mind a few times during the week—her reception on the phone from Beth's father. Eventually she said, "So, tell me about your family."

"We're a standard family, I suppose," Beth said, not liking the disturbance of her peace. "Mom works hard, Pop is insane. I hardly ever see my two brothers because they're away at school. One stayed in New Zealand, and when the other comes home from the University of Oregon, he's with his friends."

"What about your dad?" Mindy asked gently. "I spoke with him. He seemed tense."

"Oh, you called me?"

"I called to just chat and confirm you were coming, but I guess the message didn't get to you."

Beth said, "Typical," and pursed her lips. "You should have called *my* phone. Mom was out playing bridge with her friends. The game is her solace in life." She related some of their family experiences, and Mindy listened while she sat cross-legged on the floor watching Beth's face and gestures.

When Beth finished telling about her father's breakdown, she said, "I hope for Pop to be well someday. He's a quick study. He probably knows more about psychiatry than his doctors. And they're crazier than he is, because they are so *serious*. I think some of Pop's bizarre behavior is acting, just to put us on. Maybe this is why I'll probably major in drama. It's a family tradition. Acting. What's your major, anyway?"

Mindy did not want to drift from talking about Beth's family situation, but she felt reticent to say what she really thought. Answering Beth's question seemed to be an easy change of direction. "I'm majoring in Mass Communications. When I finished high school, my dad wanted me to start a bakery business, but I talked him into letting me go to college. He agreed, because I promised to take fancy cooking classes, too. I told him I could star in television cooking programs."

Beth looked at Mindy quizzically. Mindy was attractive, but her braid would look quaint on television. "Really?" she said. "You want to cook on TV?"

"No, it was a joke on my dad," Mindy said, smiling. "I'm training for production, specializing in radio. Right now I produce and host a cultural history program for the University's radio station. A friend of mine is an anthropology grad student and does most of the research and writing."

"Amazing. What kind of programs?"

"We've done Native American stuff with the salmon runs coming back on the Columbia, and Steve did one program this summer on the 'moving community' of Appalachian Trail through-hikers. He flew to Georgia and hiked the trail last spring with recording equipment. He's in Maine right now, catching up with those he met at the beginning of the season. I didn't go, and much of my work is in the studio, anyway. But we mostly interview people in alternative groups in the city. Steve tries to understand their worldviews from the inside. I edit the program and narrate."

Beth was impressed, but she felt uncomfortable, as if she might qualify as an interview subject. She shifted uneasily on the hard wooden floor and asked, "How did you get started on this?"

"Well, I always was interested in different kinds of people, and Dad had a CB radio when we were children."

"There's something I was wondering about. You live in Vancouver, but attend school in Portland. Doesn't the commute bother you?"

33

"No, it's routine. I listen to audio books or music. I often have riders, or when other people drive, I study. The University has the program I want, and Dad has a special relationship there. I did live on campus my first two years."

"Is Steve your boyfriend?"

Mindy blushed. "No, he's happily married, and he and Angela have a baby. He's just a friend and co-worker."

Beth looked closely at Mindy and said, "There's more to this story. I can tell."

"Not necessarily, but yes, there's more. When I was a freshman, Steve asked Dad if he and I could date."

"Well?"

"Dad said, 'No.'"

Beth was incredulous. "Wha— What did you think? You accepted this?"

"Yes. Dad was right. I was too young to be thinking about marriage, and Steve had a lot of growing up to do. Dad's bluntness helped him change, and afterwards Steve found the right girl for himself."

Beth wore shock all over her face. What Mindy described was alien to her, but she was not sure she wanted to learn more. She held back from saying, "I suppose you've never kissed a guy!"

Realizing that she had advanced toward the subject she wanted to discuss, Mindy steered directly. "You know, my dad isn't a psychiatrist, but he is a doctor, and he's helped people find focus and purpose. I've seen people become friends with him and they change."

Mindy considered this after she spoke. Her life was full of mystery that she had learned to accept from childhood. Dad had many acquaintances, and people were drawn to him for reasons she didn't understand. Her father, while warm, personal, and involved in the details of her life, was often remote and secretive. Many times when she approached him while he sat reading a book or writing, she saw his mind travel to her as if from a faraway place. As a little girl she would run to him, and he would turn toward her, and for an instant he looked through her, unseeing. He always had a life of his own, the meaning and richness of which she could only guess.

In this present moment Beth began to feel impatient. Her father's internal life often bubbled to the surface, and it was unpleasant. The dreamy feeling she had been experiencing was slipping away. With irritation she answered Mindy's suggestion. "Pop won't see anyone else. Mom has tried to get him to stop seeing this couple, but they amuse him. He argues with them about his medications. They are counselors, husband and wife, I think. She's a psychiatrist, and he's . . . he's a spiritual advisor. I went to them once, and they suggested I do something disgusting—don't ask—to reward myself for getting through a day without depression. I walked out of the session instantly and never went back."

Mindy found what she had been searching for, and she spoke suddenly, ignoring Beth's irritation. "I have an idea. Dad conducts regular book discussion groups in our home in Vancouver. They're open to anyone, but the unwritten rule is people only come when invited. Let me talk with him and see if we can invite your father. His knowledge in foreign affairs would add to the discussion, and it will give him a chance to meet my dad."

Beth listened, but through her own tensions now, and so her response came out in hard, loud tones. "What do you think your dad can do? Your family is just so, so disgustingly nice. Your father, with the last name Sterne? Stern!?" Bitter tears came to her eyes.

Mindy's heart raced at hearing this sudden fresh outburst. She stood up and was tempted to walk away. But she resisted leaving, and her eyes looked down to the rough handrail before her. She reached out to touch a place on it, while Beth wiped her eyes with the short sleeves of her shirt.

Mindy spoke, "Please, Beth, I want to show you."

Beth began to calm down, but she had committed herself to rejecting this family, and she stood up and began gathering her things. At this point she did not care if she saw Mindy again, or if she ever came back to this place. She was embarrassed about her outburst, and besides, her life was full enough. She didn't need more friends.

Mindy repeated softly, "Just look at this for a moment. Please."

Beth thought she could look just from curiosity before she left, and she stepped to the handrail.

She had expected something impressive on the ground below. What she saw seemed unconnected to anything Mindy and Beth had been discussing, but the fact that it was unimpressive caught her interest. Had it been related, she would have flared up again, taking it as an argument.

Mindy's finger touched the side of a heart figure carved into the handrail. It was a good carving with high relief, and across it and extending on both sides were the initials "ES & JM". The ampersand was in the heart's middle.

"Hold up. What's this?" Beth asked quietly—though still irritated—as she leaned closer to the carving.

"May I tell you a story?" Mindy asked, hoping her heartbeat could not be detected in her voice.

"Sure, why not?" Beth plopped down on the floor again, leaned back against the side wall, and slapped her hands on the wood beneath her. "Fire away."

Mindy took a deep breath. "My dad went to high school on the west side of Portland. After football games or school dances, the kids came here for adventure. They'd come in groups, park at the bottom of the hill and sneak past the 'No Trespassing' signs to explore the house in the dark. Stories about a watchman who'd shoot rock salt made it exciting. Well, like any of the other rambunctious kids, Dad came out with the crowd, but afterward he began coming alone or with a few friends. One time he brought up two girls and lit a fire in the fireplace on the second floor—the room with all the windows looking south— and the three of them shared a bottle of wine. Dad even brought candles and wineglasses. The second set of initials is one of the girls. Dad loved this place from high school and this is why he bought it, eventually. Grandfather knew the Mollicoats, so there's a family connection there, too."

Mindy stopped speaking and Beth said nothing, waiting. She thought, *Is this all?*

"That's it. That's the story," Mindy said, answering the unspoken question.

Beth had listened closely, and as she did, all her anger and resentment slipped away. She had expected to hear a dramatic tale about unrequited love, murder and mayhem, forlorn hopes and a struggle back to sanity. She thought J.M. might have fallen or jumped from the balcony as a girl full of potential and promise. The plainness of this story amused, charmed, and softened her. Why should she injure this new friend of hers because the young woman's life had been stable, her family wealthy and supportive, while her own family had been a disastrous ruin?

Beth said, "You know, I do have to go soon. Walk me to my car and let's talk on the way."

The girls worked their way down the stairs and out onto the forest floor.

"So, your father married J.M.?" Beth asked.

"No."

"J.M. is your mother?"

"No."

"J.M. got pregnant here on the balcony and you have a famous half-sister somewhere, or J.M. had an abortion and ran away and died?"

"No no. Dad didn't marry J.M. and he behaved as a perfect gentleman. And Dad was Best Man in her wedding. Not many people his age would consider the beauty of this property, or be bold enough to trespass and build fires and bring girls out here, and behave honorably. He's like this now. Dad can be remote sometimes. Austere—you've noticed—but he cares more about people than you'd guess. If you need something, he gives more than you'd think possible. He takes risks and succeeds. He's a person your father would like. You would, too."

"Maybe."

With Mindy beside her, Beth walked away from the woods and into the relative brightness of the field where she had caught the horse and met Mindy. She recalled running into the field and hearing the cheers ring out, and how she felt a release of stress and an explosion of strength. *This is a winsome family,* she thought. When she reached her car, she turned to Mindy and said, "You're right. I do like you, all of you. OK, talk to your father and see if he wants to invite Pop; I'll convince him to go to the book discussion. Hey, I'm sorry for the tantrum."

"That's OK."

"You have a beautiful family, and mine is, well, it's screwed up."

"We're not perfect, either; we have our skeletons just like everyone else."

"Thanks for inviting me. I'd like to come back."

"Sure."

"Oh, I want to say, it was quite elegant how you handled that aggressive guy before the race."

"What? Oh, that. I have brothers, and I'm not intimidated by boys."

"Hmm . . . You were . . . too kind. I would have busted his bit—his nose."

"Well, goodbye."

"Cheers." Beth got into her car and drove away.

Mindy waited until she could not see the car anymore. Then she jogged across the field and walked up the hill to the house. She continued around the house to a rock outcrop and sat down. The sun had just set behind the mountain range, and the valley below was sprinkled with scattered lights. She felt a rush of happiness to be part of this family, and she looked into the darkening sky. Seeing a few faint bright points overhead, she remembered something that she wished she had mentioned to Beth: her last name, Sterne, was German and meant, "Stars." She sighed, stood, and walked back to a utility door of the house.

We are walking along the edge of a row of trees. The sun is intensely bright on the surrounding grassland. A huge bull elephant comes into view and I am terrified. Everyone in our group wants to keep walking, hoping that he will not notice us. I stay behind the others and climb a tree, but, unluckily, the elephant's path takes him through the trees and he stands under me. He can easily pluck me from the tree and fling me to the ground. But he moves on. I climb down and run to a nearby house. Even there it is not safe because the elephant returns. He can smash into the house without difficulty. The sight of a human will enrage him. He is now immediately outside a window of the ground floor room that I am in. The window and blinds are open. I try to close the blinds stealthily, but when I do, they come crashing down. The elephant snakes his trunk inside the room intending to kill me, and I wake up sweating in fear.

-from the dream journal of Stan Timmons

Chapter Three
Saturday Morning's Game

Tommy left his revolver in his grandfather's pickup, but he kept a folded locking blade in his hat. Made by his grandmother, his hat and sweater fortified him against the chilling night. He paid for the football game ticket and stood in line for the security check. When his time came, he sauntered through the metal detector. The detector beeped and the school resource-officer, scanning him quickly with his hand-held unit, found his human-skull belt buckle and let him pass inside. Tommy's relaxed smile, natural charm, and his northern Mediterranean good looks usually put everyone at ease.

The people here for the homecoming game thronged around him, filling the stadium bleachers. This was Tommy's first association with his high school as a graduate, and he looked around for old friends. The kickoff came but Tommy did not watch the game; rather, he visited with several groups of people and caught up on news.

Tommy's interest in firearms came not from the need for defense in city gang war, but from his father who hunted with Tommy's grandfather. When Tommy was in elementary school, his family returned from living in Salt Lake City and moved in with his grandparents at their large farmhouse outside the town of Battle Ground, Washington. He and his father went into the woods every weekend the year around. Tommy was in middle school when his dad got a job in Portland, and the family moved to Oregon where he would be closer to work. After this, Tommy's dad gave up outdoor activities. During his last two high school years, Tommy again stayed with his grandparents.

His parents' divorce was finalized last year, but they had been separated for a long time. His father had met a girl at a business conference and followed her to Knoxville, Tennessee. Tommy's mother had moved to a neighborhood in the West Hills of Portland and remarried. Though Tommy went to high school on the Washington side of the river, he qualified for Oregon's in-state tuition because he gave his mother's address.

One person he wanted to find at the football game was his former English teacher, Stan Timmons. Stan had not really been a teacher, but only a student teacher during the previous spring term, and Stan had become his best friend through events when Tommy had almost been kicked out of school.

After school one day, the Vice-Principal had stopped Tommy in the hallway and said, "Mr. Duckwitz, I've been told that you brought some practice shotguns to school for your musical, *Brigadoon*. The Superintendent's office said replica shotguns can only be used during dress rehearsals and performances.

"Yes sir, and Mr. Timmons, the stage manger, told us."

"But, dress rehearsals are weeks away."

"Yes sir," Tommy said, emphasizing "sir." "I didn't bring replica shotguns to school, sir. They are only long garden stakes. I painted them. It's important to handle the guns genuinely, sir, and thus, early practice with stakes is necessary, especially for the other actor who is not familiar—"

The Vice Principal raised his voice. "You know, Duckwitz, I don't like the way you're acting."

"You don't? Then I apologize. Ah . . . Mr. Timmons said—"

"You'll have to take those sticks home today."

"Sir, I have the lead role in the musical, and there's another gun-handling actor. Mr. Timmons rented realistic shotgun replicas for dress rehearsals and performances. When they arrive, they will be locked up. The replicas can not fire. Have you ever seen movies when actors unconsciously point their guns at each other—their friends? We need to learn good habits now. The sticks I brought don't look anything like guns."

While Tommy was speaking, the Vice-Principal maintained a blank look, and then said, "They're black. Where are they? I want them now."

Tommy coolly stared at the Vice-Principal without blinking and the Vice-Principal blinked and tried to stare back. Several moments passed and then Tommy turned and began walking away.

The Vice-Principal followed him. "Are you going after the guns? I could call the police and have you arrested."

Tommy did not speak, but kept walking toward the exit.

"Are you going after the guns?"

Again, Tommy did not respond.

The Vice-Principal snapped; he spun Tommy around, shoved him into the concrete wall and slapped him across the face, yelling, "Give me those damned guns NOW!"

Tommy had scarcely flinched, and continued to stare. The Vice-Principal backed away and said, "Oh, God, I'm in trouble. Come with me to the Principal's office."

The Vice-Principal turned his back to Tommy and began walking away, and as he did, Tommy flew at him and threw him against the wall. The Vice-Principal's head hit with a crack and he fell to the floor. He did not move. Tommy took out his phone and called for an ambulance.

School authorities intended to press charges against the student until the Vice Principal recovered sufficiently to confirm Tommy's side of the story. Afterwards, officials offered a cash settlement to Tommy, who would be allowed to finish his senior year, provided that he serve two weeks in-school suspension, and thereafter, an hour a day in after-school detention. The Vice-Principal was to be transferred to the Superintendent's office. If Tommy did not accept the deal, the school would expel him and press assault charges. The school system was adamant—the attack against the Vice-Principal could not be forgiven.

But Tommy refused suspension/detention, because he would have to quit the musical—rehearsals ran during drama class and after school; and if the school expelled him, Tommy said he would sue the school and have the Vice-Principal charged with assault. He told the Superintendent, "To hell with your money," and the tension mounted—until Stan Timmons, student teacher, presented a possible solution.

Mr. Timmons usually ate lunch alone in his classroom, and said he could conduct a lunchtime detention for Tommy. Tommy agreed to give it a try. Timmons also convinced him to accept in-school suspension with a provision that he could be released for drama class—which Timmons taught. The Superintendent agreed with the deal and challenged Mr.

Timmons with seeing that Tommy "controlled himself and followed school rules."

During the lunch detention, Mr. Timmons at first maintained silence, but eventually he and Tommy began talking about the musical, Tommy's acting, his family situation, what he was reading, what he did in his free time. Stan encouraged him to work hard in drama. All went smoothly and the Superintendent hired Stan at that same school.

This past summer, Tommy had played roles in two successful regional theatrical productions. Currently, he was in rehearsal for a lead in a significant Portland community theater and was enrolled as a freshman at the University in Portland.

At the football game Tommy did not know where Stan would be, and no one had seen him, not even the Principal, Mr. Cooper, when Tommy asked. Cooper said that Mr. Timmons would be serving refreshments during halftime, so he was sure Mr. Timmons was around. As soon as Tommy left him, Cooper called Security to watch Tommy. Tommy walked along the main aisle of the bleachers in front of the cheerleaders and looked up, scanning the crowd. In the corner of the top row he spotted Stan. Tommy ran up the concrete steps.

As he worked his way past the knees of the fans, Tommy noticed that Stan's eyes were red behind his glasses, and his face looked sullen and drawn.

"Hey Mister, how's it going?" Tommy asked as he sat beside him.

"Fun, funny you should ask," Stan murmured, and looked toward the parking lot outside the glare of the lights.

"What I can't figure out is why you came to the grand-happy homecoming game looking like your mother died."

"Worse," Stan said dully. He stood up, stepped around Tommy, waded past the legs and walked down the concrete stairs.

Tommy sat a moment wondering if he should follow. This was a turn-about in their relationship. Until this moment, it had been Tommy who was always in trouble.

Tommy caught up with Stan outside the gate.

"Hey, let's talk. OK?"

They walked along toward the nearby soccer field.

"There's no good way to start," Stan said. "My sister was raped. Three weeks ago. Someone at the University. I just found out."

Tommy was not stunned by this news because the lives of people around him had been filled with similar events, but his thoughts turned coldly toward vengeance. "Who is the bastard? I would like to give him my regards."

"His name is Talus Schenk. He gave Sarah a ride after a cross-country meet someplace west of Portland. They were going to eat and he was supposed to bring her home. On the way, he pulled down a dirt road and raped her. Right afterwards, he tried to talk her into liking the experience, but she became hysterical and ran into the woods. He drove away and left her. She sat beside a creek alone for a long time and eventually wandered back to the highway. A family driving by picked her up and took her to a hospital emergency room. She refused to check in and instead called me, but she didn't tell me what it was all about until tonight. I wouldn't have come to the game, except I'm substituting for Mr. Hansen at the refreshment stand."

"Hmm. How's Sarah?"

"She's pregnant."

"Oh. Pregnant? How is she otherwise?"

"Not good. She's been sitting around at my parents' home crying all day. She stopped going to classes and cross-country practice. She won't go to the doctor about her pregnancy, and she refuses to talk with our priest. I don't know what to do."

Tommy knew Stan well enough that he should not mention his solution to her pregnancy. But dealing with the rapist Schenk was another matter. "What else is this reptile up to in these days of uncertainty and recession?"

"I don't know him, except Sarah said he's a drama major."

"Oh, yes! I know who he is," Tommy said, nodding.

Stan said nothing and looked up. The sky above glowed with the blazing light that poured over the adjacent football field and obliterated the stars. The air was cold. The crowd roared and the band struck up a fanfare. Tommy waited patiently until Stan continued.

"At first after the rape, Schenk called Sarah every day and offered money for an abortion. She stopped answering the phone and my father is taking his calls. Schenk's been threatening, too, to Sarah and my parents. They're scared. Sarah made a big mistake by writing to him saying she was pregnant. Now I'm worried what he'll do."

"He won't leave her alone?"

"No. She's so unstable now, I'm afraid he may push her over the edge."

"She won't go to the law?"

"No."

"Let's talk with Mr. Schenk tonight. We'll persuade him to stop annoying Sarah."

Stan knew Tommy's reputation as a street brawler, and though it contrasted with his own pacifistic personality, he welcomed Tommy's support. Without resorting to violence, he thought confronting Schenk might back him away from Sarah.

"But, I don't know. I have the refreshment stand."

"Let me take care of it."

"I don't know where Schenk lives. In Portland somewhere?"

"I'll take that job, too. You go home, hang up your coat and tie and dress dark and comfortable. If I find the information we need, I'll be by around midnight."

"Why can't we wait until tomorrow?"

"We could, but then you won't go through with it."

Stan was upset enough over the news about Sarah, and his anger at Schenk overwhelmed his prudence, so that he felt satisfied with Tommy's plan. He had no idea that Tommy carried a gun.

As soon as Stan drove away, Tommy went to work. He reported to the refreshment stand as halftime arrived and performed with zeal and good humor, talking non-stop to his acquaintances while he served up sodas and chilidogs. After the half, he trotted to his granddad's pickup and pulled out his computer. In a short minute he had linked with his home computer. Next, he put on his headset and called his underworld buddy, Franklin, a computer hacker who always kept a few steps ahead of the law. They selected one of Franklin's telephone scrambling codes and began their conversation in earnest. A few minutes later, Franklin had entered the University's rosters and found Schenk's entire file, which he downloaded to Tommy's home computer for future use. Schenk did not live on campus but in a nearby upper crust fraternity. In 20 minutes, as he and Tommy talked and laughed, Franklin had circumvented a local server's security and replaced the frat's home page with a poster for Schenk, complete with an unflattering photograph of him wearing Elvis sideburns and a fat lip ring. As a final touch, Franklin loaded onto the fraternity's website a nasty worm that wiped the first 36 visitors' hard drives, except for the poster as wallpaper. Under Tommy's instructions, Franklin set the worm to launch at 1:30 Saturday morning.

Tommy skipped the homecoming dance and picked up fast food. He arrived a little early at Stan's small house in a lower middle-class neighborhood in south Vancouver. Stan's restored '48 Chevy Fleetmaster sat in the driveway. Tommy exited his grandfather's truck and walked around the car to admire it while he finished his french fries. Then he went back to the truck, retrieved a soft bag from behind the seat and got in the passenger side; he flipped down the sunvisor and turned on the mirror light. From under the seat, he pulled a portable makeup kit and considered what disguise to wear. The possibilities were limited. If he had been at his apartment, he could have assumed any of a dozen different identities. Tommy had exhaustively studied makeup and disguise. He had invented his own moldable material for nose, cheek, and ear enhancements, and he had an adhesive that would last through hours of sweat and not rot his skin. Add a hat, or a cigar, and a foreign or regional accent, some practiced movements, and he could become a new person—even, with the right equipment, a passable woman.

In a few minutes, he had painted white-face patches on his cheeks, with apple-red bullseye centers: in between protruded his round red nose; underneath, his lips, thinly lined with red and white, curled at the edges into a fixed frown; further down flared his orange bow-tie, and over the top hung a gaudy, orange wig and a railroad engineer's cap. Thus transformed, he tucked his revolver into its hidden holster and walked onto the porch. A light was on in the front room and Tommy soft-stepped to the picture window and looked between the curtains. Stan was sitting in a rocking chair, holding a book upright in his hands. His eyes were closed and his head was leaning over. *He needs to get married,* Tommy thought. Through the glass, Tommy could hear meditative jazz. He sat down on the porch swing. There was traffic rumbling a few blocks away, a dog barking nearby. From the netherland a man shouted, "I'm not going to talk anymore, you stupid bitch. I'm going to bed!" He watched the night until the chimes of an invisible church struck twelve. Just after the last bell, Tommy heard Stan's book drop to the floor inside. Tommy got up and knocked on the door.

Stan came to the door squinting, looked at Tommy, said, "Cute," and stumbled to the couch and flopped down, covering his head against the light with a pillow. A few moments later he sat up, lifted his book from the floor and began searching for a bookmark; finding none, he fished a gum wrapper from the trashcan next to his desk.

Tommy walked straight into the kitchen, flipped on the lights, and quickly brewed up coffee the way his grandparents liked it. "Mix two teaspoons of grounds into a Mason jar half-filled with bottled water and stick it into the microwave." Once the water was boiling, he removed the jar with a glove hotholder and poured the liquid through a tea strainer into a mug. After adding a little cream, and a little sugar, he had Stan on his feet clutching the fragrant brew between his hands and marching out the door to the pickup.

As Stan sipped, his eyes brightened by degrees. Tommy drove onto the interstate and across the bridge to the Oregon side. "Your grandparents always made coffee this way?" Stan said. "With a microwave?"

"My recipe's not *entirely* traditional. My grandparents boil their coffee on the wood stove in a cast iron pot. Where did you get the car, anyway?"

"Nice, isn't it? Well, I'm not into restoration—I just keep it clean and polished. I should park it in a garage . . . The car was a gift from my grand-uncle. He did all the work."

"Your uncle must be a wealthy and generous man."

"He was generous, but not particularly wealthy. He had a good salary. He never married and had no children, and he gave the car to me through his will last summer—a sort of present for my college graduation."

"Oh? Sorry to hear about his death. What did he do with his life?"

"Army. He enlisted for Vietnam in the late 1960's and afterwards went to a military college, signed up again for life and worked his way up. He was a motorcycle enthusiast and was killed in a wreck. Not long ago."

"He died young?"

Stan nodded in the dark, saying nothing.

Tommy began a narrative about his older cousin—his only first cousin—who was in the Army. He proudly told about the unit he served under and the shooting conflicts he had been engaged in. His cousin was stationed in Afghanistan and had not been home for more than a year. Tommy described an earlier time when he and his cousin had wandered together on his grandparents' farm with the .22 caliber rifles their grandfather had given them for Christmas.

My grand-uncle had been a Major General," Stan said. "I . . . I hope that's not boasting. I never did know him very well. He didn't keep a real home and seldom came to see my parents. I have childhood memories of him in uniform with the red and yellow ribbons. Bright stars, him reaching down to give me a man's handshake.

Tommy kept silent awhile, remembering also, and finally he spoke. "What shall we say to Schenk?"

"I don't know. Just ask him to leave Sarah alone."

"It won't be that simple."

Tommy knew his way around Portland streets and intended to avoid the slow-wheeling party of motor vehicles. For decades, on Friday and Saturday night, young people had driven certain stretches of downtown roads to display themselves.

Despite Tommy's efforts to work around the cruising section, a recently engineered traffic flow forced them to make a right turn into the middle lane when they left the freeway. Up ahead on the one-way street, which gained in elevation, they could see columns of red tail lights in the three lanes going on forever. Traffic barely moved.

Tommy muttered a curse and rolled down his window. The booming noise of warring stereos, which could be felt through the pickup's glass and steel, clarified. There was nothing to be done but stay calm. Tommy took a deep breath of the cool air. He loved the acrid smell of exhaust blanketing the city. It reminded him of childhood trips out of the rural country to the Portland zoo. To the left, a Mustang convertible with three young men eased parallel to Tommy's pickup. The fellow in the front passenger side leaned out and shouted to Tommy, "It's beautiful, isn't it?" He was wearing dark glasses and a colorful shirt. He did not seem to notice Tommy's clown face as being out of the ordinary.

Tommy tried to scowl in his frowning fool's makeup.

The fellow shouted his explanation. "The lights, the cars, girls, and this night! We're swimming upriver to spawn in the shallow tributaries!"

Tommy did not reply to this biology lesson, but the traffic moved ahead, and he swung around the corner to the right, accelerated, and swerved past an easy chair lying flattened in the middle of the street. In a few blocks he had the pavement to himself, while Stan peered at a city map. This was a section of older homes near the University. It was not difficult to find the fraternity because unmistakable sounds of a late party in progress emanated from the building, a looming structure surrounded by coniferous and bare deciduous trees, rock walls, and a wrought iron fence.

Tommy leaned over and lifted the makeup kit up from the floor under Stan's feet. "Let me fix your face. Somebody might recognize you. What's your clown?"

"What clown?"

"Everyone should have his own clown face—a design that suits his peculiarities. You never know when you might need a clown."

"I don't want anything. The people here are not who I knew at school."

Tommy and Stan got out of the pickup and stretched. They leaned against the fender and looked through the fence that extended from the top of a low stone wall—the pickets of the fence ended as upward jabbing spikes. A *No Trespassing* sign hung nearby. Tommy muttered, "Prosecutors will be violated." Small groups of students left and arrived at sporadic intervals, but most were leaving. A sudden crash of broken glass and laughter shot through the air from the house. The sky was growing thick with clouds.

"Now what?" Stan said, feeling a chill.

"It's the right time. Let's go in."

"Are you sure?"

Tommy swung through the cumbersome gate and Stan trotted to catch up. Inside the heavy front door, inset with stained glass, a large, sleepy man asked for their invitation cards. Stan panicked and turned to leave, but Tommy began patting his pockets and asked, "What's your name?"

"Garry."

"I have the invitation here somewhere, Garry The Bouncer, Garry The Doorkeep," he said cheerfully, and pulled out his wallet. "Ah . . . I found it." He offered Garry a $100 bill. The fellow, only a hired hand, appeared alert now and glanced over his shoulder. While his head was turned, he grasped the money and said, "I'll need to see your student ID." Stan had his wallet in hand, searching for his old student card.

Tommy gave Garry a fake student ID that had him as Lawrence McLaughlin. The bouncer glanced at the photo, then leaned forward as he attempted to see Tommy through the makeup. Finally he gave up and handed the ID back. He then turned to Stan and said, "Where's *your* invitation?" meaning he wanted another bribe.

Tommy took Stan by the arm, muttering, "Mine counts for both of us," and without looking back, moved him from the foyer.

The bouncer called after them, "No weapons. OK?"

People in the main room were scattered around, some in unnatural, uncomfortable postures. Some were moving, some unconscious. Some alone, others closely entwined. The room smelled of alcohol and marijuana. Stan tried not to attend to the details. It looked like someone had sprayed the room with shotgun fire. By this time, Tommy had walked to the end of the room, and Stan followed him through a dining area into the kitchen where they found a servant staircase. Tommy said, "We should be able to reach the rooms from here."

They wandered up through the floors, and guided by information provided by Franklin, they found Schenk's room. Tommy motioned for Stan, and they retreated into a bathroom at the end of the hall. Tommy punched numbers into his telephone.

"Hey, Talus, this is Garry, the bouncer. There's someone here who wants to see you. I don't know who it is, but he says it's about . . . a winning lottery ticket. How soon can you come? He's in a hurry—OK, thanks. I'll tell him."

Tommy snapped his phone shut. "Let's go."

He exited the bathroom with Stan behind. They stood tense outside Schenk's door. Stan had no idea what Tommy would do, but all he could think about was how Schenk had violated his sister, and that they would warn him to stay away from her. The blank door clicked and cracked open. As soon as Schenk appeared, Tommy lunged forward and shoved him two-handed in the chest, pushing him back into the room. Schenk tripped and fell onto the carpeted floor. Stan closed the door. The three of them were alone.

Schenk warily rose and eased himself onto his bed. He was wearing a bathrobe. He had been drinking beer throughout the evening, and while not having had enough to make him intoxicated, it had made him drowsy. Schenk was larger and stronger in aspect than Tommy, but he trembled under this shock.

"What's this all about, anyway?" Schenk said in a high squeak that surprised him.

Tommy sat on a chair and leaned forward. The skin of his face was pale around the makeup. His eyebrows lowered and his lips pressed together before he spoke. His voice shook, as the crisply pronounced words hammered onto Schenk's head. "Leave Sarah Timmons alone now and forever. Listen closely to me. As God is my witness, if you ever speak to her again, or look at her, or come near her, you will regret it as much as a man could regret anything. Leave Sarah Timmons alone."

Schenk was more scared than he had ever been in his life. He also was wide-awake now, looking for a way to escape this humiliation, and was building up anger at the bodily assault and invasion of his room. He did not know what these men knew, or if official rape allegations might be following in the wake. All this amounted to confusion that he found impossible to resolve. He looked from Tommy to the other person in the room, who up until this moment had been only a vague, intimidating shadow. He recognized Stan, and his tangled situation slipped into the background as his arrogant personality and habits reasserted themselves. Seeing Stan, he felt relief, and had, as he thought, found a way to reclaim his dignity and gain control of the situation.

"I know you. I debated you about God in front of the cafeteria. I don't remember your name, but let's see. You said you were a Christian, didn't you? Let me ask: Jesus said to love your enemies and all that crap. What kind of Christian love barges into my room, shoves me around, and makes slanderous accusations? I should shoot you for your two-faced pretensions. What is your name, anyway?"

Stan was bewildered and did not know what to say, but Tommy stood up as Schenk slid off the bed, turned onto his knees, and proceeded to fumble under his mattress; but if Schenk had a gun hidden there, he couldn't find it.

"Listen to me, Schenk, and believe," Tommy said quietly, his hand near his revolver, "If we didn't have Christian love for you, you'd be dead."

Schenk blustered back, "I wouldn't be the only one." He rose from his knees and sat on the bed again, defiant, but empty-handed and still afraid, too.

Tommy smiled grimly in his false face and reached into a pocket. With a quick movement of his fingers, he flicked an empty revolver cartridge through the air and hit Schenk in the chest. Schenk yelped and fell back. "You'd be dead, Schenk. Now. Believe it! Leave Sarah Timmons alone."

With that, Tommy snatched up the cartridge case and abruptly left the room. Close behind him, Stan shut the door.

"We need to hurry," Tommy whispered.

Their feet clattered down the steps to the kitchen and out the back door. In the dark, Tommy vaulted the fence near a stone pillar, and Stan clambered after, mindful of the spikes.

When his room door had closed, Schenk remained stunned on his bed. After a few seconds, he got down on his knees and probed under the mattress again, more deeply this time. He found his gun at last, checked to see that a round was chambered, and put the gun in his bathrobe pocket. He walked down the main staircase to the front door as Stan and Tommy were finding their way out of the yard. The bouncer nodded from his perch on a barstool that he had pulled into the foyer.

"Did two male students just leave here?"

"No, sir."

"Then call the police right now. Now! We have two dangerous thugs in the house."

At this moment, one of Schenk's frat brothers walked up to him. "Talus, you need to see . . . upstairs," the brother said.

Schenk ran up to the other resident's room, and the bouncer chased along. The room was full of young men and a few women. Before them on the computer screen was Talus Schenk's embellished picture under the heading, "WANTED FOR RAPE & KIDNAPPING."

Schenk looked back to the bouncer who stood in the doorway with his eyes wide open. "I changed my mind," Schenk said. "Don't call the police. By the way, *Garry*, you're fired, you idiot."

Meanwhile, Tommy and Stan made their getaway in the pickup truck. The traffic had thinned while they had been at the fraternity. The streets Tommy took were desolate, and wet from rain just beginning. Tommy put in a disk of some rich electric guitar music and cranked up the volume.

Stan reached over and turned it down to a buzz. He inhaled a deep breath and let out a moaning sigh. "Was it necessary to shove Schenk? What did you throw at him? I should have worn a clown face. I remember debating him . . . It was the week before the rape."

"No kidding. Who could forget that caca-head? A name like that. Phallus? What were his parents thinking? He recognized *you* tonight."

"I had gone to check on a problem with my scholarships and university bills and stopped for lunch. Some students were arguing, and I jumped in the fray. Schenk and I took over and a crowd gathered. He was weird and taunted me, smiling the whole time."

"It adds up. You want to hear something *really* strange?"

"What?"

"I haven't hit a red light in three days running. I swear. It's been all greens and yellows." Tommy turned the music up again, but not as loudly as before, and zoomed through a flashing yellow light in a long column of flashing yellow lights continuing to a vanishing point.

"I'm afraid of Schenk," Stan said. "Did you hear his threat?"

"No. I was watching what he might pull from under his mattress, and planning what to say next. I wouldn't worry. He's a coward. A zero. A person like him doesn't hear reason. But you're right, I need to listen better."

I am watching a movie in a theater. Suddenly I see that the scene is in front of our old house near the river and also that I am inside the movie. The camera cuts to a nearby Indian burial site and then back. There is a ladder against the house and someone is tearing the house down. I climb inside the structure, which at this point is mostly a skeleton with a roof. Inside there are several people removing beams and rafters. In the back I can see part of a new building, and hymn singing is coming from it. I ask a worker what's happening here. He says they are using the building material to construct a church. I am so moved by being at my old home again, one rich with memories, but so far away now, that I begin to cry. I ask the worker if I might have some of the lumber to build a table for my wife.
-from the dream journal of Stan Timmons

Chapter Four
Thomas & Elisabeth

January term had begun the week before. Tommy's *Macbeth* audition at the University would be at 2:00 p.m. today. In preparation, he had memorized speeches from the King Duncan murder scene and rehearsed them in the park near his apartment several mornings before his classes began.

A few sunrise joggers glared at Tommy's antics; most smiled to themselves and pretended not to notice. Removed from the context of the play, his actions appeared irrational. *Another crazy homeless person,* they thought. *This one looks potentially violent.* Those who listened to the words shuddered without knowing the source of the spiritual coldness. If it had been in the afternoon when people hung out at the park, Tommy would have walked up and delivered his soliloquies personally. It was an odd and barbaric city, world, and age, when the abnormal was to be tolerated and celebrated. Tommy's clothing—dominated by black and linen—matched the play; and his practices amounted to quality enactments. A bench sitter waiting for a bus walked up tentatively and left a five-dollar bill on Tommy's backpack. The bill blew off in the gusty, warm wind uncommon in the Northwest this time of year. Tommy snatched it up, crumpled it, and stuffed it into his pocket. He hated litter.

Tommy sometimes practiced drama on his grandparents' farm. In the country no one was there to stare, not that he minded staring. Once as he hiked along a road in-between fields and pastures, he shouted, "Look at me!" to a group of cows, who did indeed look at him. He remembered attending symphonic concerts in Portland. At a quiet moment, he would imagine jumping up on the stage, raising his hands, and shouting.

Despite his hidden weapons, despite his convincing portrayal of the murderous Macbeth, and despite his vengeful ways, Tommy's heart was not wholly black. Inside he hurt at small, perceived rejections from others; he carried weighted burdens of fear, and most importantly, he aspired to purpose and meaning. The plays, the costumes, the anger against the unknown, and the "vaunting ambition" only meant that he had not found meaning, or that it did not exist. He valued friendship—he had few real friends, but many acquaintances. Being young, he did not often see the pain of people close to him, unless it was larger than life. Being young, it was easy to be pleasant, when it suited him. Life was a game, a play. Nothing really mattered. But he was a human being after all, and he had to do something, and better if it made him happy.

On this particular balmy winter morning of his audition, such matters were far from his conscious mind. Today was first in what would be a row of those rare January days when, after rainy weeks and a solid month of cold weather, it seemed winter had fled forever and spring had marched in with triumph. With daylight lengthening a few minutes each day, Tommy felt optimistic—the new term was bursting with promise.

His practice complete, he hurried from the park and jumped on a bus to the University. Tommy entered the library and unloaded supplies from his backpack at his study carrel. The carrel, which really was not "his," might as well have been. He often lived there during the workdays. It served as a locker, and sometimes as a dorm room. In the evening, if he did not go to his apartment—usually over-populated with the gang of people that he associated with—or if he did not go to a pub, he would stay through the night. For such a contingency he kept a rolled-up blanket and a pad at the carrel, along with food and necessities. Overlooking a central square of the campus, the carrel had a window—a slit of glass running up to the ceiling. This was his suite and the only space he owned.

Today's classes were elementary, and made an unfocused backdrop to the main action of his mind—which was contemplating the audition. When the library tower chimes rang a quarter till, Tommy slipped out from Biology early and ran to the theater. The air was warm and breezy. He hesitated before the door, and, as if on cue, walked inside the lobby. The drama department Chairman—who had attended graduate school in London and who, as a condescension, was to be the Director of the play—and several upper class Fine Arts majors looked up and saw their Macbeth with a leather jacket thrown over his shoulder, striding through the glass doors. They did not like what they felt, but they knew instinctively that they might not have a choice about the part—if this young man would study his lines and if departmental politics could be ignored. Tommy gave them a folder containing two typed pages and photographs depicting his dramatic credits—three high-school leads, a main role in community theatre, stagehand work, and parts at the Oregon Shakespeare Festival. Without waiting for them to finish looking at his portfolio, he asked if they were ready for his audition. They were not. They were less ready now than when he appeared in the doorway.

The Director asked him to go inside the theater and wait. Tommy said, "Fine," but did not go inside right away. Instead, he paced around the window-lined lobby and inspected posters from University plays of previous years. Having been busy in summer theatre elsewhere that had lingered into fall, he had not taken drama classes in the fall term.

Behind the long ticket counter were the rooms of the theater office. Tommy sat at a counter stool. The chimes of the library tower outside rang a melody and then struck two. Tommy reached over and tapped the little bell on the counter twice in mimicking echo. The Director and his advanced students stopped their murmuring to stare across the lobby. Tommy bowed to them.

A form walked up behind the counter. "May I help you?" a female voice asked.

The doors to the auditorium opened, and closed with a low-pitched thump. The department Chairman/Director of *Macbeth* and his students no longer stood in the lobby.

Tommy fell in love with the voice's accent before he turned around. The girl was different, too. Her dark hair was pulled back from her face with a woven headband. Her features formed a pleasing whole—child-like, but mature and alluring. Tommy smelled a sensual, vanilla scent.

"Umm." He leaned an elbow on the counter, cradled his chin in his hand, and said, "What's your perfume?"

The girl laughed, and her brown skin flushed faintly; her teeth were white and perfect. "It's not your damn business." Seeing

Tommy's comic frown, she laughed again and whispered, "It's classified."

"What I really want to know is, how much are tickets for *Macbeth*?"

The girl turned a seating map around to him, and leaning so that her arm touched his, she said, "Where will you sit?" Tommy perused the auditorium layout. He shook himself, stood— pushing back the stool—and said, "On the throne of Scotland." The girl leaned back an inch at this, and he abruptly changed tempo, "But my audition! Sorry. Must run." He smiled, and after a slight bow and flourish of his hand, whisked away.

He entered the theater, and another student had begun her audition in his place. Tommy's name had been called, and he had been bumped from his time. He sat at the end of the front row to watch. When this audition was done, there were a few quiet minutes, and Tommy was called again. Shunning the stairs, he leapt to the stage from the orchestra pit, and went through his prepared routine. Everyone in the room thought, *Effective, authentic.*

The Director then asked him to read from another scene of the play. After this, the Director said to pick up a stage sword and walk. Tommy peered at the audience and asked, "Walk?"

Tommy not only not walked, but began an unaccompanied mock-sword fight with tumbles, sound effects, and a complete repertoire of combat moves. At the end of this choreography, he died, casting his sword—which grated across the stage floor— and he fell face first.

Embarrassed silence followed. The Director was bewildered at this startling presentation. Tommy stood, and, concealing his rapid breathing, waited for further instructions.

To cover the awkward moment, the Director asked him to alter how he played the final few lines of the murder scene. Tommy complied, and the Director pretended to write notes.

"Thank you, Mr. Duckwitz. Callbacks will be Thursday, starting at 4:00 p.m., and the list will be posted outside my office and on our website no later than 9:00 that morning, but possibly as early as Wednesday at 4:00 p.m." Duckwitz was not Tommy's real name, but his chosen stage name.

Tommy returned to the theater's ticket counter where the girl with the accent had been. She did not answer the bell, but presently emerged from the auditorium.

"Hi," she said, "Your audition. I couldn't believe it. You're really good."

"If I were good, I couldn't act well, but thanks."

"My name is Elisabeth."

"Hi."

"Are you an incoming freshman?" she asked. "I don't remember seeing you before."

"Yeah. Last fall." Tommy paused. He did not want to go through the rituals of student chitchat as in, "What's your major?" and so on, but he did want to know where she was from. "I may have seen you before. You speak so beautifully. Tell me your life's story."

She laughed a sultry laugh like one of Tommy's favorite movie actresses, Lauren Bacall. "My family lived in New Zealand for five years. Pop taught Political Studies and International Relations here at the University for many years and then was called into the diplomatic corps. I attended public school there, in New Zealand, and then some classes at the University of Wellington. When Pop retired and returned to the States, I came back too."

"I always wanted to see New Zealand," he said in a dreamy voice.

"It's decadent. The climate is the same as here, and they have mountains, too."

"Where did you go to school here, before you moved away?"

"Cascade Middle School."

"No kidding? Just a second. Elisabeth? You were Beth. Beth Telford?"

"How do you know?"

Beth Telford had been the prettiest girl in school. She had been a cheerleader and was popular. Tommy remembered how good she looked in the cheerleader's sweater. Once in the sixth grade, he held her hand during square dancing. She had been a frequent object of his daydreams—in one of them, she fell down a flight of stairs that descended from an outdoor play area, and he caught her. She rested in his arms until the medivac people came. She had long dark pigtails then.

Tommy revived from his momentary reminiscence. "I went to Cascade, too, when we moved from Battle Ground."

"That's cool. But I'm sorry, I don't remember you."

"That's alright. I was invisible."

They moved over to a window bench and sat and talked. Sunshine poured in. Every once in awhile she had to jump up to the counter to help someone, but always she returned to the bench.

"Aren't you afraid of being fired?" Tommy asked.

"No, I'm only volunteering for today. Susan, the regular secretary, has the flu and I'm filling in. How did you get involved in drama?"

"As a child, I had a proclivity for imitating people's voices and moves—impersonations. My parents thought it was hilarious. And I fell into drama when I was a junior in high school. The English teacher assigned each student to learn a few lines from a classic play. I selected the 'All the World's A Stage' speech in Shakespeare. The speech captured my own impressions of life. It reminded me of lying outside in a field looking at the remote stars, waiting for an answer to my prayers.

"I had long hair then, and what should I do with my hair? The solution was a turban. Who wears a turban? I would make Jacques be from India. A few hours of research and I had the character in saffron-orange, brown and green, with a Sikh knife. Grandma helped with the sewing and dyeing. I even found out there'd been a British colony in India early in the 15th Century. It all fit the character of 'strange suits and accents.'

"The recitations were to be done in front of all the English classes of that period, and students filled one side of the gymnasium. At the end of my speech, at 'sans everything,' my arms went numb, but my voice hadn't failed. The moment I quit, the students responded with cheers, and a standing ovation. I was stunned. I hadn't anticipated any reaction. It was funny, because I darkened my skin and learned an accent, and everyone thought a new foreign exchange student had done the part. From that experience I decided what my life would be, and the next semester, I signed up for drama class."

Beth gazed at him askance and said, "Did that really happen?"

Tommy looked to the floor and ran his hand over his hair. He looked back up at Beth. "Well, yes. The story is over-rehearsed, I guess."

The two of them continued talking for an hour. The time passed quickly. They each learned that the other was lonely, despite having talents and activities. Tommy learned that Beth also had auditioned for *Macbeth*—she wanted only a small part. He was amazed for such an attractive girl to be friendly with him and Beth was impressed by his attentiveness. They briefly discussed marriage, in general. Because of his parents' bickering and divorce, Tommy said that he did not believe in marriage. Beth kept her opinions about marriage to herself, but joked, "Mom keeps Pop as a pet."

When closing time arrived, they got up to leave, donning their bookbags. Beth held a flat, long package.

"I have an idea," she said, flushing faintly. "It's lunatic, but I was going to fly my kite after work. It's such a right day. Want to join me?"

"Sure, I'd love to."

They walked to the athletic fields.

Because of its topography, the Northwest gives a person the feeling of being in an amphitheater. The mountains give perspective to the land, and a frame and scale for distances. In the plains a person looks to the horizon and sees the earth drop away, or in the Appalachians, layers behind layers of rounded ridges disappearing toward infinity. But higher mountains define infinity, showing the sky to be bigger than it appears in the flat lands, or amid humbler ranges.

The air blew freshly from the south and the paper kite pulled north toward thin, high clouds. The picture on the kite of a full moon with a jolly face became blurred. They walked slowly and talked about the moment. Like a puppy on a leash, the kite towed them along, and they paid it little heed. Not having an attachment to any other girl, Tommy fell in love this afternoon, though he had not yet given his feelings the words. She, however, had not made up her mind. She had a date for the coming weekend with an older theatre student who had recently distracted her.

Evening darkness drew down, and it was time to leave. The kite was far away. Tommy wanted to reel it in, but Beth pulled the spool from his hands, laughing. She removed a penknife from her pocket and cut the line. Tommy felt crushed. Waves of gloom rushed over him. Insignificant as the loss was, her action seemed cold and senseless.

"I always cut kites loose," she said. "It's a ritual of freedom. I have liberated the kite, and her moon will float into the sky."

Tommy did not believe she really thought this. The kite grew smaller and seemed to rise; then it faded. They returned to the main part of campus in silence. Tommy left Beth at her dormitory door, forgot about the bus, and ran to his apartment—a couple miles. He was so charged that he did not tire or notice the distance. He would see her tomorrow, he thought, elated.

The next day flew by, and as soon as Tommy was free of responsibilities, he dashed to the theater, weaving through trees and students. One student heard his footsteps and turned to glance behind. Trying to avoid Tommy, the student miscalculated and stepped right into his path. Tommy veered, nearly crashed into a wall, recovered, and kept running.

Beth was working again at the theater, the regular secretary still out with flu. Again they sat in the sunny window and talked. Tommy found courage to ask what he had planned since morning.

"Will you go with me to a concert or a movie this weekend?"

"I'm sorry; I have a date with Talus for Saturday night. Do you know him? Talus Schenk."

Tommy's heart froze. Since the encounter with Schenk back in the fall, Tommy had watched Schenk closely whenever he was near. What could he say to Beth to warn her away from this sick swine? He thought of Sarah, who had not improved since Schenk left her alone, but had admitted herself into a mental hospital.

Tommy's mind burned, but he managed to say, "Oh, I see. How about Friday or Sunday?" *How thick can I be?* he thought. *I have to warn her about Schenk.*

Beth paused, considering. "I don't think so this weekend. My parents have a social event on Friday that they expect me to attend, and Sunday . . . I have to study. But the next Saturday's free."

"OK. Saturday after next—Wait, I can't. It's Grandfather's birthday. I'm working with him all day on the farm, and then we have a party planned. Both my parents will be there."

"Maybe another time, then," Beth said. They both felt disappointed and did not have the heart to try another arrangement.

Tommy had been watching students on the mall outside the window; something caught his eye and he turned. The Director passed them, and he did not look happy about Tommy beguiling Beth from work. The Director pinned a paper to the bulletin board. Tommy jumped up, ran, and skidded to the board crying, "Are we on the call back list? Yes? Good. I'll see you tomorrow afternoon!"

"OK!" Beth answered. "Hooray!"

Tommy left as the Director gave Beth papers to staple.

The next day, Tommy came to callbacks and read from the script with four different Lady Macbeths. Talus Schenk read for *Macbeth* too, and with Beth. The Director let the latter two continue for a long time, making Tommy angry and jealous. And when it came his turn to read with her as the evening grew late, the Director perceived the genuine affection that Macbeth had for his lady, and he liked this element that would add a complexity to the visionary and ambitious character. Imagine, making *Macbeth* into a love story!

After auditions, Tommy spoke with the Director, who asked him about his interpretation. Then Tommy rushed into the bathroom to rinse his face with cold water, and when he returned to the audition room, Beth was gone. A backstage crewmember told him that she had left with Schenk.

Tommy's apartment was in a five-story building south of the University. He and two of his acquaintances rented one large high-ceilinged room with windows all along the east and south walls. Brick columns separated the window sections. When Tommy arrived later in the evening, the room was empty of persons, but signs of recent occupancy lay in abundance on the floors, furniture, and on his bed. In despair, he cast himself onto the bed, on top of papers, books, and a pizza box. For the first time in his life he had found someone who would be a fulfillment for him, but he was losing her already. More than this, he felt an urge bordering on panic to protect her. He jumped up and searched the online student directory, found Beth's number, and dialed. His heart pounded and suffocated him. "Stage fright, that's all," he said as the phone rang on the other end.

"Hello." It was Beth. Thank God she was not with Schenk, or was he in the room? Her *Hello* had been a whisper.

"Hi, this is Tommy."

"I know."

"Are you alone? Can you talk?"

"Sure. My roommate's asleep. She won't wake though. Are you OK?"

"Yeah."

"You called to tell me you're OK?"

Tommy paused, and blurted out his burden. "I love you, Beth."

Beth paused. "Ah . . . thank you."

Tommy was embarrassed. He didn't want her to feel uncomfortable, but it was too late. "Please, I want to tell you . . . Don't go with Talus Schenk tomorrow night."

"Why not?"

"He's . . . "

"Really, he's harmless."

"No he's not!"

Beth waited for more.

Tommy bit his lip, mulling. "I shouldn't talk about this on the phone. Can we meet somewhere?"

"It's late."

"But it's important. How soon can you meet me at the Humanities library?"

"About five minutes."

"OK. I'll be there in five minutes. No, ten. Just wait for me; I'll be right there."

"Hurry. The library closes at 11 o'clock."

"I know."

65

Tommy crammed leftover pizza into a bag and snatched his backpack and jacket. He heard stomping up the apartment steps and voices in the hallway, and knew that some of the roommate crew was returning. Not willing to risk a delay, Tommy scrambled onto the fire escape. He worked down to a tree branch near the corner of the building and leaned over, grabbing the branch and swinging his body out. He wrapped his legs around a trunk and inched down to smaller side branches. The rest of the descent was easy. The buses had stopped running, and he selected a loose bicycle with chipped paint from the dayroom of the building. The bicycle's owner would not miss it, or would borrow someone else's. It was an informal communal arrangement that rarely broke into tempers.

In seven minutes he wheeled up to the library and hid the bike in the shrubbery. Beth was waiting on the front steps. He walked up to her and took her hand.

"Thanks for coming," he said. "I don't want to keep you long, but I have to tell you . . . "

"Like, you love me, again?"

"Yes, but not in so many words," he said and smiled. "Come on, I have a secret to show you."

They slipped into the library. At that moment lights flicked off and on, and a screechy voice filled the building saying, "The library closes in ten minutes. Ten minutes." Tommy and Beth eased up the steps to the second floor and he deposited his backpack at his study carrel.

From floor three, Tommy led Beth up a narrow staircase to the fourth floor, which had only two rooms. A locked door guarded the room on the right. The left door was open and the room empty, except for chairs and a desk, an ancient computer, and a file cabinet.

Tommy walked to the outside window that was higher than his head, and shifted a chair to a position below it. "Shhh . . . and follow me."

Tommy stood on the chair and lifted the window. The heavy weights inside the sash rumbled down as the window slid up. He put one knee on the sill and disappeared into the darkness outside. His head popped back in and he said, "It's worth it."

Beth found herself on the roof. The window they had just clambered out of was a dormer set upon the slope. Tommy walked up to the ridge and Beth followed. For a few seconds they stood still, and then Tommy turned in a circle, breathing in the warm wind. Overhead loomed the bell tower. Down on the other side of the roof was an identical dormer window. This window did not have a lock—and soon they stood inside the locked door that they had met at the stairtop. Tommy switched on a flashlight from his key chain.

This room led up a short staircase into an attic chamber. To the side were wooden steps set into the wall.

Tommy looked at his watch. "Let's wait."

Soon the chimes began tolling 11:00 p.m. He and Beth clapped their hands over their ears until the vibration passed into the hills. More steps led into the bell room. Through the midst of the mammoth bells, more steps zigzagged higher. These steps were narrow and had no handrails. Next, at the end of those steps, through a door, was the bell timer room, and a ladder. At the ceiling of this room Tommy pushed up a trap door, which when opened, leaned against the inside of the rounded cap of the tower. They had reached the end of their climb. On one side, Tommy pulled open a panel on hinges, eased through, and carefully sat down outside. Beth followed and sat beside him. He took her hand and they surveyed the scene before them.

They were overlooking the entire campus, hanging their feet over the edge and smelling the soft air. The sky was deep violet. Tall separated clouds rolled over them from the southwest, thinking of rain, but not delivering. Sections of the Portland skyline were visible. Tommy pulled out the pizza and offered some to Beth.

She shook her head. "No, thanks. How did you find this place?" she asked, excited and charmed.

"I have a friend who worked in the physical plant. It was part of his financial package. He needed to clean the gutters last fall and stumbled onto this route to climb up here without a key."

Beth gazed out and hummed a sound of satisfaction. "OK. What do you want to tell me?"

"I hate to sully this place, but . . . a friend of mine . . . I may have mentioned him before . . . He has a younger sister who dated Schenk. It was their first date, not really a date; he was taking her home and, and . . . " Tommy shuddered. "Talus Schenk raped her. That's it. The bastard raped her."

"I don't think so."

"He did. Afterward he laughed and asked her what did she expect? Didn't she know he was a stud? That's what he said. She ran into the woods to hide. She lost her emotional balance afterwards and dropped out of school. My friend was crushed, and we wanted to confront the bastard to scare him away and we sat him down to talk . . . Did he take you home last night?"

"No, we just left the building together. He reminded me of our date and went a different way."

"You have to believe me. Schenk is a rapist. Don't trust him."

Tommy waited to see what Beth would say. Frogs peeped in a nearby pond, lulled out of winter slumber by the false spring.

"What's her name?" Beth asked gently.

"Who?" Tommy still thought about Schenk.

"The girl? Your friend's sister?"

"Sarah Timmons."

Beth made a gasp. "No! I know her . . . How can that be? But it makes sense. She quit the cross-country team, and no one said why." Beth paused, thinking, and then she recounted slowly, "At the last race that she ran I saw her leave with . . . oh, it was Talus! This is horrible."

Tommy then related to Beth the remainder of the circumstances that Stan had told him.

Beth thought for a few moments. "How is Sarah doing now?"

"She checked herself into Steilacoom Hospital near Olympia. Her doctor didn't want her to go, but she insisted. She's undergoing therapy."

Beth shivered, and muttered, "The ratbag."

"My friend and I are visiting Sarah on Sunday. Would you like to come with us?"

"I don't know. Those places give me the creeps."

"The hospital isn't bad. Our high school psych class made a field trip there. It's a cool campus."

"I have to study on Sunday."

"Bring your books. Monday is a holiday, too. Martin Luther King. No classes, remember? I would enjoy your company.

Listen, you might collect behavior effects from patients—for Lady Macbeth."

"Oh, I won't get the part. But . . . I'll come anyway."

"Good. Great, I mean. It will be nice to have you along."

"Yes. What's your friend like?"

"His name is Stanley. He's a school teacher—English. Wears glasses. Dreams big and has a tiger's courage if you push him. He visits his parents every weekend. And he's never had a girlfriend."

"Really?"

"He's old-school, but loyal. And a lot of fun, if you don't show him drugs or deranged behavior. You should see his car."

"I know someone perfect for him," Beth said as if she had a scheme. "She's prudish and a lovely creature. Smart, athletic. Her father's a wowser though—a dictator; she's never dated."

"How old is she?"

Beth answered, and told him about how she and Mindy met.

"This sounds interesting. I have an idea. See if your friend Mindy will come with us to Steilacoom on Sunday. If this doesn't work, we can try something else later. We'll introduce them and see what happens. It'll be amusing."

"Will Stanley mind? He might not want people crowding his sister."

"We'll improvise. He's used to my games. Anyway, we won't go to her room. We'll keep Stan company during the drive and explore the grounds. He'll love it."

"And a mental hospital is so idyllic, so romantic," Beth cooed sarcastically.

"Uh, yes. You will invite the girl, right? And keep it a surprise?"

"Right."

They sat silent a few moments, pursuing their private thoughts. Tommy's body tensed, and then he asked the question that still burned in him.

"What are you going to do about Saturday, and Schenk?"

Beth grunted. "Are you kidding? What do you think I am?"

"What will you tell him?"

"I've contracted a contagious terminal disease."

Tommy laughed and said, "He may not back off easily."

She scooted up close to him, her thigh touching his, took his arm and said, "I'm not worried. You'll help me, if I need it, right?"

Tommy felt dizzy. He longed to kiss Beth on the mouth, but this was too soon after warning her about Schenk. He did not want to be Schenk. He softly cleared his throat. "Well then, come with me to the Oregon Symphony concert. Do you like classical music?"

"I haven't given it any thought. I'm tired. I'll tell you tomorrow."

"You'll like it!"

"Tomorrow," Beth said.

"OK. Let's go."

"Thanks for bringing me here," she said, not moving. She then sang softly, "Some days I peer into your soul."

"What's that?"

"A line from my favorite song. It's sorrowful."

"It is. What do you see?"

"I don't know what you mean," she said.

"When you peer into my soul, what do you see?"

Beth had not altogether applied the line to Tommy, but she thought for a moment and said, "A beautiful human being."

Tommy tried to dismiss the compliment. "I'd like to hear your song."

"Some-day," she sang.

They slid back from the edge, then retraced their steps down through the wooden tower, over the roof, and back into the dim illumination of the library. Tommy led the way to the basement and a service entrance. Near the door on the wall was a white box with a series of lights. Tommy flipped up a cover and punched in numbers to disarm the door's security. "My physical plant friend," he whispered over his shoulder.

"You have a bundle of friends, but I've never seen any yet." Beth stepped outside and Tommy let the door stop, nearly closed, on a piece of brick. The two of them walked back to Beth's dormitory and Tommy stopped at the door.

"Good night," Tommy said, giving her a quick kiss on the cheek. "We hear about our parts tomorrow. And don't forget to invite your friend for Sunday, and you can meet mine. Let me know what she . . . Her name is Mindy? Let me know what she says."

He handed Beth a white-on-black business card with his phone number. "Call if you need me," he said as she perused the card. With that, he turned and loped away.

Back snuggly in the library, he rolled out his pad by the study carrel, folded a towel into a pillow, opened the window a crack, pulled the blanket and his jacket over his shoulders and composed his mind for sleep.

Talus Schenk was not inert, and had been creating plans and marshaling forces to fashion his designs into reality.

Some few months ago, after the rough October visitation in his fraternity room and humiliation before his fellows, Schenk had made a list of people who might have been the clown and his chubby compatriot. Tommy moved to the head of list during auditions because Tommy resembled the threatening clown, and because he had become a competitor.

While Beth and Tommy had been dangling their legs from the old library tower, the Director for *Macbeth* worked in his office long after supper. Darkness had arrived. The assistant director had left only a few minutes before. They had made up several casting option lists, but finality escaped them, and the assistant left without them making a decision about the leads. Schenk ambled into the office without knocking and sat down on an upholstered chair, throwing a leg over the arm. The Director put aside his notes, thinking he might hear something to help finish his work, and he listened to Schenk's version of the clown encounter, and to Schenk's suspicions. The Director soon figured out that Schenk was attempting to stir up calumny against Tommy.

"Duckwitz is interfering with my private business because he envies my success," Schenk said. "I even heard he's trying to steal my girlfriend. Because of his tendency toward violence, I'm worried about him hurting somebody. He's scary enough as is, and it wouldn't help him to be cast as Macbeth and delve into the soul of a murderer. And Duckwitz has been spreading an ugly rumor about me."

71

"How about you, Talus?" the Director said. "Can you play a military hero who goes bad?"

"I can play anything."

"I have kept this a secret so far," the Director said. "I'm putting *Macbeth* right here in the Northwest, say, 10 years from now. But here's the zinger. The office Macbeth covets is not King of Scotland, but Governor of Washington State. And at the beginning of the play, Macbeth will be a county commission chairman. I'll have the Space Needle painted into a night background and Mt. Rainier in moonlight. I hope to portray our society devolved to where 'dark magic and scantily concealed murder have become the means to accomplish political and personal goals.'—that's how we will bill it."

Schenk understood the dangers of such an artistic statement in publicly-funded theatre. Primarily, he was pleased because he thought that the Director's confidences foreshadowed himself receiving the Macbeth role. In a further attempt to impress the Director, he raised a problem that the setting might present.

"How about fighting? Are you going to remove the swordplay? I hope not, because I'm good."

"The offstage war in the final scene will be done with private armies using modern weapons. Political mobs, really. But the onstage fighting will be performed with swords. Macbeth will be a hobby collector of ancient weaponry, which will line the hall of his mansion where the action will take place. Maybe I'll tweak the script to make it fit. I'm looking forward to building costumes. A friend of mine in Milan is a fashion designer who'll throw her latest concepts to us. We might be creators of the next vogue. Lady Macbeth will be exalted and stunning, and I plan to send out tantalizing press releases. This play will be noticed."

Schenk had listened with fascination. He absolutely must have the part of Macbeth, but he could think of nothing more to help himself. He did not want to push too far and become a nuisance. It might be better to retreat from the office now.

But before he left, Schenk gave a hearty recommendation for Lady Macbeth. "The girl from New Zealand was faultless in auditions," he said emphatically. "Her accent is fabulous. We've been dating, as I mentioned, and we get along well."

When he was alone again, the Director considered the "act" he had just witnessed from one of his fourth year undergraduates. The Director had heard the rumor about a girl Schenk dated who inexplicably dropped out of school last fall, and he knew that Schenk exaggerated and concealed truth, and yet what Schenk said about Duckwitz made sense. Duckwitz might be uncontrollable, and what about violent tendencies? Anyway, life would be smoother in the department if he did not give a freshman the lead. Schenk had worked hard. It was his senior year and a role like this was due him. The Director pondered and settled at last on Schenk for Macbeth. In the same mood, the Director cast Lady Macbeth. She was a graduate student who, while merely an adequate actress, needed the experience for her MFA . . . *Oh, my costumes from Italy . . . yes, she certainly has the body for the part.* She would do well enough.

Once resolved that Schenk would get the role, he struggled with the lost benefit of having Duckwitz, who was highly gifted and ready for professional theatre. The Director wasn't this student's advisor, but he'd have to talk with Duckwitz about his career plans.

The Director seesawed in his mind for a minute as he leaned back in his chair. He rose, walked the few steps to his open window, and let his mind go empty.

Outside, circular patches of light illuminated the grey turf, tree trunks, and walkways under the lamp posts. A breeze rustled the clinging leaves of a nearby beech. The library bells chimed half past 11:00. Damp odor rose from the soil. Next to the Director in the corner sat a barrel full of practice swords. He abruptly struck a solution. "A hit, a very palpable hit," he murmured, and he laughed at his ingenuity and deviousness. He would give Schenk the part of Macbeth, and build into the story a passionate love element between him and Lady Macbeth. The untested and cute Beth Telford would be Lady Macduff who was murdered along with her children by Macbeth; and Tommy Duckwitz . . . he would be Macduff, who, in revenge, killed the bloody Macbeth and cut off his head.

"There's justice for you," the Director said.

He scribbled the casting list under the department's letterhead; into his assistant's box in the outer room he tossed these notes— to be typed in the morning. He switched off the lights, strode from the office, slamming the door as if exiting the stage after a climactic scene.

The country is at the verge of a civil war. I am a member of an underground army dedicated to defending ourselves and overthrowing the government, which seeks to jail or kill us. My job takes me into the house of the leading General of the rulers. I am a busboy and dishwasher. I also have another job at a manufacturing plant because I do not make enough money at the General's house. The factory is a night job. The government plans to round up those it suspects of disloyalty, and at the plant many of us have been ordered to report to a certain room. They plan to flood the room with water and a toxic liquid to burn and drown us all. Commotion breaks out along one wall, and a door opens. We all scramble to escape, and once outside we scatter to hide. I run to the General's house and crawl into a tight space under the porch. I push dirt into a mound at the opening to prevent anyone from seeing me. Also, I pull a broken chair in front. A soldier looks into the hole, but sees nothing and goes away. Later, I fall asleep. When I awake, it is dark again. I move carefully through neighborhood alleyways for several miles until I reach the house where one of our leaders is hiding. At that time I have a pistol. Few of us have guns. We are not connected with the well-armed rebel militia groups.

I enter the house where our leader is engaged in earnest conversation about new developments. The house has cardboard taped up on the windows so that no light can be seen from outside. His plan is to raid the General's house and hold him hostage. I am a key to this operation because I have access to him, since the guards still think I am loyal. We must draw up maps so our people can move on foot secretly through the city to the target house. We must also clear trails through brushy areas. I can hear tanks rumbling nearby, coming this way. We all leave the house and disperse into the night.

-from the dream journal of Stan Timmons

Chapter Five
Worlds Meet

Friday was another miracle, weather-wise, full of shirtsleeve promise and hope. Tommy's hopes turned on whether or not he got the lead in *Macbeth*, but his blooming relationship with Beth filled him with a heady madness, and satisfaction from rescuing her from dangerous exposure to Schenk. He almost did not care what else the future might hold, as long as he would see her again. He was a newly wealthy man that no loss could injure.

When he dashed into the theater building in the afternoon to see the cast list posted outside the Director's office, Tommy suffered a letdown. He sat in a chair in the lobby to think it through. As his initial disappointment faded, it was as if he could interpret the Director's selections.

Knowing what I know, he thought, *I would have cast this play exactly so.* He was relieved because, really, he hated the play. But at least now he could act out the avenger against Schenk. Tommy was not surprised that Beth did not get the Lady Macbeth part, but he wondered what meaning there might be in her being Lady Macduff.

Tommy did not see Beth all day and the next, except once to wave across campus. They talked briefly on the phone about their parts. In the happiness of anticipating their Saturday evening date, Tommy could wait to be with her. While the previous few days had been sunny and uncommonly warm for January, a dense cloud cover crept overhead—rain and normal winter weather approached. With his dark jacket over his arm and sporting his best California shirt, Tommy arrived at Beth's dorm with enough time to catch the bus to the Performing Arts Center and be seated before the beginning of the concert. However, he found that Beth had not arrived at the dorm. In a few minutes she came running up the front stairs in a "muck of a sweat," as she said, from an exercise routine. Tommy paced back and forth in the dorm lobby—he only had one ticket—given to him by Stan Timmons—and he would need to wait in line to buy a student ticket.

He thought it ironic that a girl who was obsessed with time in racing and athletics would be lackadaisical when time really mattered. When Beth at last emerged from the elevator, she was gorgeous in a black evening dress with a knee high slit. She smelled delicious. Sensibly, at least, she had on flat soled shoes. But exasperating Tommy further, Beth had to return to her room for a coat, which made them later, and they hotfooted it to the bus, which dropped them in front of the auditorium. Tommy leaped off first and rushed to the line.

Beth caught up and stood next to him.

"Did you ask your Mindy if she would come to the mental hospital tomorrow?" he asked.

"I did. She's coming. Maybe to do me some good. She wants to meet you. She'll attend early church and we'll collect her at her parents' house and go to Stanley's. She's in for a surprise!"

Tommy shifted his weight from one leg to the other, expending nervous energy about the admission ticket. "Good. Good. I hope this matchmaking doesn't explode in our faces."

The line shortened quickly until Tommy was one back, and suddenly the ticket window slammed shut. He shoved around the person in front of him and rapped on the window. The woman inside shook her head and disappeared behind a curtain.

Tommy hacked his arm in the air and blurted, "Shite! Now what will we do?"

Beth had no idea.

"OK." He pushed back his hair and fished into his shirt pocket. "Here, you take my ticket and I'll sneak in. Hurry; the music starts in minutes."

Beth passed through the tall glass doors and Tommy followed a short distance. He saw from the watchfulness of the ticket takers that a direct assault wouldn't work.

Shit, he thought, snapping his fingers. He forgot to arrange to meet Beth and he did not know where her seat was. He shrugged his shoulders and walked around the building, methodically trying each door. They all were locked. He walked around the entire block and could find no way inside. Giving up, he sat down at the fountain in front of the center to wait until intermission. The fountain was a collection of waterfalls made from poured concrete.

Out of the lounging crowd there, he noticed few people whom he recognized. People drank beer, smoked marijuana, and played drums. He watched a professorial type try to pick up girls with the bluntest of lines. While repulsed by his coarseness and stupidity, Tommy was impressed with his audacity. Ten girls or so turned him down. There was a jeer, a shake of the head, a bluff slap, profanity, laughter, and a silent stare and a long middle finger among other signs of rejection, but after all this, one female and he walked away arm in arm.

Time passed slowly until intermission when cigarette-hungry concertgoers streamed into the night air. Looking straight ahead, Tommy walked into the building; no ticket-takers spoke to him. He spun up the spiral staircase to the first balcony. There was no use trying to find Beth in this crowd of several thousand. He leaned against a blue carpeted wall, kept his nose in the program, all the while watching. When the lights dimmed, Tommy headed for the empty box in the middle front of the balcony.

The best seat in the house and a whole box to himself! So much for a sell-out.

He fingered the brass plaque on the railing, and looked over the grey heads below, in case he could pick out Beth. The musicians tuned their instruments, and shortly afterward, the audience applauded as the conductor took the podium. Tommy leaned back, put his feet up on the rail, took them down because they were too conspicuous, picked up a white spot at the edge of his vision, and turned to see a man with a goatee glaring at him over the short wall from the neighboring box. The man was alone.

"You're not a van Fleet!" Tommy said, sitting up.

The man seemed confused by hearing the exact words he had formulated. "Wait. You don't belong there," he said.

With the music beginning, the man started up and went to an usher. The usher and he bent their heads together while they looked in Tommy's direction. Tommy tried to listen to the music, tried to ignore the irritation behind him. Apparently, the usher convinced the man that it was not worth creating a scene, and Tommy's opponent returned to his box—the far side of it—huffing. Tommy crossed his arms over his chest, sat back, closed his eyes, and let the music carry him away to his favorite daydream—riding the oceans in an unsinkable wooden vessel under towering white sails.

Sometime later he felt someone squeeze his arm and he opened his eyes to find Beth sitting beside him. The music still played. Tommy must have dozed off in his sailing ship.

Beth whispered, "I saw your feet."

He avoided looking across to his irritable neighbor. Beth and Tommy snuggled together for the remainder of the final piece, and the concertgoers stood and applauded. Some cheered, and the lights came up. People began filing from the auditorium. Tommy again noticed the white spot in his peripheral vision, and he turned his head to the goaty neighbor standing on the other side of the low wall.

Gone was the anger, but now he smirked. "You're lucky to not have been thrown out tonight," the man said. He turned his eyes to gawk at Beth up and down. "You and your heifer."

Tommy felt a spurt of blood flood his brain. He vaulted the wall and landed deftly in a clear space between the moveable chairs. The man had stepped back a pace, but now he stood his ground. His knees were bent and Tommy saw a blacked steel blade in his hand. Tommy had intended only to intimidate the man, but seeing the threat, he reflexively kicked him in his wrist as he heard Beth cry, "Tommy! No!" The blade found Tommy's flesh. The man let loose of the knife as it twisted from his grip by the downward force of Tommy's leg, and restrained by another cry from Beth, Tommy stopped from throwing the man from the balcony. Only in his imagination did he see the man hurtling down to the seats below. The man grabbed his coat and trotted up the steps toward an exit. Tommy picked up the knife, unlocked the blade and put it in his pocket. Concertgoers above waiting to file down the stairs who noticed the brief upheaval turned their heads away. Tommy sat down, pulled up his pant leg and inspected the wound. It was not bleeding profusely—a good sign—but he would need stitches. Beth found a small roll of purple duct tape and a bandanna in her pack, and he made an impromptu bandage around his calf.

The usher came by and asked, "Is everything all right?" Beth tilted her head sweetly and assured him it was.

The usher moved on. With haste and difficulty, and Tommy hanging on to Beth, they left the concert hall, caught a taxi to Tommy's apartment, and climbed the stairs. He flung himself on the bed and said, "Call the third number down on the list near the phone—on the table. Ask for Franklin. Get him to bring his medical kit."

"Who's Franklin? A college student?"

"No, Franklin is not a college student. Just call him."

Beth made the call and Franklin had asked no questions.

While they waited, Beth wandered around the room. She picked up a soft porn magazine and began leafing through.

"My roommate's," Tommy said, frowning. "I cleaned the room, but—"

"Uh huh." Beth seemed engrossed or unbelieving, and then she clucked her tongue and tossed the magazine on the floor. "Boring. I see that everyday."

Franklin lived upstairs; he charged into the room carrying a black case. He examined, cleaned, and sewed up Tommy's wound, while Tommy told him the story.

When Franklin had finished the bandage, Tommy said, "Thanks, buddy. It's good to have friends."

"You're, you're welcome," Franklin stammered. "Certain kinds of friends, you me-mean. Who's this guy that cut you? Why dih-did he pull a knife? You-you, didn't threaten him."

Tommy rolled toward Beth who sat in a nearby chair. "Franklin's only awkward when he's polite." To Franklin he answered, "I aim to find out who he is."

Franklin reached with his hand. "Leh-let me see the blade."

Tommy slid the knife from his pocket, inspected it under the light, and then gave it to Franklin.

"Expensive," Franklin said. "There's gold. Eight or nine hundred bucks, wholesale. Engraving." He bent closer to see the etched lines. "Says, 'To Dr. Mark Ponder, in recognition of your noble work.' Uh, do you wa-want to sell it?"

Beth picked up the phone book and began leafing through the yellow pages. It took a minute before she said, "No Mark Ponders here."

"I'll find him." Tommy propped up a pillow, slowly lifted his leg onto the bed and settled back.

"Are you going to call the police?" Beth asked.

"What for? I stay far away from the police."

"You're smart." This was Franklin. "Check him out online."

"There's one thing," Tommy said. "I need to train to defend against knife attacks. I want moves. I don't like being stabbed."

"When your leg heals, seh-set an appointment and we can train upstairs, in my gym-gymnasium."

"Change of subject." Tommy signaled toward the far corner. "I have some fancy blades of my own. Under the cabinet there is a case. Bring it over. Careful, it's heavy."

Franklin slid the long wooden case out from under the metal storage cabinet, and brought it to the dining table at the foot of Tommy's bed. The box was aged, but did not have scratches or gouges. Beth came nearer. Franklin flicked the brass latches and lifted the top. He removed the velvet blanket, and underneath rested two matching swords.

"Take one," Tommy said excitedly, as he sat up.

Franklin lifted one of the swords and felt an edge. "It's not sharp."

"Not yet."

Franklin waved it around. "Where did you find these? They're proper. They're beautiful."

"My father gave them to me for my eighteenth birthday. His father made the case. The swords are replicas from one of his—our—Scottish ancestors. Don't look at me that way. My face came from my Roman mother. They are real combat weapons from an antique armory in Texas."

Beth took out the other sword. "Look at the fancy metalwork. These would be incredible in *Macbeth*."

"Over four and a half pounds each. I might loan them to the play as props, for ornamentation in Macbeth's mansion. They'd have to be insured."

Franklin kept waving the sword pensively.

"Go ahead, put them away now," Tommy said.

"Can-can you fight with them?"

"Yeah. Trade broadsword lessons for knife-fighting lessons?"

Franklin leaned back, frowning. "I'll show you-you defensive moves for free. I'll move this junk out of the way. Since you're injured, Beth wih-will be the attacker." He went to a kitchenette drawer and removed a butter knife.

Tommy fell back against his pillow. Beth returned to the chair, and the room was silent except for traffic noise from outside.

Franklin stopped in the middle of the floor. "OK. I got it. I'm leaving. Uh, may-may I take a beer?"

"Why not?" Tommy said as a stab at hospitality. "Beth, do you like beer?"

"A bit."

Franklin took a bottle from the fridge and left its door open for Beth. He tossed the bottle cap toward a trash basket. "You beh-better find crutches for the next few days. Your leg will take five days to knit. Longer." No one spoke for a few seconds, and Franklin cleared his throat. "Oh. Talk to you later. Uh . . . if you nee-need anything . . . you know where to reach me." He exited the room, gently closing the door.

Beth skipped across the floor to the refrigerator and removed a beer.

"You'll find mugs in the freezer," Tommy said.

She removed the cap and poured down the inside of a mug, but too fast. Foam overflowed onto the counter. She gave the mug to Tommy, set the bottle on the bedside table, walked to the door, threw the deadbolt, and turned and asked, "Do you have roommates?"

"Ah . . . yes. Are you staying?"

Beth smiled, nodded. "What will your roommates do? I mean, where will they stay?"

Tommy laughed and said, "They'll survive. I told them I needed the room, just in case."

"I see," she said, exaggerating a difference in pitch between the words.

Beth sat on the bed close beside Tommy and picked up the bottle, which showed only a mouthful in the bottom. She twirled the beer and said, "It's all I want. I'm in perpetual training, remember? Soccer?"

Tommy reached to the bedside table and picked up a remote control. Light dimmed to a faint glow, and he said, "Perfect."

Clouds thickened and lowered in the night. Rain began to fall slowly, and then fell heavily—pure distillations of the Pacific Ocean descending upon saints and sinners alike; the wet winds swept into every unprotected corner. Long before daylight, the door rattled and there was a discreet knock from the outside. No one answered from within.

In the grey light later in the morning, when Tommy and Beth left, there was a person curled up in a sleeping bag on the hallway floor. Tommy leaned up closely to Beth and breathed in her ear, "My roommate. He keeps his camping stuff in his car." Holding on to each other, they hobbled down to meet the cab they had called to take them to Beth's dorm and car.

When Tommy, Beth, and Mindy arrived at Stan's doorstep an hour later, Stan was dumbfounded. It was not because he thought Sarah might feel that a crowd was invading her privacy, but that Mindy was attractive in every way he could have envisioned. He loved her softly tanned complexion, rosy tinted at her cheeks. He well remembered seeing her on campus when he had been a student, and her image fed his daydreams about a wife, though he had never worked up the courage to speak to her.

While the girls waited on the front porch, and as Stan scrounged in a storage room for an old set of crutches, Tommy leaned against a door frame and said, "She's probably a virgin. Your type, exactly. Clean, pure, faultless."

But Stan's own discernment already told him this. She was what he thought did not exist in real life. Her appearance reminded him of a maiden princess from a Grimm's fairy tale, misplaced in this 21st century. Her humble but confident manner might have put him at ease, but from the moment he shook her warm, strong hand, he knew that he wanted to marry her.

In the back of Stan's car, Tommy and Beth sat cemented to each other. Because of his leg, Tommy would have preferred to cancel the venture. And since last night, Tommy's emptiness had been filled by an ecstatic focus upon the young woman next to him; he was impatient for when they could be alone again. But the amusing plan of introducing Mindy and Stan would make the day worthwhile. He and Beth sniggered, trying to hide their glee in watching the awkward scene in the front seat.

Mindy was calmly aware of the happenings around her. She consulted the map, noted the mileage and exit signs through the rain-jeweled windshield, and conversed with the two in the back; other than driving, Stan functioned solely in the world he and Mindy occupied. It was like a Sunday afternoon chess game between personalities of opposite types. Stan spent every second plotting his next moves. Mindy paid no attention to the game except when it was her turn, and then she looked at the board for a few seconds. By the time they reached the hospital, the sky brightened and they could see the outlines of fractured clouds. By then Stan and Mindy knew each other's tastes in music, the best radio stations, favorite movies, their ideas on race relations, theological leanings, and such things that people share with passing acquaintances.

Stan drove up to the security gate at Steilacoom. The guard smiled and waved them through. Stan's car was unforgettable, and the guard had recognized it from previous visits. The grounds and buildings formed a pleasant picture with spires and cupolas, tall trees, fountains and courtyards, and crocuses breaking through the turf. There were tennis and basketball courts, but not many people outside. Those tramping along the sidewalks and carrying folded umbrellas possessed the self-assured countenances common to college professors and other educated people.

Stan parked near the building where Sarah stayed. "I'm not sure I want people mobbing my sister."

"I can wait in the car." Mindy said.

"I have to go to the bathroom." Beth announced and opened the door.

"We're going for a stroll to find a lady's room," Tommy said, smirking. "We'll see you in, how long?"

"One hour," Stan said.

Beth, and Tommy with crutches, retreated before anyone could say more.

"Well, it looks like we're together," Stan said to Mindy without looking at her, "Will you come in? Or, you can wait here and study, if you like."

"I'll come in," she answered cheerfully, resigned to being set up with Stan by Beth, and determined to make the best of this visit to the hospital.

They checked with the front desk and climbed two echoing flights of stairs. The interior smelled flowery. Stan was glad that they did not use pine disinfectant, which always reminded him of the ammoniated urine it was intended to mask. The handrail shone dark—a rich, polished oak. Above each landing, set in the brick of the outside wall, hung an intricate stained-glass window with a bright angel as the focal point.

The inside of the building teemed with people. At the third floor, the stairs opened at the end of a hall, and on the left was a large common room where a television flickered, and women sat alone or in pairs. Away from the TV and near the windows, residents engaged in a painting class. Most were copying photographs from books or postcards.

Stan turned to Mindy. "Is it OK if you wait here? I want to find out if Sarah will see a stranger."

"Sure, that's fine."

Stan was amazed with how serene she appeared, and he hurried down the hall toward Sarah's room. He slacked his pace to absorb the behavior of a woman coming in his direction. Wearing a flimsy nightgown, she shuffled staccato-fashion along the floor in slippers. With lips pursed, she breathed in and out noisily. A stream of dribble worked down her chin. Both her hands pushed tightly across her protruding belly. Her eyes exhibited no human qualities; she glared at the world without recognizing anything. Stan passed her warily, and she turned to follow him, blowing in and out. He resisted running. Arriving at Sarah's door, which was ajar, he knocked softly. He heard a weak, "Come in," and entered. The steam engine—as Stan uncharitably thought of her—pivoted and resumed shuffling toward the common room.

Stan found Sarah sitting in a rocker and looking toward the window. She turned toward him and rose. He hugged her and she shuddered under his arms, then removed herself and slowly walked to her bed and sat down. Stan could not understand how, after these many weeks, she still could be crying.

"This is my new roommate." She motioned with the back of her wrist across the room. On the other bed lay a figure wearing a pink dress, with her face to the wall. "She's undergoing electro-shock therapy."

"I didn't know they still did that. How barbaric!"

"It helps relieve their depression. I wonder if I should try it."

" . . . How's the baby, Sarah?"

She put her hand over her womb and said nothing. She was three months along and not showing.

Stan sat down. "Oh Sarah, why don't you come home? You don't belong here. I know it's hard, and Mom and Dad are not sensitive enough to you, but we want you to be closer. You could help Mom in the garden and cut firewood. You wouldn't have to go anyplace or see anybody. What's here for you?"

"I can't cut firewood while I'm pregnant," Sarah said, her voice flat.

Stan glanced around the room, and his eye fell upon the painting on an easel. "This is yours, right?"

Sarah nodded. The scene was the view outside Sarah's window, but she had painted an iron grid over it all. Through the lattice, the nearby trees were symmetrical and trimmed with white and gold. A fictional road climbed hills to the horizon that was lined with a military tree-front ready to advance. Those trees were veiled in gunpowder-grey smoke, and set against clouds boiling into the stratosphere.

"How beautiful. And powerful." Stan stood up to have a closer look and bumped the other bed frame. The bedbound figure did not stir. "This is nice. But you *can* come home. You'll be safe there, I promise. Tommy and I will keep Tal—"

"Don't say *any*thing!" Sarah said, fiercely hissing. "He held me down and raped me!"

Scanning the room in frustration, he said, "Sarah, where are the flowers I sent you the other day?"

Sarah rose and made her way to the window. Stan moved to stand beside her and looked outside. Below them were two women: one an older lady sitting on the bench, crocheting; the other, an athletic figure who made contorted faces as she set up and shot baskets.

"See the girl dribbling the ball? She ate the flowers."

"Noo!" Stan said, sliding his voice from a high pitch to a lower. "She *ate* them?"

"Yeah, stems and all. Last weekend she broke into a freezer and ate two packs of fish sticks."

"That's disgusting. Can't they control the patients better?"

"She isn't a patient."

"What? Then what is she? She should be a patient."

"She's a visitor. Her mother's a patient. The woman knitting."

Stan held his nose, laughing into his hand. He closed his eyes while jagged bursts of air escaped his rocking body.

Sarah smiled.

"The visitor ate the flowers?" Stan said, his voice higher pitched with suppressed chortle. "I wonder what they have for an Easter feast with the whole family? I could see them at a funeral. They would decimate the memorials. In lieu of food, send flowers!"

Sarah said nothing but still smiled.

Stan said, more soberly now, "Sarah, there's someone here I want you to meet—" Her smile disappeared and her eyes darkened. "No, it's not some man. It's a girl."

"Really, Stan?" Sarah brightened, taking interest.

"Yes, you won't believe this, but she's the most beautiful girl I've ever met."

"Is she your girlfriend, Stanley? I want to see her." Sarah began straightening a pile of magazines. "Go and get her, Stan. Where is she waiting?"

"No, she isn't my girlfriend. I just met her. But, I'll be right back."

Steam Engine was not puffing along the floor. Relieved, Stan went down the hall. His gaze roved over the common room, and he could not find Mindy. He was about to leave to see if she had joined Tommy and Beth, when he realized she must have gone to the bathroom, so he decided to wait. He spotted an empty chair in the corner, just beyond two residents on a couch facing away from him. When he moved around them and glanced at their faces, to his astonishment the residents changed into the blonde-braided Mindy sitting next to Steam Engine and holding her hand. The disturbed woman's eyes closed and opened like a relaxed cat's, and she breathed normally. She wore a smile at the corners of her mouth.

"Oh, there you are," Stan said quietly, shaking off the optical illusion, and afraid to stoke up Steam Engine.

Mindy stood up, bent over and kissed her on the head. "Goodbye, Esther. I love you, sweetie. Remember, we'll pray for each other."

Stan and Mindy strolled toward Sarah's room.

"In the summers in high school," Mindy said, "I worked at a camp for handicapped people. It was on a river near Mt. Hood at a former labor camp. We had all kinds of disabilities."

They stopped outside Sarah's door. Esther had followed them without making the bizarre sounds. Stan did not address the subject of her unwanted presence, but said to Mindy, "Talk Sarah into coming home with us today, OK?"

"I don't know. Let me just feel this out."

"OK."

Stan entered the room with Mindy following him. Esther came in behind them and sat on the roommate's bed.

"Sarah, this is Mindy. Mindy . . . Sterne."

Sarah held out her hand to Mindy. Without saying a word Mindy gave Sarah a hug. When the girls stepped apart, Stan saw Mindy's eyes and they were wet. A heavy tear dropped from each cheek to the floor.

Mindy looked up at Stan and said softly, "May we have some time alone, Stan?"

Stan glanced at Sarah, who nodded that it was all right with her. He left, leaving the door ajar, and went to locate the two who had arranged all this. Esther had remained, making no noise at all.

It took Stan a few minutes to find Beth and Tommy around the corner of the building. Sitting on a bench, Beth was bursting with giggles and spasmodically shifting on her seat. The crutches leaned against a tree. Stan stared down toward the road. Near a parked bus stood a conglomerate of people. They were, as Sarah told Stan later, Midwestern aficionados of Kirkbride architecture*, which had been popular for asylums in the late 1800's. The group was touring the country to see Kirkbride structures remaining in existence. For the moment they were otherwise occupied, because Tommy—his colorful shirt inside out, pants rolled up over his knees showing the bandage, and tennis shoes tied around his neck by the laces—was entertaining them. Tommy had found a little bell, and he walked under the trees and rang it incessantly, looking up. His jaw hung loose and his eyes bore a queer, cross-eyed cast, and his gait was so lurching that Stan almost could not recognize him. He wondered if he should have his eyeglasses checked. While Stan observed dumbstruck, Tommy coaxed two women from the group into joining him. They looked into the trees and called, "Kitty, Kitty." Meanwhile, the group leader was calling the women back so they could continue the tour. The majority of the tour members clustered before the bus and watched with fascination, refusing to load.

The bus driver yelled up to the women, "Ladies, ladies, he's lost his mind. Come along, now!"

On stubby legs that chopped up and down as if they had not been much used for their given purpose, the driver started up the incline toward the trees. Tommy dropped the bell, screamed, and raced away barefooted, hopping off his hurt leg, behind the next building.

Beth at last mastered her hilarity and Stan plopped down on the bench. A hospital security team arrived on a green golf cart and in a minute it sped in the direction Tommy had run, and when it disappeared, Tommy sauntered up, dressed and in his right mind, as if nothing had happened.

"Are we ready to leave so soon?" he said, hands in pockets and bouncing his head jauntily.

Stan muttered, "Oh, you're staying."

Beth heard this and began her hysterics again, interjecting, "Bravo, Bravo!"

"You were supposed to stay off of your leg," Stan said. "You probably tore your stitches. Is it bleeding?"

Tommy pulled up his pant leg, stuck his finger under the bandage and said, popping his p, "Nope."

Stan sighed, heaving his chest. "A miracle, Tommy." Without waiting for a meaningless answer, he continued. "Mindy is trying to talk Sarah into coming home with us. She's afraid to leave. She's lonely and the people are weird, but she feels safe here. I don't like this place."

Neither Beth nor Tommy heard Stan because they were standing together, breathing each other's breath, and ignoring heaven and earth. Stan smothered in his own thoughts. When sufficient time had passed for Mindy and Sarah to talk, he shrugged and said, "Let's go." He trudged up behind Sarah's building. Beth, and Tommy again on crutches, followed. When the Chevrolet came into view, Stan found Sarah sitting in the passenger seat and Mindy lugging suitcases from the building. Stan held back his curiosity long enough to unlock the trunk and help load the suitcases, and he stood as close to Mindy as he dared, to ask, "How did you convince her?"

Mindy moved closer, and Stan's heart pounded when she put her hands around his arm, leaned in toward him, and whispered toward his ear, "She'll live with me and my family."

With Mindy's feminine presence so near—too near—Stan entirely missed what she had said.

Mindy stepped back, smiled, and said, "Sarah is coming to live with me at my parents' home."

On the return trip to Vancouver, Stan and Sarah talked about his teaching work. In the back seat, Mindy concentrated on a text book. Beth also studied. Tommy's leg began to ooze blood—he could feel cold wetness dripping into his shoe—but it stopped after a half-hour.

Sarah seemed encouraged about living with the Sternes. "Dr. Sterne might see me through the pregnancy and deliver the baby when the time comes." Sarah also chatted about the Sterne children—what she had heard about their projects and personalities—and relished the prospect of being amongst them.

When they arrived at Stan's house, Sarah began to doubt that the Sternes really would welcome her and asked Mindy, "Will you call your parents to be sure?"

The battery on Mindy's phone was dead, and Beth, standing a little away from the Chevrolet, was using her phone, so Stan volunteered his home phone.

Tommy limped to Beth's car while Mindy ducked inside the house. Stan hovered near her, and from the front porch he heard her ask Mrs. Sterne to prepare a bed for Sarah. After the call, Stan followed Mindy down the porch steps, and when the two of them approached the curb, the nearby traffic noise dimmed, and the whole world stopped to listen as he blurted, "Uh, Mindy, will you see a move, movie with me next weekend?"

Mindy did not answer. Instead, she leaned into Stan's Chevy where Sarah sat alone, and said, "My mother would love to have you. There'll be a nice, private room waiting when we arrive."

"Thank you very much," Sarah said softly.

Mindy now walked away a few steps with Stan trailing behind. There was only shadow-laced illumination from the street light.

"I'm sorry," she said, "You asked me to a movie?"

"Yeah. I wondered if you would go to, with me to 'Clouds Fall to Earth.' It's about a people who have lived in dirigibles for a thousand years. The sound track is supposed to be incredible."

"No thank you, Stan, because I don't date. It sounds like a remarkable story, though."

Mindy put out her warm, dry hand for him to shake. "Please don't take it personally," she said. "I'm glad I met you. It was an enjoyable day, and I liked riding in your car. I'm sure Sarah will let you know how she's getting on. She may need some of her things brought to our house and possibly I'll see you again."

Stan and Mindy transferred Sarah's luggage into Beth's car. Beth had started the engine and was ready to go. Mindy climbed into the back seat, and Stan closed the door for her. Everyone exchanged "Good Nights" with Stan. They pulled away and from the front passenger's side, Tommy grinned at the shock hanging all over Stan's face, raised his eyebrows, and winked. Stan read Tommy's mouthed words, "Well done, man!"

Stan shook his head and dragged his feet onto the porch. Before he touched the doorknob, he stopped and wheeled around, exclaiming, "Why didn't *I* drive Sarah and Mindy?"

But it was too late. Beth's car and the enchanting, illusive person it carried were gone.

*Footnote to Chapter Five:

Dr. Kirkbride's progressive therapies and innovative writings on hospital design and management became known as the "Kirkbride Plan," which influenced, in one form or another, almost every American state hospital by the turn of the century. Dr. Kirkbride created a humane and compassionate environment for his patients, and he believed that [a] beautiful setting... restored patients to a more natural balance of the senses.

- *from* the Pennsylvania Hospital Newsletter of the Friends of the Hospital.

Dr. Kirkbride spoke of his plan as linear. Buildings were arranged en échelons. *The center building was more imposing than the others and had a dome, in agreement with the classical tastes of the time. From the center building, used for administration offices, extended wings right and left for patients. From the ends of the wings short cross sections dropped back to connect with more buildings, for patients, which were parallel to the original wings. Each ward was enough out of line so that fresh air could reach it from all four sides and it was not under observation from the other wards.*

- *from* Dr. Kirkbride and his Mental Hospital, *by Earl D. Bond, 1947.*

A creature is in the back yard of our old house—I guess it's a rat. It scampers up an old wooden bookshelf that leans against the shed. It's a plump rat with short hair and round transparent ears. I pick up a sharp stick, and the rat jumps down and scuttles under a pile of smashed cardboard boxes. I see the rat at the edge of the boxes and I jab hard with the stick, impaling the rat. The stick's tip passed through the animal's body and bumped into the wall behind it with a thunk, but the rat is not killed. I look around for another instrument and find a garden hoe. With the hoe I push aside the boxes and start chopping at the rat, but it isn't a rat anymore, it's a kitten. I chop and chop, but the kitten doesn't die. All of a sudden I feel really bad about killing the kitten. He was cute with a soft coat like a rabbit's, and now he is a bloody mess. I should stop and try to nurse it back to life, but it is so badly hurt it might not survive. I decide to finish killing it. Then I woke up.

-from the dream journal of Stan Timmons

Chapter Six
The Play

Talus Schenk was ambitious. He believed in rewarding his friends, punishing his enemies—which included anyone who insulted him—and when possible, eradicating all obstacles.

Schenk gloated over his masterful sabotage of Tommy's chances with the Macbeth part, and cursed Tommy's achievement in robbing the luscious Beth Telford, and percolated ideas of how to punish Tommy, but he had no designs on revenging the incursion made upon him by Stan Timmons. Schenk guessed Timmons early, because it was simple to scan for Sarah's relatives in University information resources—and there was an internet yearbook. He knew where Stan lived and where he worked as a benign high school teacher. It was Stan's sister Sarah who could create for him pressing problems, and for her he had developed a plan.

Sarah had not aborted, and had insisted she would not prosecute for rape, nor would she seek patrimony. She adamantly said she wanted nothing from him, ever. But Schenk did not trust her; she might change her mind and sue for child support, and he constantly fretted about this. To protect himself against the possibility that she might not keep her word he had hired someone in the medical community to steal the newborn baby. With this arrangement, not only would he avoid years of financial obligations, but he could turn a decent profit. His helper said the baby would bring $60,000 from a couple who could not have children of their own. Minus the commission to the helper, the money would give Schenk a living while he broke into theatre in New York or into film. Or, he might attend a better school and earn his MFA.

This helper was Dr. Mark Ponder, whom he had met the previous spring when Schenk brought him a client. Schenk had been careful, but this girl must have been particularly fertile because she conceived, and afterwards convinced him he was the responsible gentleman. He argued, but she insisted it could be no one else. The ad for Ponder's Vancouver clinic had been the largest in the Portland yellow pages, and it occurred to Schenk that traveling across the river to another town and state would afford better privacy. The girl concurred and they made the appointment for the following Saturday morning.

Schenk had not gone inside the building with her, but stood on the front porch. The security guard rocked back and forth on his heels, swinging his arms, tapping his hands together.

Schenk nodded to him. "How ya doin'?"

"Just great. Just great. How about you?"

"Oh, you know."

"Yeah. Tough, huh?" The guard raised his lower lip in a sympathetic frown, then popped his neck with a head jerk.

Just then a man and a woman who had been waiting in their car walked up the steps, shadowed by an escort wearing an orange vest.

"OK," the guard said loudly, "you'll need your ID. No weapons. Please step inside."

The guard and the couple went in the door and Schenk watched through the window as the guard searched the girl's bag and waved a metal detector up and down their bodies. The guard quickly stepped outside, picked up a clipboard, and made a checkmark.

Schenk leaned on the brick wall shielding the ramp going up to the front door. "Have you been doing this long?" he asked.

"Oh, yeah. Couple years."

"Does it take much training?"

"Not much. Basic weapons. I've learned a lot on the job. Women ask you questions when they're waiting. They need to feel safe. Yeah, I know a lot about this business. I have to."

"Like, safe from them?" He tilted his head sideways toward the protestors who loitered on the sidewalk.

"Oh yeah."

"The guy with the black beard, camouflage cap, and boots?"

The guard laughed. "Don't worry. We know them all. They won't try anything. We stop most of their crap with the fence and cameras. If they get too frisky, we just call for a police officer to park nearby."

"What about that dead fetus picture?"

"It's fake." The guard looked at his watch and said, "Probably everyone's here that's coming. I need to walk around and check on things."

"Can I come with you?"

"Why not?"

The guard toured Schenk around the building. "Note the bubble lenses mounted on all four roof corners. Remote controlled gate. Hidden cameras under the eaves. Motion activated alarms for afterhours. We've got bullet proof glass."

"What about land mines?"

The guard laughed.

A protestor yelled in a jarring voice, "How can you laugh when babies are being butchered? How can you laugh? How?"

Schenk had jerked his head to look down to the sidewalk.

The guard smiled and began swinging his arms again. "Those people put on a show of compassion," he said. "They look innocent and make the police believe it, but they're devious. They have friends we don't see—the dangerous ones who carry out their dirty work. We've seen it all. Yeah. Three weeks ago someone locked our gates to the posts and it took an hour to find a bolt cutter big enough. We've had acid attacks, bomb threats, and envelopes of white powder. Except nobody's been killed. There's a funny side, too. Tubby men like that guy who bellow about Jesus and the women who squat in the bushes when they think no one sees."

"I believe it."

"Think you could do this work?" the guard said.

"Guard work?"

"Yeah. This place."

"Of course. Why?"

"Can you pass a background check?"

"Of course I can."

"Hmmm. I need a substitute for next weekend. You'd be paid $259. Five hours work."

"That much?"

"Yeah. What about it?"

"It's tempting." Schenk looked down at the protestors.

"Don't worry about them. You're a big guy."

"But, I don't think I could learn the job by then."

"Yeah you can. I'll train you while you wait for your lady. You've already got a start. There might be other days I need someone, too. Weekdays. In the future."

"Well, I'm free next Saturday. OK, I accept the position."

Filling in once or twice a month became a financial boon. Not only this, but Schenk had a lot of fun. Many of the girls were withdrawn and scared, some hard and angry, but a few bounced in saucy and sexy—the voyeurism tantalized him. When the need arose, he took it upon himself to advise patients on intimate details, such as how far along they were, or the symptoms of pregnancy.

One day in the fall of his senior year Schenk received a call from Ponder himself.

"Yes, Talus. I need you to come in this Wednesday."

"Ah, Dr. Ponder, I can't. I have a . . . I have something."

"Well. I've heard good reports about your work for me and I want you to be my regular security guard."

"Really? What happened to Neil?"

"He quit."

"What happened? Did the anti-choicers get to him?"

"It's nothing to worry about. I need your help, Talus. I'll pay what you're getting for substituting. More than Neil got."

"Excellent. But I need to know all the risks of this job. What happened to Neil?"

"Alright!" Ponder blurted. "I suppose you'll hear it anyway! Last Saturday when Neil left home to drive to the clinic, he heard clacking under his car. He had backed over square-headed roofing nails that someone had placed behind his tires."

Schenk stated the obvious. "The protesters found where he lived."

"Yes. It wouldn't have been so bad except for what happened afterward. When he pulled a nail out, the air hissed madly and he stuck it back into the hole and drove to a service station. By the time he had the tires repaired, he was an hour late. The protestors had extra time to harass the patients, who were rattled, which made the whole day tense. The worst was when a woman began blubbering, after her boyfriend demanded his money back. We called the police."

"So, Neil quit over that?"

"He didn't want to move to a new apartment. I told him we couldn't have him late anymore."

"So, you fired him?"

"You could say that."

"Too bad. But good for me."

"You can work every weekend now and whenever else you're available. How's your class load this year?"

"Pretty light."

"Can you come in on Wednesday?"

"I think so."

Schenk found the atmosphere exhilarating, and he reveled in the knowledge that he was performing important work for a good cause. His duties included meeting Dr. Ponder at his car in the staff parking lot when Ponder arrived, and walking him into the back entrance. It was only a few steps, but as the former guard had explained, "You're being paid to stop a bullet, or a baseball bat, or whatever might come for the doctor." The clinic supplied Schenk with body armor.

The relationship between Schenk and Ponder had grown. Once he began to feel comfortable, Schenk became loquacious, and Ponder had warmed to his robust, edgy greetings. When Ponder learned Schenk was in theatre, being an art and music patron himself, the doctor took interest in the promising student. They began meeting for breakfast, and each sensed in the other a kindred spirit. Ponder invited Schenk home for dinner once and introduced him to his young wife, Barbara. Schenk found her intriguing. Ponder noticed Barbara's flirtatious responses, and because he did not object, said nothing. In tending their budding acquaintance, Schenk and Ponder understood the other's nature and how far he could be trusted.

While they had not worked up the details of how to take Sarah's child, Schenk had prepared the ground with Ponder. Ponder said he had done this before, "providing children to loving families," and Schenk comforted himself by knowing that he was taking responsibility for his progeny. As the idea of kidnapping became fixed, any issue of child support became irrelevant. Schenk laughed at the reversal: he, the stud dog, would be paid for sporting a pup, instead of the bitch.

Schenk thought it best to leave Sarah and her brother Stan alone in the meanwhile, as to not arouse suspicion.

As far as the clown was concerned, Schenk squelched his desire for further retribution. Schenk had no immediate designs on Tommy, now that he, Schenk, had received the role of Macbeth. Of lesser importance was Tommy interfering with Schenk's now forgone female quest, Beth Telford. He was annoyed with her, but not angry—there were other women to conquer. He did not resent women who got away as much as the men who got *in* the way. Only the defeat galled him.

When Talus Schenk was alone in his room, he mulled all this over and it made perfect sense.

+   +   +

The weather lost its balmy flush and resumed a clammy progress toward spring. The extravagant days of the Northwest's tropical daring slid into a timid swamp of February. Busy preparing lesson plans for each day, Stan monitored Sarah from afar. She had settled in well with the Sternes, but her relationship did not provide the expected openings for Stan to see Mindy. One afternoon he got directions to the Sternes' Vancouver residence and brought items that Sarah had requested from their parents' place. The Sterne house overlooked the Columbia River from a neighborhood of expensive homes.

"House," Sarah had called it. *It's more of a concealed, understated castle,* Stan thought.

A castle taking up a quarter block, and surrounded by arched walls, an iron fence with severe spikes, and a solid fire-thorn hedge. From the sidewalk, Stan could not make out the form of the house, because it was set back amid stairways, trees, and decks. Stan picked a likely entrance, on the side rather than the formal entry at the crescent driveway.

A child answered the door, saying, "Neither Sarah or Mindy are home." Stan set the box and an armload of dresses inside and did not linger.

A few days later, he picked up Sarah at the Sterne residence to take her to his parents' house for Sunday dinner. Their parents strayed away from any subject touching Sarah's "unfortunate situation." Sarah seemed morose and did not talk about her experiences living at the Sterne home until late in the evening on the way back. Discussing this, her personality changed.

"Stan, it's Heaven! I've never been in such a place. The harmony and peace is overwhelming. They have such love for one another. With so many children around, fun happens all the time. There *are* small conflicts and arguments and noise, but where else but in Heaven would such things do no harm?"

"What about Dr. Sterne? Is he helping you?"

Sarah paused to consider. "Um. I'm not exactly counseling with him, but he and I and Mrs. Sterne talk in the evenings when he's home. I've learned so much about myself, and about God, and I'm seeing how to accept and offer forgiveness. I'm provided for, and I can begin to release what's keeping me from happiness. With the children especially I'm learning to give and be appreciated."

"Do you like Mindy? Tell me about her."

"Mindy is busy, but loves being at home. I like her a lot. I wouldn't say I'm her best friend, but she's mine right now. She is reserved, but she's thoughtful and brings me presents, like perfumed soap, or pistachios. When I feel like facing people, we go out on weekends. She'll drive me anywhere I want, but not to checkups with the midwife, because they're during a weekday."

Sarah stopped speaking momentarily and then said, as if musing to herself, "I believe I should have a C-section." Resuming her happy narrative, she said, "We went grocery shopping for the family last Saturday, and once we went to a dance at the Mollicoat Estate."

"Dance?" he asked. "What kind of dance?"

"Not exactly a square dance, but formal and elegant; we wore long dresses, and the music . . . Mindy said it was traditional English. A violin, a guitar, and accordion, and flute. Think of Jane Austin—*Pride and Prejudice*. It was so much fun. It was a potluck, and the room was decorated with banners and candles, and full of people—most our age. Parents and the children dance, too. I didn't, but I might at the next one."

"When will that be?" Stan asked with a vague hope that had more in it of hopelessness.

"Oh Stan, I didn't think. You like Mindy, don't you? And you're jealous because I see her. Why don't you come to the dance? I'm sure you would be welcome as my brother. I invite you. It's a Valentine's Party."

"I don't know how to dance. Not square dancing."

"The dances are easy, most of them, and the caller teaches them."

Stan cheered up. This looked as if he might see Mindy. In the week before the Valentine's dance, he took satisfaction in the pleasures of daily life. In the evenings, he listened to classical music on the radio while reading and grading papers; and most nights he fell asleep on the couch, only arousing himself after midnight to brush his teeth and change into pajamas. He immersed himself in work.

When the dance date arrived, Stan dressed in his best suit and picked up Sarah at the Sterne house. Mindy was already at the Mollicoat Estate, decorating. At the event, Stan stood back, uncomfortable, watching the proceedings, which were like nothing he had ever seen before. It was a sweeping, weaving, orchestrated symphony of richly costumed bodies, moving in circles and lines across the gleaming wooden floor, holding hands, spinning, swinging, bowing, smiling, laughing, and smelling sweetly. Mindy was in the middle of this, and Stan could not fathom how to plunge into the schools of people swirling around her.

He was leaning against the wall behind a refreshment table.

Another man who had been watching walked over. "Why don't you join in?" he asked.

"Oh, I don't want to appear a bumbling fool."

"It's all foolish. You might as well be having fun with the rest of them."

"You're some kind of policeman, aren't you?"

"How did you guess?"

"The way you're standing—your posture. You notice everything happening in the room."

"You're observant, yourself. I'm an off-duty deputy sheriff. Just keeping an eye on things."

"Are they expecting trouble?"

"It's standard at Chinook Assembly events. There are a lot of important people here."

Stan had been watching a refined, tuxedo-decked man, who, like a discreet waiter, kept near Mindy, but without intruding. "Who's the Asian fellow in a tux?"

"That's Dr. Uchida," the deputy said as if Stan should already know him.

A dance had concluded and the caller announced the next one. People scurried about looking for new partners.

"You should get out there," the deputy said. "This one's a simple dance. Ask your sister. She's not taken yet."

Stan wondered about the deputy knowing who he was. He walked across the floor and tapped Sarah on the shoulder. She turned to him, surprised.

"May I have this dance?" he asked.

She smiled and said, "Sure."

The dance was not as hard as he had supposed, and the other dancers forgave his occasional mistakes. Stan tried another simple one with Sarah, but, for the complex dances, he resigned himself to being a wallflower.

Near the end of the evening, Mindy asked him to join her for "a mixer." He clasped her hand in the correct way and they walked onto the floor and assumed places in the outside of two concentric circles. Stan's hopes fell with mercurial speed when he learned that after one dance figure, Mindy would be passed to the next male in line. The dance began and she was swept around the circle. Stan failed to follow her progress because he was too engaged with keeping up his part. However, Mindy cycled around to him, they danced the figure once more, and the music ended. She made a lovely curtsey and walked away.

By the evening's last dance, a "free waltz," Stan had to face reality: he would not be able to talk with Mindy. He asked Sarah to waltz with him, but feeling dizzy and clumsy, he quit before the music concluded. As he helped Sarah with her coat, he could see Mindy gliding around the perimeter of the room in the arms of the Tuxedo. They formed one dervish of two persons in perfect step: the Coat's tails and Mindy's dress arching away in graceful curves.

All through the winter, Stan saw little of Tommy, who gave no thought to Stan. Tommy's leg mending and heart swelling, he floated as one who remains constant in the flexuous state called romantic love. He carried off perfunctory requisites of life, but his heart was consumed with Beth. While in her presence, the contemplation of her was ecstasy, and in her absence his only wish was to be with her again.

He saw her frequently, since she was in the cast of *Macbeth*, and his primary hours apart from her were morning sword combat practice in the park, weekends when he visited his grandparents on their farm, and when she began informal outdoor soccer. They decided against her moving into the apartment with him, since this would certainly end her parents' contributions for school, but for Beth, her financial dependence was the lesser concern: Tommy had not met her parents, nor had she talked about them much yet.

But one night, as they walked hand-in-hand in the park at the foot of Mt. Tabor, Beth told him about her dad's condition. She hoped, she said, to keep her relationship with Tommy a secret from her parents and from everyone else.

"If Pop knows about us, he might kill you," she said.

"From what you've told me, I like him. I wish I could study his character."

"He's not happy. You'd have to observe from a distance. I'm serious. He worries me. I think he would hurt you for showing up at the door. We have a gun in the house—a shotgun."

"I have a gun."

"You're joking."

"I wouldn't joke about that."

"Where is it? I've never seen—"

"Right here." He patted the place under his shirt.

Beth touched the place and pulled her hand back slowly.

"Why?" she said, mystified.

"For the same reason some people wear a cross."

"Would you kill someone? That's what guns are for."

"I'm ready for the chance it might be needed. I've spent enough time shooting silhouettes and practicing gunfighting moves to be lethal in any situation."

"Tommy!" Beth said, stepping away from him. "I don't want to hear this."

"A gun might prevent the loss of those I love." Tommy moved to Beth and put his arm around her shoulder. "It's part of my heritage, my persona, my chosen character; it's my secret treasure and security. Like you."

"Tommy. Please. I don't like guns. Just—just keep it away from me. Why haven't I ever felt it? I don't want to see it, OK?" She shook her head. "You and my father are a lot alike."

"Has he ever hurt you?"

"No. No. I am glad about that. Some girls I know have abusive fathers. He's never really done anything like that. He's never been violent to me or Mom. But he embarrasses me. He talks lewd, and he tries to pat me as if I were a child."

"You should tell him to stop."

"I do."

"If I were to speak with him, I'd insist."

"All the more reason for you to stay away from him, Tommy."

"What about your mother?"

"Pop's smart, and paranoid. If she knew about us, he would guess she was hiding information."

"I suppose you're right."

"Please, I *am* right. I want you to respect me in this."

They left the park and walked on a trail the short distance to the summit of Mt. Tabor to watch the Portland lights. From then on, Tommy became scrupulous about Beth's parents never seeing him, or even knowing about his existence.

$$+ \qquad + \qquad +$$

During the weeks of *Macbeth* practices, the self-esteem of Talus Schenk swelled like a super-nova and annoyed everyone. In the middle of a scene he would pitch a tantrum over a dropped line or a mis-step by another actor. He would suddenly yell at the Director, or hurl an insult to an imaginary scapegoat—insults such as, "What, you egg! Young fry of treachery," or "Fit to govern? No, not to live." He flirted mercilessly, even with Beth, who offered him no regard, her dreamy heart occupied with Tommy's attentions.

When not on the stage, Schenk stormed or alternately crept through activities and classes. As with some vain amateur actors, he found circumstances to pitch an *apropos* one-liner from his part, with chilling effects, considering *Macbeth's* bloody context. And he scared silly his fellow fraternity residents with ravings, or else he swung to the opposite extreme with deadpan recitations during dinner. In later rehearsals, he began taunting the superstitious cast members by whistling backstage, which is frowned upon in Shakespearean theatre. Tommy was the only one who dared to jibe Schenk: a rude comment here, a soft sword-poke-in-the-ribs there. Whenever this happened, Schenk fell out of character and glared at Tommy. The Director refrained from intervening as long as real violence did not follow. In spite of Schenk's antics, he had talent and worked hard, achieving a solid character, so at the end of February, the play was falling together.

The Director released sensational press teasers with photographs of Lady Macbeth wearing the revealing Milan costumes.

As the opening approached, the cast became jittery. In the days before dress rehearsals, the technical people began testing lighting and special effects as they coincided with the action, and the Director kept the auditorium dark. Realistic fight rehearsals being added, the cast suffered strained muscles and bruises from tumbling stunts and mistimed sword strokes. Actors bumped into one another backstage and cracked into wooden studs. The Porter sprained his ankle when he stepped upon an upside-down stool. Once, a roll of duct tape inexplicably dropped from the fly loft and hit an actor on the shoulder.

The first days of dress rehearsals were punctuated with curses and mutterings. By now, the schedule allowed no margins, and there was so much work that the Director had to endure the tense ambiance. He regarded it as adding to the play's dynamic. Wednesday evening, the last night before the opening, the problems eased and the play ran without a break.

Attendance was thin on Thursday. Beth's mother came. Friday presented a sold-out auditorium of audience members in high spirits and wearing eccentric clothing and the occasional animal relic. On Saturday a reasonable number came for the matinee and evening performances, the attendees being from the customary Shakespeare-loving culture, and there was an all-important writer for the *Oregonian*, who came because of the Lady Macbeth photos. The evening crowd included Stan Timmons. Afterwards, he and Tommy and Beth went out for beers. Tommy asked Stan about his "girlfriend, the blonde ice princess" and Stan said, "I don't have one—a girlfriend." When Tommy pressed, "Why didn't you invite her?" he answered, "I was afraid."

The Director was excited by a rave review in the Sunday paper. The writer said the play was "brilliantly executed" and "especially pertinent to the political climate of the day." The "immense power of the production," the reviewer wrote, "was buttressed by small parts threatening to upstage the whole, such as Thomas Duckwitz playing Macduff." With the review, the Director hoped for the next weekend that the play would receive the audience and wide acclaim it deserved, and in fact, the review was picked up by the wire service and the Director had received a call from the *LA Times* asking for an interview.

But events were coalescing that would bring more attention than the Director wanted—the wrong kind of attention.

Early on, the Director had introduced a creative concept to complement the atmosphere of the play. For the three apparitions in *Macbeth*, the Director placed children into those roles. They were filmed in costume, the voices and images distorted to give them a horrific appearance, and then the images were back-projected through screens on the set—screens painted to blend with the background.

The daughter of Dr. Prochaska, a faculty member in Math and Engineering, played one of the apparitions. March often provides perfect snow on Mt. Hood, the weather alternately giving heavy snowstorms and mild temperatures, and the Prochaska family had planned a skiing trip over the weekend. Since the child, whose name was Garland, had been recorded, her bodily presence on stage was not required. The family had attended the play on Thursday night. On Saturday they left home early, planning to ski all day and stay the night at a lodge;

but they never reached the mountain. A log truck plowed into the corner of their minivan. The van lifted up, rolled down an embankment, and rested against a tree. One child and the mom were thrown from the vehicle. All six of the family members were killed.

Officials did not immediately release the names of the family, and so it happened that *Macbeth* had played Saturday night without anyone realizing that one bloody apparition truly spoke from the dead. However, early next week a debate fumed among the cast members and school administrators—the same time as a memorial was being conducted at the University—about the use of the image and voice of the deceased child. Tommy said that the remainder of the performances should be cancelled out of respect for Garland. The Director tended to agree, but he was worried about having to return sponsoring money and give refunds. Beth's view was, "The performances could be dedicated to the family." Schenk commented, "People watch movies with dead actors in them all the time."

However, the real issue was the horror and shock they all felt.

Minor casualties resulting from the Prochaska tragedy were the Porter and a stagehand. Both resigned, saying they were frightened. "The Scottish Play is bad luck," they said. The Director was forced to hire a professional actor who had played the Porter recently in another production.

During the late week rehearsal, Tommy and Schenk engaged in a silent stare down.

As it turned out, the play was sold-out on Friday night and they turned people away. Despite the crowd's enthusiasm, the cast was depressed and nervous, fearing a new tragedy, but they did their jobs well. The audience roared riotously at the professional Porter's comedy and gave the play a frenzied standing ovation.

Another minor casualty was the cast party, which followed the Friday night performance and was held at the home of Lady Macbeth. Nearly no one came. Schenk surfaced and inspected the food and drink. The other few cast members who were present felt uncomfortable, having stumbled into a shunned event, and when the music shut down early, they all slipped away. Left alone, Lady Macbeth and her parents wondered how they would dispose of the refreshments.

On Saturday evening the cast members arrived at the theater not later than an hour before curtain. No one except Schenk had his heart into performing again, and there was yet one more blow to come. The chairman of the University Fine Arts program had called the Director and told him that the President of the University had called him. Two parties had contacted the University President on Saturday morning—a member of the press, and an FBI agent, bringing the hammer of power politics down on the Director. He had to tell the cast and crew, and he called a meeting at the staircase on stage left.

"This won't take long," he said when everyone had assembled in miscellaneous states of dress and makeup.

"I don't know if you've seen the news late last night or today."

Most had heard it at least by word of mouth.

"Doubtless, you know that the newly inaugurated governor of Oregon, Mr. Farrell, has been assassinated. Last night a sniper shot through his bedroom window and killed him. Rumors are running wild that this was politically motivated. The University President said our play hits too close to the facts, and he ordered me to cancel tonight's performance. At risk to my tenure, I told him to take a flying leap. The idea that our play is connected to the governor's assassination is preposterous. But here's more pressure. The press will attend the play tonight to write a new perspective to the Prochaska story. The family now has asked us not to use the film of Garland—word came to me this afternoon. I think this is untrue, since no one from the family contacted me—it was the FBI agent who relayed the demand. But someone called the press, and it looks like they will tell the world about how callous we are in our theatre department, not to mention associating the University with the assassination. I don't wish to back down. We should stand firm for free speech and artistic license, but if we try to perform the play—I'll be arrested, for trespassing."

Some students spoke up saying that they should cancel the show. Only Schenk said, not loudly, that it should go forward. Tommy thought, but did not say, how the assassination—the real-life replication of the play—could launch the play into a national spot-light—that they should cut Garland's image and voice out, put in a live actor—he could do the part—and run the play tonight and schedule another week. Then take it on the road.

"I need you to help me decide. We'll vote," the Director said. "We don't have time to discuss, so let me count hands. How many conclude that we should kill the play?"

Nearly everyone raised a hand.

"To be fair, is there anyone who strongly feels we should perform?"

There was silence except for a disgusted mummer of, "Oh, come on."

Schenk and Tommy said nothing. They both had abstained from the vote.

"We'll handle this with dignity," the Director said. "Quietly, get out of makeup and change into street clothes. Pack up costumes and hold tight. We won't begin striking until the audience is gone. I'll step out at eight and make an announcement, and I want it absolutely silent, as if we were about to open the curtain. We'll see—I may walk you through a curtain call for a final closing of the show." The Director's voice had begun to fail.

There was silence and no one moved. The Director's eyes grew larger, magnified by tears. "I'm sorry. Thank you—everyone."

While everyone had been dragging like senescent grasshoppers when they expected to perform, there was now communal relief in knowing the play was terminated. An efficient bustle ensued.

As 8:00 p.m. approached, the Director knew that the auditorium remained empty. He peered out from the side of the proscenium. It had not been necessary to vote to cancel the show. The public had already decided for them. This was more weirdness. What had scared them? And yet in the front row sat a dad and three children. *An appalling play for children,* the Director thought. Near the central doors in the back stood two men in suits: FBI agents. He had been told that members of the press and a few police officers waited in the lobby.

The Director walked down toward the family who was pouring over the playbill. "I hope you won't hate me for telling you we are canceling the show."

The father looked up. "Actually, I'm relieved. It would have been uncomfortable to have the play put on only for us. We were thinking of leaving."

"Well, thank you for coming. The box office will refund your money, and for your trouble, we'll give you a set of complimentary tickets for any play we will be staging this spring. Thank you for coming."

The Director ran up the steps to the stage. He opened the curtain and fired up the house lights from the backstage controls. The FBI agents scuttled out to the lobby, like cockroaches on a suddenly blazing kitchen floor. The Director would no doubt be seeing them later in his office.

Everyone commenced working.

The dismantling of a set after a beloved play's conclusion is like the sorrowful discarding of a child's worn out, broken toy house. The parents delay as long as possible before they begin the task. They wait until the children are asleep and they stand side by side, shedding a few tears, lingering, remembering the joyful hours of play. But the cast and crew of *Macbeth* assaulted this playhouse as if it were a despised fortification whose gates at last have been breached. There was noise and dust and revelry. They exorcised its ghosts not with prayer but with hammers and by total obliteration—razing walls and towers and packing salvageable parts to the storage area. Someone threw open the backstage doors and flooded the putrefied country of Dunsinane with a purifying breeze of Spring, and the true and loyal forces of Scotland began building a junk pile near the dumpster.

Later that night, leaving their respective vehicles—his pickup and her car—parked behind the theater, Tommy and Beth walked arm in arm to the pub four blocks away. After an enjoyable hour talking with cast members, and listening to a Scottish fiddler, they returned to the theater. In the dark next to Beth's car, they embraced for a minute.

Beth left to go home. Tommy then recalled his matched swords locked in a cabinet inside the theater. He meant to take them home tonight, but had not wanted to leave them in his pickup, lest they be stolen.

He had the key, but the backstage door was unlocked. It should not have been. Tommy pulled the door wide and left it open, adjusting the door's self-propping mechanism. The misty night air flowed through again. The soundless backstage area of the theater was caliginous with its lofty ceiling, and dark, except for the Running Man exit signs and a light from the theater's technical office. Its door was partially open, and through it, across the oaken stage floor, thrusted a long, sharply angled beam of light. Tommy recalled the Prochaska family and shuddered. He smelled cigarette smoke. He glanced into the fly tower. The demons who were cast out had returned in greater force, and they swirled in the air around the catwalks above him. Tommy did not wish to disturb them. He quietly made his way to the properties cabinet, unlocked it, and removed the sword case. During his next breath, a female voice from the office said "Stop," and the sharp triangle went black—the light in the office had been switched off. Again he heard "Stop!" cried urgently. Tommy crept closer with the sword case under his arm.

"I'm not that kind of a girl." There was a stifled scream, and Tommy reached inside the office door, flipped the lights back on, and pushed the door open.

He beheld a frightful sight. On the floor lay a struggling mass of black cloth and then two upturned faces, one scared and wretched, and the other ferocious and lustful. It was Lady Macbeth and Macbeth. Talus Schenk leapt to his feet and adjusted his clothing, his eyes glittering with hatred. Tommy felt tension drain away, leaving him alert and calm: a clear purpose and charged adrenaline forming a harmonious force. Schenk held an unsheathed knife—one of Macbeth's props. Lady Macbeth crawled to Tommy's feet, rose up, and slipped behind him. Her clothes had been torn or cut.

Tommy spoke to her, "Get away, quickly."

The Lady ran, stumbled, and ran again to the exit and the safety of outdoors. Tommy backed away slowly from Schenk and undid the latches of his sword case. Schenk had the light at his back and Tommy could only see him in sable silhouette. Tommy set the case on the floor and flipped up the lip. Schenk rushed forward with a yell and Tommy flashed up a sword. Schenk halted the charge and stood frozen, but breathing hard. Tommy put his foot on the sword case and slid it over to Schenk. The case stopped a foot from where Schenk stood.

"Let's stop pretending and fight a real match," Tommy growled. "You'd best pick up the sword and defend yourself, because I will cut off your head with your knife. I've warned you before about terrorizing women."

Tommy did not have it in mind to kill Schenk, because if he had, he would have just shot him; nor was he completely bluffing. The swords were dull, but could damage. He wanted Schenk to feel and remember pain. He held his sword in two hands.

Schenk croaked, "Oh, I see—we should stop . . . *clowning.*" With his chest heaving, he added a foul obscenity.

Tommy replied calmly, "My voice is in my sword."

Chin held up, eyes fixed on Tommy, Schenk jerked down and picked up the other sword. He weighed the weapon in his hand. With his other hand he replaced the knife into its sheath. Schenk was wearing Macbeth's costume—a suit with a black velvet cape—and Tommy felt goose bumps. Here was Macbeth, and he was Macduff once more. Schenk lifted the sword over his head. Suddenly he yelled and charged, chopping the sword in an arc toward the crown of Tommy's head.

Tommy ducked and sidestepped the blow, a move never required in the play's fight choreography, and therefore unexpected. Schenk's sword tip hit the floor, jarring his arms. Tommy was turning in a half circle, pirouetting, and with a step forward, in one continuous motion, he swung his sword hard across Schenk's back. The sword thudded. Schenk howled, dropped his sword and fell forward. In a fraction of a second he was on his feet, facing Tommy and snarling like a cornered dog. Schenk tugged out his knife. Holding his sword over his shoulder like a baseball bat, Tommy advanced a step for another strike, but accidentally kicked the sword on the floor, and the sword spun around. His arms tingled, as if thousands of sharp needles prodded his skin.

Schenk drew back his arm and flung his knife at Tommy, who flinched away blindly. The knife clattered behind. When

Tommy recovered and looked for Schenk, he heard him running for the backstage door. Tommy trotted after, his sword held to the side. He reached the top of the stairs and saw Schenk flying down the alley like a madman.

Tommy returned inside, his heart still banging against his lungs, which he had not noticed until now. He recovered the other sword, packed them both into their case, and decided to have them sharpened soon. He picked up Schenk's knife. It was an expensive one, long and razor sharp. He rummaged around in a box, found a piece of leather, wrapped the knife, and tucked the bundle into his belt. As he locked the door of the theater and subtly strutted to his truck, he felt strong and indomitable. He patted the leather-clad knife and said, "I'm starting a collection of these."

As he neared his fraternity house just after midnight, the badly bruised Talus Schenk called Dr. Ponder. Ponder was irritated, but he had been awake anyway and asked Schenk a few questions. The injury not life threatening, Ponder told him to apply a local antibiotic where the skin was torn and sleep on his stomach. "Do you have an all-night pharmacy close by? Good. I'll call in a prescription to make you feel better."

Schenk had an additional subject on his mind. "I need to talk. Can we have breakfast tomorrow? I want to finalize our business plans—the ones we've been discussing."

Ponder paused a second and said, "Good," vaguely complimenting Schenk about being obscure on the telephone. "But I can't see you that early. I have a golf appointment and a colleague to meet on Lovejoy Street afterwards. Let's convene for a late lunch, say, at the Hung Hi Wei restaurant in old China Town. Near Union Station."

Schenk produced a bemused laugh. "My father went there when he was in high school. It was the cool place to eat."

"Fine. Let's meet at 4:00 p.m. I'll treat."

Later that night, the flesh around Schenk's wound swelled, the throbbing increased, and he gave a buddy his driver's license and sent him to pick up the medication at the 24-hour drugstore. The drug stopped him from groaning and relaxed him, but despite the narcotic effect, he slept fitfully. In the late morning when he sought food in the kitchen, he made a crude joke to his lounging fraternity brothers to cover up for his stiff and crippled condition. "What a plum!" he concluded. After breakfast, he walked to a bookstore near campus and drowsed through the early afternoon in a reading chair. At length, he rose from the chair with a bad headache. He was hungry by now as well.

He grabbed a taxi for the short distance to China Town. Ponder had not arrived at the restaurant by 4:00, and while he waited, Schenk admired the high-powered sport cars parked along the street. Ponder walked up, and after a brief question and answer session about Schenk's condition, they entered the restaurant's bright red doors. An old Chinese man led them upstairs to a tall room darkened by tapestry-like curtains. Having just opened for the day, the restaurant was empty except for the cooks, servers, and the owner's family members, who were sitting around a table finishing a meal.

Schenk and Ponder took a corner booth and asked for beers from an unsmiling Chinese girl. Schenk watched her walk away. Bending close over the table, Schenk said, slurring his words from the narcotic in his system, "Her name is Miss Ooh La La."

"Not for you, jackass," Ponder replied laconically over the top of his menu.

The girl returned with bottles and glasses. Schenk glugged half his beer. He then rolled his head around to look over the room; the beer plus the drugs made his brain swim. "They keep it dark to hide the dirt. But the drinks are jet fuel, and the food will give you a heart attack. I love it."

Ponder motioned for the waitress to return. She had just perched primly on the edge of her seat at the table with the dining Chinese restaurateurs. When the waitress stepped up, Ponder said, "We're ready. I'd like your favorite dish from what you've been enjoying."

Schenk smirked at Ponder, expecting him to hint at a double entendre. He didn't.

The girl scribbled without saying a word and looked expectantly at Schenk.

Schenk folded his menu and said, "Shrimp. A big plate of stir-fried shrimp in a garlic and ginger sauce. Nothing else. No rice."

When the girl left, Schenk leaned forward and said, "I want to know your specific plans."

"First, tell me more about how you were injured."

Schenk narrated the backstage duel, except he said nothing about Lady Macbeth. He explained that the reason Tommy attacked him was because he, Schenk, had been flirting with Tommy's girlfriend. "But this is connected with our discussion," he continued. "You see, Duckwitz's friend is the brother of Sarah, who is providing the product we intend to sell."

Ponder had to think about this. Schenk's story sounded similar to his confrontation with the young man in the balcony box at the symphony. He passed it off as a coincidence. Society had become increasingly violent in recent years, and it was not surprising for two such incidents to land close to home. "This business sounds more complicated than I like," he said. "I don't know if we should go through with our scheme. There's too much exposure. Will you report the assault to the police? That could create problems."

"I guess not, then."

"What reason will Duckwitz assume for you not telling the police? Won't he become suspicious? He could raise questions when the baby turns up missing."

"Duckwitz is insane. He imagines I'm a rapist. That's what he'll think when I don't report his attack against me. To protect myself."

Ponder watched Schenk's eyes as they wandered around the room. "Well, whatever you do on your time is not my concern, but stay away from trouble if you want to make some money. Let this thing go with Duckwitz. Stay out of his way. Don't try to even the score. You'll feel better with heavy cash in your pockets."

Schenk picked up his fork and examined it. "Oh, I have designs, and I'll manipulate them behind the scenes. He won't know I had anything to do with it. But I'll be nice. The most important thing in acting is sincerity. Sincerity. If I can fake that, I can fake anything." He laughed.

Ponder violently slapped his palms on the table causing everything on it to jump. "I would drop plotting revenge if you want to work with me! I mean it!"

Schenk recoiled. The Chinese family looked up.

"OK, OK." Schenk waved his fork. "I'll forgive him, if only to make you happy." He took a deep breath. "Now, if you'll el-u-cid-ate how to pull this bunny out of a hat."

"Alright." Ponder lowered his voice. "My plan depends upon everything working perfectly toward the most predictable scenario. There's a good chance that the mother will want the baby in the hospital nursery during her stay. If she breastfeeds, the nurse will bring the baby to her room on a schedule. When things are quiet overnight, you call away the nursery attendant with an emergency page. As you know, I keep a private office on the uppermost floor and have access to all hospital systems. You will be posted there. As soon as the floor is clear, I'll descend the stairs with a tub modified for carrying a live newborn. It has heating strips, thermostat, ventilation holes, micro-fans, and is powered by a battery. Picking up the baby is the easy part—"

At that point the waitress appeared with the food, deftly placed it before the diners, and left. Schenk lifted the stainless cover of his dish and dug right in with his fork.

Ponder ignored the food. "The difficulty is evading the security implements. This nursery system has two components. The camera system and a leg-mounted transmitter for each baby. The transmitter alerts hospital security and signals nurse stations if it breaks contact with a baby's skin. I'm not worried about the transmitter because I know how to crash this and make it look accidental—I helped order the system in the first place. What bothers me is the camera. I can't enter the nursery and approach the computer terminal to shut down the contact alarms without being photographed. This is what I came up with: the recording will only show the nurse or nurses leaving and then babies sleeping—I'll have myself electronically scrubbed."

Schenk was savoring each chunk of shrimp, which he studied and then forked into his mouth.

"Are you listening to this?" Ponder said.

"Yeah, ah . . . electronically scrubbed. How will you do that?"

"Leave this to me." Ponder decided he would charge the prospective family more for this sale and not tell Schenk.

"This is sounding expensive. It would be cheaper to snatch the critter with low-tech force. Shove and grab."

"I'm allowing for improvisation. If something goes wrong, I can abort the plan and pick the baby up in a conventional way."

"Conventional?" Schenk said.

"Don't worry about it."

Ponder recalled how he had profitably stolen babies before; and as easy as it was, it had downsides—baby snatching was traumatic and risky for the goods, and knocking down a parent raised attention, which increased the chances of being caught. Besides, the brute force repelled him. Despite not having all of the bugs worked out, he was excited about this new method.

"My mother was a social worker," Ponder said. "She saw a lot of abused and neglected kids. By deadbeat parents."

"Really?"

At last, Ponder served himself a portion of the complicated dish that never appeared on the Hung Hi Wei menu. He undid the chopsticks wrapper and ate a couple mouthfuls. Schenk had already finished his meal and used his finger to sluice the sauce from the serving plate. He licked his finger and asked, "What will happen when the baby is missed?"

Ponder sniffed, and perceived a fetid odor. He looked on Schenk with disgust, pushed away his plate and opened up a fortune cookie. "Hey, this is your fortune!"

"Why?"

"It says, 'Your good manners will bring you long life.'"

"Are you implying . . . ?"

"OK. Let me see the other one."

With some trouble Schenk tore the plastic wrapping. He cracked the cookie and read the white slip silently.

Ponder pulled out his wallet. "Well?"

"It says, 'You will never be without excellent comestibles and generous patrons.' This one is mine, too."

"You know, you've gained weight lately. You're too fat for a young man. You need exercise."

Schenk patted his belly. "The other day, I was sitting on the edge of the bed, leaning over to tie my shoes, and my own flab bit me. It pinched and I yelped. And I've noticed how when I walk, everything revolves around my middle. But I get exercise, at night, when I sleep. I toss and turn. My problem is, I feed too well."

"So, you *are* claiming my fortune!" Ponder smiled and tossed down a cash payment and a large tip.

"Yeah, I want the food and patrons. I opened it. Obviously, it's mine."

"I don't think so."

Schenk nodded and winked to the waitress who ignored him, and the men left the restaurant while discussing whose fortune was whose.

As the due date of the salable baby approached, Ponder became nervous. Nearly everything was in place, and Schenk was invaluable in learning who the mother's doctor would be; from this information, Ponder confirmed the baby would indeed be delivered at the Vancouver hospital where he himself was on staff and had a small top-floor office. He began monitoring admissions and learned that she was scheduled for a C-section, and he was ready to move, except he was afraid. No matter how careful he would be, there was the existential problem of a missing baby that would provoke an investigation. As an intelligent and philosophical person who had spent hours imagining how to perform the abduction, Ponder was troubled that he could not erase the reality that he would have taken the baby, and this would leave detectable traces. A lower class criminal would not cogitate on this level, but Ponder writhed over the impossibility of eliminating all risk. If only he could steal the baby by witchcraft . . . He put the plan on hold, and Schenk began to worry.

However, one week later, a solution presented itself that Ponder had not considered before. As was their custom, Ponder and Schenk discussed their undertakings over a meal, this time a fast-food breakfast before Saturday clinic. Schenk kept yawning. Ponder was satisfied with the brilliance of the resolution, as he described it to Schenk.

"Occasionally I have a genuine hard case. Not long ago a woman came wanting to abort late in her pregnancy. With such cases, I usually say everything possible to persuade the patient to carry the baby to term, even when there are fetal abnormalities. I offer to refer the patients to specialists, who could treat the fetus surgically, but with this woman I haven't succeeded, and ethically I have no problem in providing the service requested, as distasteful as it may be. Also, whenever this situation comes along, I offer to perform a memorial service at discounted fees."

Ponder paused and Schenk nodded approvingly. "This sounds good to me."

"So, this woman requires a hysterectomy," Ponder resumed. "The procedure will leave an intact, nearly full-term fetus, one that has some anomalies. I'll bring this fetus, alive and at body temperature, into the nursery in my special tub and switch it with the healthy one . . . switch the fetus with your baby. They are both male, as I found out. I'll hide the tub in my office and carry the healthy fetus—baby—to my car in a vented sports bag. The defective fetus in the nursery will expire or grow cool in a short time. When the nursery—"

Schenk had grown pale and stopped chewing his sausage biscuit. He took a drink of orange juice, chewed more, and then attempted to swallow. The food caught in his throat as if he had downed a whole walnut, and he began glowing red.

Ponder laughed. "Here, take more juice. Listen, I have an important job. I wouldn't say this to anyone, but putting it bluntly, I'm a paid executioner. People want the service. Society wants not to be burdened with handicapped children. We can't let emotion sway us from the logical conclusions of our beliefs. I believe in choice, and as a practitioner I have to deal with messy situations. Look at the positive side. A single mother like this girl of your acquaintance will have it tough raising a child on her own. She shouldn't be burdened with an unwanted child. Just because the girl is stupid shouldn't rule us. I know a wealthy couple who will love and provide for this child in ways beyond the girl's imagination. The demand is great and suppliers rare enough that I, and you, deserve good money."

By this time Schenk had negotiated the lump in his throat. "OK OK. That's enough of your sucking blarney. How will this substitution work?"

"I'll tweak the hospital computer, entering the dying fetus's weight and length info—and Apgar results—into the living baby's files. I'll steal the paper records. With newborns, genetic identification is seldom done. I'll lose profit from the whole fetus or its parts, but a dead fetus never brings as much as a living baby. If the patient insists on a burial, I'll steer her toward cremation and give her fireplace ashes. In fact, to facilitate the realism of our substitute, I'll schedule the procedure to suit our timing. The hospital frowns upon late-term procedures because they are illegal except under excruciating circumstances, but the hospital never looks closely. The law and policy are flexible enough to suit staff members' needs."

Schenk thought a moment and said, "There's a fault in your plan."

"What is it?"

"The nurses and the doctor aren't brainless. They'll know that the dead thing won't be the one born to the mother."

"Probably. The pediatrician might. Any suggestions?"

"Blackmail. Bribery. Drug their possets—their coffees."

Ponder suddenly tilted his head sideways and shook it violently as if wax had shifted and bubbled in his right ear canal. He took out his car keys and dug in the ear with one of the keys. "I'll come up with something," he said.

"The mother will know."

"Nobody will believe her. Anyway, no one will suspect me."

So, the matter was settled, and Ponder and Schenk individually began dreaming of how to spend their shares of the expected cash windfall.

A dark night. The enemy is approaching my position to capture or kill me. I run to the home of people who support our side. With their help, I hide my combat gear and weapons, but I am not so easy to conceal—my body dirty with stains of blood, mud, and gunpowder; and so I strip, stuff the clothing into a cabinet, and climb into a bathtub with bubble bath and mountains of suds. An enemy commander barges into the room and begins to interrogate me. I act like an emasculated dandy. He orders his men to search the house. Seeing a penknife on a close-by table, he jams it into my arm that rests on the edge of the tub, as if he is measuring fat on a pig. The flesh of my arm separates. The commander jerks out the knife. The wound does not hurt, pumped on adrenaline as I am, but I scream and moan exaggeratedly and put my finger over the slit. The enemy soldiers do not find my gear, and they leave. I am safe.
-from the dream journal of Stan Timmons

Chapter Seven
The Melodrama of Self

Neither Mark Ponder nor Talus Schenk had nurtured their protective male instincts. The baby poised to be born to Sarah Timmons did not have a real father, and their schemes did not figure on someone else filling this role.

As Sarah's mood improved, Dr. Sterne cancelled the C-section, which he did not support anyway, and Sarah's midwife assured her that she could give birth naturally, as long as she employed a few simple practices that women had used for centuries. Sarah's confidence increased to where she hoped to give birth at home, that is, at the Sterne residence, but Dr. Sterne recommended that she be in the hospital for her first baby. This change of allowing a regular delivery stressed Ponder considerably, because he would have to arrange the late-term extraction with less than eight hours notice to the surgical scheduler and to the family. But the lies were working, so everything was prepped, including the relevant hospital personnel.

Stan's year since January had been uneventful, except that he could not forget Mindy Sterne. There had been the usual teacher difficulties—hours spent in lesson preparation, grading papers, following through on discipline problems, and performing extra duties. But he endured, class by class, day by day, and rejoiced at every week's end. Opportunities to see Mindy had been non-existent until Stan learned that Sarah wished to deliver naturally and he began taking her to birth classes on Thursday evenings. This was his opening. When he arrived to pick up Sarah or drop her off, he exchanged small talk with Mindy if she came to the door or was studying in the family room when he stepped inside. Stan eagerly anticipated these brief meetings.

+   +   +

May turned into early June, and the latter month promised to continue a delicious spring. And so, one evening after the birth class, in the heady air, Stan drew Mindy onto the deck overlooking the river—the private family entrance to the Sterne home. Sarah had gone up to her room.

"Thanks for coming out." Stan said. "I wanted to talk with you about Sarah."

"That's fine," she said, smiling. "Let's sit at a table. How have you been?"

"Really well."

"And your teaching?"

"It's tough, but summer's almost here."

"What are your plans for summer?"

"I'm taking a graduate class in fiction writing and I'm helping my parents. They grow a big vegetable garden. They freeze and can stuff for winter. Kind of boring."

"I don't think so."

"I'll probably hike a lot—maybe around Mt. Hood. What about you?"

"Oh, our family is taking a trip. Summer vacation. I have to help with my brothers and sisters."

"Where are you going?"

"Ah . . . we're going on a fishing and boating trip."

"Very nice. Where?" Stan was thinking of the Oregon coast.

"Starting in the North Sea in the British Isles. We'll be sailing up the Norwegian coast, cross to Iceland if the weather permits, then down through the Shetlands."

"Oh." Stan was taken aback because he was humbled by the family's prospective adventure, and because Mindy had been holding back information to prevent him from feeling this way.

"Sarah said that you are attending the birth," Mindy said, steering away from the vacation.

"Yeah. My job is to coach her and massage her neck and back during labor."

"That's impressive. I'll be in the birthing room, too. I've attended the births of my younger siblings. All of them have been home. Sarah wants me by her side for comfort. Yesterday she said that she wants to move back in with your parents after the baby is born."

"Oh, that's what I wanted to talk with you about. She doesn't want to move. She wants me to tell you that she's changed her mind." Stan feared that his enthusiasm might show.

"Why, I wonder?"

"She said it was awkward—changing so suddenly."

"I mean why doesn't she want to move back home?" Mindy leaned forward to listen with focused absorption.

"She wouldn't tell me," he said, "but I know it's hard there. My parents always had difficulty accepting the fact that Sarah would be a single mother, and I don't think they quite believed she had been raped. But they seemed to realize that they were on the threshold of grandparenthood, and bought a crib, baby clothing, disposable diapers, and a quilt."

"That's good."

"Well, yes, I was happy with that, but it wasn't good enough. I was upset because Mom and Dad didn't support her for her own sake, so I told them to take Sarah out to dinner and buy her a pretty post-maternity dress. After that she said she wanted to move home. Our parents were thrilled, and talked about redoing her room and fixing up the house. But today, Sarah inexplicably changed her mind. My parents will be disappointed. I'll try to help them understand that it must be for a good reason."

"She likes it here," Mindy said.

"That must be it. I like it here." *Whoops.* Stan was afraid that he had spoken too openly. At least he did not say that if Sarah moved, he wouldn't get to see Mindy any more.

Mindy smiled. "You have a great evening, Stan. I have to study for finals now. See you later." With that, Mindy touched him on the arm, walked inside, and left Stan alone to return to his empty house. On the way, he wished he had asked her more about her sailing trip.

On Saturday afternoon, after hours of widely-spaced contractions, Sarah's waters abruptly broke. Mindy called the midwife, then Stan and her father. Sarah's night bag was packed, and Mindy drove Sarah to the hospital.

The delivery went normally; for Stan it was frightening, and embarrassing—especially in Mindy's presence, and for Sarah it was painful, exhausting, and thrilling beyond expression. For Mindy it was an ordinary, joyful part of life, and she found herself developing respect for Stan. She observed him closely while he concentrated on Sarah. During the hardest labor, Stan gave his entire attention to his sister. Mindy saw his eyes open with amazement at the rounded mountain of Sarah's belly bearing down on the infant inside. Once, between contractions, he stood up to stretch his back and whispered, "I never realized how the uterus is the strongest and most gentle muscle in the human body. It puts a man to shame." Dr. Sterne stood in the corner watching during the delivery's final 10 minutes. As nothing transpired that required his attention, he left shortly after the baby boy slipped into the midwife's hands.

Meanwhile, Dr. Mark Ponder, having gotten word of Sarah's admission to the hospital, had scrambled to get his patient in for the "emergency" surgery. Sarah brought forth her healthy baby boy in a room decorated with flowery wallpaper and furnished with a real bed, a homey bedcover and soft chairs. One floor above in a sterile, cold, surgical room, Ponder sewed up a mother from whom he had removed an unhealthy baby. While Sarah taught her baby to nurse, Ponder weighed and measured the other baby and made a footprint. While the midwife and nurses weighed and measured Sarah's baby in the nursery under Stan's watchful eye, Ponder placed the other nameless baby boy—still struggling for life—in the plastic cooler he had engineered in his basement. As Sarah announced that the baby would be named Guthrie after her father, Schenk was camping out in Ponder's office—a tiny room on the northwest corner of the hospital. He had opened a window and smoked one cigarette after another. His face damp and pale, he sat up in a chair and stared toward the city night-lights; his elbow rested on the arm of the chair and his cigarette-holding hand was turned palm up and flared away from his head. The ash fell on the floor.

Long after midnight, Dr. Sterne and Mindy at last left the hospital. As they walked to the parking lot together, Sterne asked, "Well, what did you think?"

"It's wonderful."

"Do you want to be a mother?"

Mindy was tired, though exhilarated. "Of course, someday. With the right person."

"What do you think of the Timmons boy?"

"Stan? He's . . . I can't think of a word. He's intelligent, reserved. There's nothing *wrong* with him."

They arrived at Mindy's Volkswagen and stopped.

"Will you . . . " Sterne paused, and then finished asking, "Will you invite him to the book discussion?"

"Why me? Are you trying to put us together?"

"You should get to know him better."

Mindy made a face of amused interest and said, "OK, I'll ask him sometime."

They drove home in their respective vehicles, in tandem. By then the hospital had shifted deeply into sleep mode, while some stayed awake to watch the sleepers and attend to the restless.

Ponder rode the elevator down one floor and pushed a cart to the nursery. A plastic cooler rested on the cart. The room, according to his and Schenk's contrivance, was empty except for three small persons in clear bassinets. His heart racing, Ponder glided through the grid of these warming beds, pausing to look at the records of each occupant. When he reached the last bed, he swore. The Timmons baby was absent. What should he do? His mind went numb. Should he switch with one of these babies? Why not?

Ponder set the cooler down roughly on the floor and opened it—he heard a faint whimper and shivered. He lifted a warming bed cover and reached down to remove the security band from this child.

"Oh my God!" he said outloud, scaring himself. The baby was wearing a pink gown. "It's a damned female," he whispered. He checked the other baby records. All girls. Another curse. He should abandon the mission . . . but there was still another chance. He dropped the lid onto the cooler and stalked out taking the cooler, leaving the cart behind. No one at either end of the hall. Assuming a business-like gait, Ponder began searching for Sarah's birthing room. He stood erect and carried the burden in one hand—his other arm balancing in the air made clockwise circles. In a few seconds he found the right room. He opened the door partway and peered inside. In the right corner, next to an easy chair, a pole lamp burned dimly. A book lay opened, print down, on the chair's seat. The mother slept on the bed. On the far side of the bed, on top of the covers, lay a man lightly snoring, his hand resting on the lump of baby and blankets between him and the mother. The man was fully clothed except for his shoes. It was Uncle Stan.

Ponder eased the door closed, and with the cooler, returned up the elevator to his office.

Schenk jumped up from the chair and tried to wave away the smoke. He could see from Ponder's head shake and by the tilt of his shoulders that the undertaking had failed.

Ponder closed the door. "God, Talus, smoking in a hospital?" He punched Schenk in the shoulder. "God!"

"What are we going to do?" Schenk said, stiffly sitting back down. "I say we kidnap the thing at a grocery store."

"Let's forget it for tonight. I'm tired. It's been a long day and I still have work."

Schenk covered his eyes with his hand. "Some of the money is already spent. I'm in debt."

"You idiot. I told you this might not work. Let me think about it tomorrow. I might be able to procure the child by a non-violent method."

Both men focused on the blankness in their heads. The air circulating system hummed louder. A mouse rustled near their feet. *But hospitals don't have rodents,* Schenk thought.

Ponder massaged the back of his neck. "I'll tell you what. On Monday I'll mail you a check for $10,000. Consider it a bonus for your security work. But there are conditions: you lower your expectations on the baby matter and you keep working for me at the clinic. Do we agree?" He held out his hand.

Schenk was expecting at least three times the money, and he was not as enthusiastic as he should be for the generous offer, but he shook on it.

Ponder picked up the cooler. "Let's leave. I have to drive to my clinic to put the day to bed."

"What about scrubbing yourself from the security videos?"

"Don't worry. I've taken care of it. Let's go."

Schenk stepped into the hall and Ponder locked up behind him. He watched Ponder carrying the cooler as the doctor passed ahead toward the elevator. Schenk looked down at his hand that had taken the doctor's and he wiped the sweat onto his pants.

Leaving Schenk fumbling for car keys, Ponder purred his black Jaguar to the clinic a few miles northwest. The doctor lugged the cooler inside, set the incinerator's timer and temperature, quickly put the baby—still wrapped in a disposable blanket— into the incinerator and tried to close the door. A corner of the blanket prevented the door from shutting, and he had to open it to poke the edges of cloth away—as he did, he felt the baby's firmness. He closed the door, turned on the flame and walked away. The baby probably had still been alive, but Ponder did not allow himself to dwell on this; he had done this sort of thing before.

When he arrived home, Barbara was sleeping. He patiently mixed a large iced gin-drink, with Madeira wine, cherry flavored brandy, and two teaspoons of orange juice, and he sipped this while preparing for bed. He slept badly. In the morning he resolved to not stay up so late again, because it disturbed his inner balance, and in this frame of mind he decided that the Timmons baby was too protected—he'd have to give this project up. Also, Ponder decided to never perform this specific type of emergency surgery again.

Later this same morning, Schenk lay in bed thinking, trying to process his sudden downturn. He was disappointed about losing the money, but the promised gift from Ponder, coupled with not having engaged in a criminal abduction, left him feeling relieved for the present. Perhaps Ponder could nab the baby later. Schenk was ready to put the matter aside; however, the insult from the Duckwitz idiot now rose to the surface and galled him anew. The pain had subsided, but Schenk's stiff back reminded him daily. Duckwitz was unsafe to confront directly, but as a breeze blew into his open window, Schenk began thinking of a covert revenge. He eked out of bed and downstairs to the fraternity kitchen to scrounge a noon-time breakfast.

Commencement was set for the following Sunday, and Schenk had finals and a design project to complete. During the week, he fretted about finding a summer job. He had intended after graduation to spend his money pleasurably and prepare for graduate school, but now he had to find an income. Ponder called midweek and offered him a job performing yard work and walking the dogs. Even though days near Barbara Ponder might prove entertaining, Schenk said, "No thanks," hoping for a better position somewhere else. He had interviewed in early spring for a choice theatre internship in Portland, but as fate determined, it had gone to Duckwitz. Schenk was second in line. He pummeled his brain for anything to alter Duckwitz's availability.

It was Schenk's nature to avoid unpleasant realities with diversion, and after his final exam, he attended several parties around the University. At one of the tamer events, he ran into Lady Macbeth. When he approached her, she was scared, but in a chastened mood he said, "Sorry for my behavior. I was a bad boy," and then he drifted away. The parties could not drive away his misery, however. His situation felt desperate and only an unusual measure would suffice. The hours of subsequent brooding about how he landed into his troubles finally produced a result. Blaming the Timmons girl's pregnancy on her failure to use contraception gave him the idea. Also, his heartfelt guilt for aggression toward Lady Macbeth could open the door . . .

During the daylight hours he looked for Beth Telford on campus. On Thursday afternoon, he found her working alone with her computer and a pile of books at a table near windows at the main campus cafeteria. Schenk had brought a plastic bag.

He smiled and said, "May I sit down?"

"Go away."

"Talking won't hurt."

She nodded, but did not look up. She stifled a yawn.

"Finals are over," he said, pulling up a chair. "What's the project?"

"I'm late— It's not your damn business. What do you want?"

"I suppose you know about the last night of *Macbeth*, the final scene."

Beth looked up at him with a sardonic expression, "You mean *after* we struck the set? I heard. How's your back, playboy? Whollop!"

Schenk cleared his throat, shifted his feet, and scratched his eyebrow with a finger. "Yeah."

"I heard you apologized—"

"I don't want to talk about this, OK? If you know I apologized to Lady Macbeth, that's all I wanted."

"You didn't for my sake, I hope. That would be stink. Did you apologize to Sarah Timmons? She had her baby the other night. It's a boy. You want to know his name?"

Schenk looked away and almost ran. It was either escape, flare up, or control himself. There were few other people in the cafeteria. He fought his anger. He was an actor, and he had been preparing for improvisation, so . . .

He spoke soothingly, "Well, you've raised a good point. You know someone connected with Sarah, and I understand what's been said about me, but you don't know the whole story. I didn't exactly force her."

"Maybe," she said. "OK. I'm not listening now. I have no idea why you're talking to me. Please go away. I have to turn this in by 4 o'clock."

From under the table Schenk lifted the white plastic bag containing small boxes. He set the bag on the table. "This might seem strange, but I work for an OB-GYN doctor—doing odd jobs. He has samples of a new birth control pill that's supposed to be very effective and safe, and I wanted you to have these, for free. They're expensive."

A spot on each of Beth's cheeks had grown pinkish. She said nothing, but leaned forward like a mantis, poised to mar his face with her fingernails. Schenk jumped up out of range. "Uh, uh, I'll just leave the stuff and the literature."

"You bloody pusser!" she spat icily and lunged from her seat. She started around the table and stopped.

Schenk took a step backwards. "There's a card of the doctor's. He does reproductive stuff. Gives a student discount, too."

Beth glowered, her temperature rising.

"Are you going to my graduation ceremony on Sunday?" He asked cutely.

"No! Graduation is Father's Day. Bugger off, wanker dumb-ass." She sat down hard and glared to the side.

Schenk laughed sheepishly. He backed up, tripped, and bumped his head into the glass doorway.

The instant that Schenk fled, in a flurry Beth snatched his material in both hands, marched to a nearby trashcan and jammed it through the flap. She returned to her seat, laughed bitterly, and plunged back into her paper.

When he was out of sight, Schenk skipped a few steps down the sidewalk, laughed at his own act, and thought, *She might not use the phony pills, but I had fun. Fooled the nigger-wench.*

After an hour's concentrated work, Beth completed her paper. She closed her computer and gathered the books into her bag. She began to leave by the glass door, and all of a sudden she grew thoughtful about Tommy. She stood unmoving for a moment, stepped to the trash can, and removed what she had previously discarded. She looked at the sealed boxes inside, tucked them into her bookbag and said, "Might come in handy."

Tommy's summer internship was with a professional theater in Portland. The theatrical group was quirky, well-financed, and focused on Shakespeare, staging three or four plays a year in the 300-seat auditorium of the city's première performing arts center. In addition to its regular season, the theater produced plays during the summer, and this with minimal sets in the park blocks near the University. Tommy's internship was as a dramaturge and he would also fill a major dramatic role in each play. It paid well and he could stay near Beth, who had a summer job at a camp. The internship was to begin in less than a week and he had already learned his lines for the first play.

The weather had turned hot and dry. Every night, cooling fog crept inland from the ocean and burned away by noon the next day. Tommy's paternal grandparents were killed by a hit-and-run driver while they rode their bicycles on a bike trail along the coastal highway north of Seaside. They had finished lunch at a restaurant and walked to the beach to digest before beginning the fatal ride back to the house that they had rented for the weekend. The local newspaper interviewed the waitress at the seafood restaurant. "They loved life," she said. "They ate a big meal and talked about their plans for a winter trip to Hawaii. They looked forward to his retirement." The police investigated, and all they came up with were cut-up parts of a blue SUV at a landfill, but no vehicle identification number and no suspects.

The day after the accident, Tommy drove alone down to the coast. He parked near the place where his grandparents reportedly were hit, and he walked around. Pieces of glass and plastic lay beside the road. He searched, and in the bushes he found a woolen shirt belonging to his grandfather. It was torn and bloodstained. He folded it and took it to his truck. Returning to the spot where the shirt had been, he pushed a black wooden cross into the ground. Before he had left home he had lettered on it in white paint, "Peggy and Cameron," the names of his grandparents. After this he bought a kite at a tourist shop and walked along the beach. Coastal clouds sank down all the way to the water and he could not see the kite overhead pulling hard.

It was time to return home. He reeled in the string, handed the kite and reel to a passing child, got into the pickup and drove back to his Portland apartment.

The next business day, wearing a white shirt and tie, Tommy sat down in the estate's lawyer's conference room in a Vancouver office. The lawyer had not arrived. On a glass-topped table was a vase holding wilted flowers. The office overlooked a noisy street. One wall of the room was made entirely of weathered brick, colored with a huge advertisement for an antique product. While Tommy waited, he suddenly took the dead flower vase and hid it in a corner. He returned to the chair and arranged himself to look relaxed. The lawyer entered the room in the subsequent moment. He was a personable man with a rolling, rather choked voice.

The lawyer shook hands with Tommy and took a seat, leaning back in the chair while he explained. "You may wonder why I'm meeting with you without your father. The reason is his share of your grandparents' estate is miniscule, and I expect he won't be happy. For your sake, and mine, I want to avoid an unpleasant scene."

Tommy, roughly imitating the lawyer's posture, had been sitting back with his feet crossed and his fingers interlocked over his stomach. Now he sat up and put an elbow on the glass topped table.

Pleased to have gained the young man's attention, the lawyer choked on. "I've been retained by your grandparents since I opened my practice. Your grandfather was displeased with his son, your father. The issues were . . . Well, they don't matter now. They quarreled. Enough to say that the dissolution of your parents' marriage was the clincher.

"Early on, your grandmother feared that if your parents received benefits from the estate, they would squander the proceeds and not provide for you, their sole grandchild. Your grandparents also believed that if they had placed their wealth into a trust that would come to you over time, it would allow for a protracted court conflict. Anyway, the best solution your grandparents could devise was to transfer their major asset—the farm—directly to you and put your name on certain custodial accounts. There's not much money in those accounts, I'm sorry. On the other hand, your grandparents were . . . well, frugal, and what you possess—the cash—comes tax-free. They did not have a life insurance policy, and this seems odd because your grandfather had a decent income. The best I can tell is your grandparents either gave away their money or bought gold and hid it under their mattress, so to speak. In any case, possibly a substantial part of their liquid assets has not been uncovered."

Here the secretary entered with a pitcher of ice tea on a tray with glasses. The lawyer paused when the door opened and he helped himself to a glass. He gestured to Tommy to have some, but Tommy shook his head and mumbled.

The lawyer glanced over his shoulder to reassure himself that the secretary was not standing near the door, which was open slightly. He got up and closed the door before continuing. "We have one principle on taxes in our firm: pay as little as possible as legally as possible. You'll have to pay certain taxes, but everything on the land, including that not known to the government, and not specified for any other individual, is yours."

The lawyer sipped his tea to let the statement soak in.

"Well," he said, "here are the papers—deeds and other documents. The farm is 193 acres and there are buildings and considerable machinery, and livestock. It has views. The farm doesn't produce much net income and its chief value would come when, or I should say, *if* you sell. Considering the location and growth pressure, even with the economy as it is, you could get, well, $25-30 million."

"That much?"

"Yes. This kind of land is rare."

Tommy was astonished, and speechless for a few seconds. Never once had he given thought to the disposal of his grandparents' property, because he never thought much about them dying. He had his future charted, and now something he never lacked or needed hung about his neck. Wealth. It changed everything. It entailed new opportunity, and responsibility.

"Wait a minute." Tommy sifted through the papers.

The lawyer chuckled. "Hmmm. You are holding oil stocks worth around $25,000. I'm afraid the funds are bound until you get married, so you can't put your hands on them yet. This, however, is separate from the property transfers."

"There were several?"

"Yes."

"Why? When did this start?"

"Um . . . you were seven when he started buying stock, but he began giving you property before you were born. He spent a wheelbarrow load on surveyors to avoid paying gift taxes. He was eccentric about this. Will you need a loan until estate benefits come to you?"

"I have money. Enough to live on."

"Are you planning on getting married soon?"

Tommy thought before speaking, "No plans, but I might get married anyway."

"There it is. Let me know if I can help. If you ever sell the land, I would be happy to advise you and do the closing. I'll protect your interests and make everything legal."

"Yeah. I don't want the government to hunt me down."

"Well, I'll help you minimize the tax damage. I can recommend a financial consultant, if you like."

+   +   +

Tommy left the attorney's office with his emotions much agitated. This windfall had changed his whole outlook. He could sell the farm. Already he was thinking about what he might buy. A new car? A gift for Beth? He felt guilty for being happy and said to himself firmly that he wished his grandparents were still alive.

The funeral was held at a large church in Battle Ground the next day. The church was full of people. Though the beach had been his personal farewell, Tommy grieved again. Stan Timmons and Sarah attended, and there was a certain luminescence present when they intercepted him because before he knew it, they put an oblong bundle in his arms and he stared into the pink face of a sleeping baby. The baby's features were tiny and perfect, and the sweet, clean baby smell rose and melted Tommy. He had never known the strength to drain out of him like this before. The baby awoke and arched his back, stretching and yawning. Tommy was afraid he might drop it, and quickly gave it back to Sarah.

Tommy's father and mother had come separately of course. His dad brought his girlfriend Rosalinda, who could not be much older than Beth. His mother arrived without her second husband. She kept away from the pair, and they all avoided eye contact. His parents were kind to him, and his mother appeared to be melancholy.

That evening at his father's hotel where Tommy and relatives gathered for dinner, his father received a phone call. From the next room his father began an explosive, spiteful rage, to the discomfiture of everyone present, who could hear him without trying, and Tommy supposed that his father had learned about the modestness of his portion of the estate. Tommy abruptly excused himself and left. Until the funeral, he had not seen his father since high school graduation—and at this juncture of his life he did believe that he needed to see him again.

He drove from the hotel toward Beth's parents' house in Portland seeking solace, and he called her on the way. She had moved out of the dorm and was beginning her summer job the next day. When Tommy's arrival drew near, Beth left the house on the pretext of an evening run. Her dad called out behind her, "Do you have pepper spray?"

Tommy parked a few blocks away at the edge of a specialty strip-mall. The coffee shop there was overcrowded and noisy, and instead of going inside, they sat in the pickup, watching traffic. There were grass and trees between the mall parking lot sections, and at the perimeter next to the sidewalk.

"That's sad about your grandparents," Beth said, snuggling up close with her head on his chest. His somber mood made her feel needed.

"Yes, but *they* were happy," Tommy said. My parents are a living tragedy."

"Wow. You have a farm now. *The* farm. When will you take me? I've never been there."

"I think I'm going to turn down the internship. It would be fun, and everything is close to the campus and my apartment, but I don't need the money—not for next year. Maybe never. I want something larger than theatre. Maybe we should get married."

Tommy glanced down to Beth, and she gouged him in the ribs with her fingers, saying, "Why?"

He squirmed away and said, "If we got married, I could cash out special stocks from my grandparents. They're worth several thousand dollars. Also, they had purchased tickets for their 40th wedding anniversary to go to Hawaii next January. The tickets are refundable. We could get married and go to Hawaii for a wedding trip."

"Why don't we pretend to marry and do Hawaii? Why get married? Marriages fail, or you get stuck with a nutcracker like my dad. Your partner dies. You get pregnant and fat."

Tommy did not answer.

Some seconds passed, and then Beth spoke again. "Have you seen Sarah's baby?"

"At the funeral. He was the only good part of a sorrowful day."

"I don't want any children."

"Really?" Tommy sighed. "My grandparents had a good life. They took care of each other. They worked hard and had friends. They cared for their land. I used to spend hours a day wandering through the woods and helping with the animals. What else is there in life? We could live like them; we could move to the farm after Hawaii. I could sell just a piece of the land and I don't need school because now I can afford to find an agent and pursue big parts."

Beth hung her arm around his neck. "Could I keep horses?"

"Sure . . . There are barns, and acres of pasture, and trees. Which reminds me, I wonder who will look after the cattle? Grandpa's neighbor is probably feeding the chickens and ducks, I hope, but he can't do it forever. I should check. I think I'm going to take off the summer and stay on the farm. It'll be fun. You can visit whenever you like."

"Fine, but you know I have a post at a camp, and it's six days a week, 24 hours a day. I thought about playing the summer soccer league with the Portland Rain, but . . . I didn't want to travel to games . . . and I have my scholarship . . . already."

Tommy said nothing.

She thought for a few seconds. "I know, I'll make excuses to my parents and spend every other Sunday with you. Maybe."

"That sounds wonderful. Now tell me all about your job."

"I got it with Mindy Sterne's help. She gave me a reference."

"Good."

"Let's get out and walk to the park, and I'll tell you about it."

They strolled in unison and talked, Tommy's arm around Beth's waist. When they came to the park near her house, they stopped at a picnic table where Tommy embraced her.

Tommy returned to his apartment after walking Beth within sight of her home—she would not let him take her nearer. In the morning, he hastily packed clothes to last him through the next couple weeks. He completed some financial business, and scribbled a letter turning down the summer internship—which guaranteed that Talus Schenk would be offered the position. He bought groceries at the natural foods store, and drove north across the big river to his grandparents' farm—now his, though the house seemed impoverished and destitute without them being there. In the evening he cooked a stir-fried vegan dinner with shiitake mushrooms and steamed brown rice, and after a refreshing night, he wrote up an inventory of what needed accomplishing, and began the chores around the farm.

I am visiting a college reputed to prepare young people for leadership in restoring the moral greatness of the United States. The lectures are held in one large room, and the college president is speaking. The students are not paying attention because they are working on papers and reading. After the speech it is lunchtime, and the students eat at long tables in the lecture room. I sit near the president while he discusses the faculty members, who all are accomplished in their fields. After lunch I go outside where it is sunshiny, but cold. The president of the college comes out and I approach him. I say, "I hear that you and your wife are divorcing." His wife is standing beside him. I say, "Your students will follow you, and their marriages will also fail. Close the school for two years and put your talent into saving your marriage. Only then will the college accomplish its purpose." The president is angry and leaves, but his wife remains. I say to her, "I'll show you that my words are true." I push off from the ground and hover there. She gasps. I say then, "Now you push off." She does so and rises into the air. She wears a bright colored dress that waves like a flag. Students in the pavilion look up in astonishment.

-from the dream journal of Stan Timmons

Chapter Eight
Light Shattering Water

Beth was excited about her summer job. She looked forward to it as an escape from the smell and intensity of the city and from college life. The camp's grounds were situated at a former prison camp along a river originating as glacial melt from Mt. Hood. Running beneath a ridge of evergreen mountains that blocked the view of Hood, the river was full of trout and steelhead. One mile below the camp was a salmon hatchery, and every spring season through the fall, some of the once tiny fingerlings returned as huge monsters—their sides flushed ruby red and their smooth heads having morphed into pinchers—to beget the next generation, and die.

The camp was not glamorous. Its awkward name, Camp Clack-Ri-Ki, did not help. A more significant actuality was that the campers had serious or multiple disabilities, and no camp activities reached anywhere near the pinnacle of technical challenge or high adventure, but every summer, on the purely human level, there were mighty rock faces to conquer, remote class V waterfalls to negotiate, marathons to run, and rearing wild stallions to tame.

Into Cabin Eight early Monday morning, Beth labored under her backpack, which contained personal items she would need for the week, including chocolate and organic foods to supplement her diet. The cabin was not a self-standing unit, but rather a large room at the end of a long building comprised of a row of other such rooms. As she entered the dimly illuminated "cabin" from the outside door, a tall young man with dark plaited hair down his back—rather like an Etruscan Apollo—jumped up from a chair near a window through which gold-green sunlight poured. He held a paperback book in his left hand and put his right in a pocket.

"Hello, I'm Theodore, the senior counselor for this cabin. You're Beth, I assume."

"You're correct. Uh, say your name again?"

"Theodore"

"Oh, Teddy?"

"No, don't ever call me Teddy. It's Theodore. Don't forget."

"OK, I won't," Beth answered with a hint of irritation.

"This is your bunk and a chest of drawers. The first campers will begin arriving in less than an hour, and I have to give you a tour. You attended the orientation, right?"

"Yes." Beth answered, her voice hissing on the "s," and she opened up the top of her backpack.

"Then follow me. You can unpack later."

They stepped out of the door Beth had just entered, and Theodore rounded the corner to the back of the building. In a clump of trees a few yards away was pitched a small nylon tent.

"This is where I sleep." Theodore waved his hand toward the tent while he kept walking. "Every counselor is supposed to keep a watch for one hour every night, and some nights your shift begins at 2: a.m. right before mine, in which case you will need to wake me at 3. I'm not sure who wakes you. It might be Emily; you'll have to check the schedule."

Theodore walked fast, and Beth had a hard time keeping up without running. He led her first to the horse barn where he introduced her to the horsemaster, Mr. Reggie Amundsen—a wiry man who smelled of tobacco, but was never seen to smoke—and she promised to come back. Then she and Theodore raced on to the river banks. Here Theodore stopped and waved his arms as he said, "I'm in charge of afternoon water activities: swimming, fishing and rafting, and the hatchery tour."

Next, they took off for the nurse's station, cafeteria, gymnasium, and garden area. At the end of the lightning-fast tour, they stopped at the climbing towers, where they met Jona, who was now inspecting climbing holds from a box. Jona was small-built, but energetic and muscular.

"Jona leads the climbing challenges, obviously," Theodore said, "but his greatest contribution to humanity is that he plays guitar and leads the campfire."

He greeted Beth with a graceful bow.

"Jona's been a counselor here since he was a high school freshman, I believe."

Laughing, Jona said, "Are you ready for Big Bertha?"

"Oh, I almost forgot." Turning to Beth, Theodore asked, "Would you like to help me play Big Bertha this year?"

"Sure. Who's Big Bertha?"

"The camp Sasquatch who performs tricks every Friday night at campfire," Jona said.

"We begin circulating the Big Bertha rumor today," Theodore said. "We give her a promotional on Wednesday nights by bugling around the camp perimeter. I'll tell you more later." He examined his watch. "You have half an hour to be back at headquarters to greet campers. Don't be late. Camp leadership makes a big deal about punctuality."

Beth nodded, said, "Nice meeting you, Jona," and ran back to the stables and found Mr. Amundsen in his office. He took her to the stalls and told her about the horses—their histories, breeding, and temperaments.

"This isn't a fancy riding school," he said in a voice low and raspy. "We show each camper how to touch the horses and brush them. The campers hold the reins—which are only attached to the halter—and we walk them around while holding the horses' heads." Beth entered the stall of the Appaloosa gelding, and Amundsen watched Beth move around and inspect him, putting her hands on the horse reassuringly, and he said, "There are trails along the river. If you have free time, you can ride him."

"Thanks! Sounds splendid. See you later!"

Beth hurried to camp headquarters near the entrance to help disembark the campers. This week, the age group was roughly 14 through 19, and was co-ed, though her cabin and wing was to be all boys. The arrival process was orderly, and excitement was high. There were wheelchairs to unload, nametags to affix, medication bags to transfer to the camp nurse, snacks of fruit juice and cookies to dispense. Tears were common, and hugs, and pats on the back abundant. An anxious voice croaked above the chatter.

Beth went around with a list, found her campers and collected them beside the central playing field under a tree, where Theodore waited and made jokes with those already gathered. When she had all eight campers assembled, and Theodore began his talk about the rules and the week's schedule, Beth surveyed each responsibility: Jesse, broad shouldered and apish, wearing a mischievous grin. There was Morgan, with a baby-like innocence, but bright, cheerful eyes. Buster was autistic, she thought. He had his shirt off, was stooped and kept searching the ground with his eyes, like he had lost something. James was the only dark brown person in the group. She watched his eyes flicker and go vacant. He was wearing a camera on a strap around his neck and a new basketball jersey. Anthony's information showed an intensive regime of controlling drugs. The other boys, Justin and Earl, appeared to be afflicted by Down's syndrome, and then there was one other boy. He lolled in a wheelchair—not really a boy, but a child in a 21-year-old wreck of a body.

This was Gene, whose retrogressive parents had neglected to have him vaccinated for polio when he was a baby. When Beth turned her eyes to him, thin and sprawling in his chair, with a jutting, fleshless jaw, she realized he had been watching her. He nodded and winked, and smiled a toothless smile that made him look like an old man. Beth nodded back and blinked her gaze away.

After all of the campers found their cabins, they moved in baggage and selected their bunks. Special Olympics began immediately afterwards. That whole morning Beth felt like a sheep dog bounding everywhere to keep them from wandering away. Once, as Jesse lumbered down a sidewalk, he began to step off into the grass, then he stopped and began hopping backward in staccato jerks. Beth ran up from behind to stabilize him, and he lurched and fell backwards on top of her, crushing her underneath his solid bulk. She was pinned to the ground and couldn't move.

She struggled for an instant and shouted, "Get off me!"

Theodore came up and rolled the laughing Jesse off.

"You shouldn't do that," Theodore said to Beth, sounding angry as he helped her to stand. "Nine times in ten Jesse catches himself, but if he falls and you're in the way, you'll be hurt."

Beth looked in wonder at Jesse, who had rolled onto his stomach, because his elbows were masses of scar tissue.

"Are you OK?" Theodore asked Beth, suddenly tender.

"I'll be just fine, thanks."
"Jesse needs exact handling and it's often contrary to instinct."
"Ooo. I'll try to remember that."
Everything about the first day was chaotic. How so many
people with such limitations could accomplish the tasks of living
and playing in these semi-primal conditions was amazing. Beth
marveled at the parchment and foil certificates made for the
campers for the "special olympics," with each camper's name
written in elaborate calligraphy. Beth ended up pushing Gene in
the "Ambulance Races." He bumped along, tied in with a sheet,
yelling "fath-er, fath-er," and grinning, and Beth and he sprinted
first across the finish line. The award ceremony, which
overflowed with applause, smiles, and hands raised in jubilation,
filled Beth's eyes with tears. An edge of her competitiveness
wore off as she understood how such immense joy could be
derived from a modest amount of love.
After dismissal for lunch, Beth found her campers and trooped
with them to the cafeteria line. She counted heads and turned to
look at the playing field for who was missing. Gene was sitting
in his chair where she had left him. He waved, and she walked
back and brought him to the front of the line that entered the
building. She made a place for him and his chair at a table, went
for the food, and put the plate before him. She stood back and
waited to see what he could do. With the hand that worked, he
picked up the napkin and tucked it under his chin and then
picked up a fork. He slowly fed himself and cleaned his plate,
making little mess. Beth ate green beans and a hotdog bun filled
with mustard, and finished on a piece of coconut cream pie.
After lunch she and Theodore escorted their campers back to
the cabin. It was naptime, and Theodore disappeared to his tent
after saying, "Call me if you need anything." Beth was irritated
at him leaving, but she soon saw there was nothing to do. The
campers settled onto their bunks and slept, all worn out from the
morning. Beth slipped outside and lay down on some grass
against a tree. She dozed for the half-hour, and when the bell
rang, she got up refreshed. The campers were already moving
and preparing for the swim. Though they scarcely noticed her
presence, she discreetly removed herself during the change of
clothes, and since she did not intend to swim, her shorts and

sleeveless top would be all she needed. Gene wanted only to watch the playing at the water, and Beth wheeled him along to the riverside.

The section of river adjacent to the camp was not deep, but wide and bouldery. Beth left Gene on the bank in the shade and waded into the midst of campers, rocks, and counselors. Screams of delight accented the stream's rushing and rumbling. The sun shone hotly. Beth scanned to be certain everyone was safe. On a rock in the middle of the hubbub sat a thin, tanned boy, with his feet in the water and wearing a loose blue and white swimsuit. His eyes rolled around in their sockets, and he was smiling and swashing his feet under the surface of the water.

Beth worked closer to him and said, "Hi. What's your name?" but he didn't answer. She saw his name from the tag he wore, but she hoped to elicit a response. "What's your name?" Beth said louder. With a sudden movement, he raised his open hand before his eyes, the palm turned to his face, and with his fingers spread apart, he waved his hand in front of one eye.

She sat down and brushed him lightly as she did so. The boy scooted away a few inches and reached both hands toward her. Beth touched him on his shoulder, and the boy took her hand and began working his hand inside hers, making shapes; it dawned on her that he was trying to communicate using a manual alphabet.

"Hith name ith Michael," came a hoarse voice from the shore.

"What?" Beth looked up at Gene.

"Hith name ith Michael!" Gene said again, shouting, and this time she heard over noise of the water.

"Oh. Thanks, Gene!" she called out.

Michael soon gave up trying to talk to Beth. But he patted her on the shoulder, and then bent over. He scooped his cupped hand down and quickly shot it up, spraying a clear water fountain in front of his left eye. Water fell on his face, but it did not bother him. He patted Beth on the shoulder again and repeated his liquid light show. Then he fumbled until he found Beth's hand again and put it into the water. With him holding on to her, she tried the geyser before one of her own squinting eyes with the other eye tightly shut. The light from the sun flashed brightly into her brain, and she could see the form and shape of the illuminated globs, the sun behind them.

"He hath a thithter! They're from Columbia, Thouth America!" It was Gene again.

"What?" Beth stood and took a few steps closer to him so she could hear.

"He hath a thithter, and thhee ith blind and deaf, too."

"Oh. Thank you, Gene." Beth turned back to Michael, but his own counselor had sat down next to him and was giving him wet rocks to feel.

Beth waded shoreward and flopped on the ground beside Gene.

Because he sat in his chair crookedly and Beth was on the side away from the direction he faced, Gene tried to roll his body in his chair so he could look at Beth. He couldn't execute the move, but he spoke anyway. "He makth me feel lucky. I can thee and hear. Michael can't."

"A brother and sister, both blind and both deaf? Are they adopted?"

"I hope they're not adopted."

"Why, Gene?"

"Becauth my little brother and thithter were put in fothter homes and adopted. I don't know where they are."

"That's sad, Gene."

"I know. I try to not think about it."

"Where do you live?"

"In a nurthing home."

"Does any of your family come see you?"

"Ummm . . . My mother thumtimeth."

"Must be tough."

"Not really. I have frienth there. And thum people come every week to thing thongth."

The conversation lapsed. Beth did not know how to deal with this young man's pitiful life. She could hardly imagine being locked inside an ugly, crippled body, and yet *he* was cheerful. She would rather die than be in his miserable condition. And he could quickly exhaust all her empathy for him. She got up, intending to visit the other campers.

Gene lifted up his head. "Do you have any brotherth or thitherth?"

"Yes. Brothers."

"I want to meet them."

"Maybe," she said, and walked away.

+   +   +

Over time, it became clear that Gene had developed a crush on her and this made her work more difficult—complex, that is. During the first days of the week, she remained kind to him, and he always spoke respectfully to her. Had he been a normal young man, she would have flirted with him thoughtlessly, and otherwise made herself scarce. She played a game in her mind as she wheeled him to the different activities—that she was a middle-aged nurse and he an invalid older man. She was thankful that Theodore dressed and undressed him.

On Wednesday she committed herself to assisting Theodore on the afternoon fishing expedition. Gene had begged to go fishing with them, but Beth told him that at their destination it would be impossible to carry his wheelchair down to the stream. There were only narrow, rocky trails to the water or long trails through the woods.

The fishing crew drove to a tributary in a van. Beth carried two fishing rods, Jesse's and hers, and walked down a path with him to join more nimble fishers who had gone ahead. The trees here on the trail grew tall and straight, and sunlight poured through gaps in the canopy, the light radiantly illuminating patches of trunks and undergrowth. At a place where the trail traversed a steep slope, Jesse mis-stepped, slipped from the trail, and slid downhill. He caught on the slope, with his head just below the level of the trail, his feet digging into the soft, black earth. Beth reached to give him a hand up, but he could neither help himself back, nor could she pull him up by brute strength. So, Beth climbed down behind him, her feet making their own steps in the earth, and putting her hands on his iron-hard behind, she urged him to crawl. He jerked his legs in good faith while she pushed, but they got nowhere. Beth tried once more to shove him up, and Jesse began laughing and straightened his body as stiff as a steel bar, and slid a few feet further down the hill. The situation was getting frustrating.

146

Beth spent the whole time allowed for fishing trying to push Jesse back onto the trail, and she succeeded at last by yelling at him, and coaching his legs one at a time. Beth was worn out, and she and Jesse were late getting back to the road. The driver had not waited, but had taken everyone else back to the camp and returned with Theodore, who was glum. All he would say was, "By the time we get back, supper will be over." At camp, when they drove through the gate, there was a cursory reprimand from the grumpy assistant camp director for being late. Theodore whispered, "The reprimand was mild, you'll soon learn why."

As it happened, during the meal, a camper eating mashed potatoes had raised her chin and began making gasping noises. In less than a minute she turned grey and fell face down on the dining room floor. Jona had rolled her over and tried to clear her mouth, and then lifted her and attempted a Heimlich maneuver. Nothing worked and the girl died.

She was Michael's sister. Michael, the blind and deaf boy.

Supper had all been put away, and Jesse said he was not hungry. Because of the death, campfire activities were cancelled for the evening, but a few counselors quietly sang in their cabins with the campers.

After they put the campers to bed, the counselors and staff gathered around the campfire for the day's debriefing. Beth shared her personal food with Theodore. The shock of what had happened was a tangible presence in their midst, and no one felt like talking. They sat in silence, watching the coals flare and glow, and the sparks flying up like flaming bugs. An ambulance came and took away the small body. Beth would have guessed her to be half her age.

Beth made her way alone back to the cabin. It was quiet and dark. Throughout the day, she had been reminding herself that she had arranged to call Tommy this evening. She rummaged in her backpack for her telephone, but could not find it. She took a flashlight and shone the beam inside the pack's main compartment. She cursed under her breath. "Did I forget to pack it? What would Tommy think?" Not being able to share with him the tragedy around her, she felt an immense disappointment. She lay down on her bunk. It was impossible not to see the suffering here. She wondered if there was life after death and if this girl who died was in Heaven. How many people that she knew had died already? Her great-grandparents who she only remembered from watching them in home movies. There was the old woman who lived next door to her once who spit phlegm into a can she kept under the bed. The neighbor kid who drowned one summer while swimming at the pool. Her paternal grandfather. The girlfriend in New Zealand who died suddenly from a tumor. A child with raven, wavy hair at the beach, recurrent in her dreams. The Prochaska child. All those people, and a hundred personages she had read about, had died, had graduated to the next stage, which was unknown to all who remained behind. In the dark, she thought of death as the only reality, and life an illusion. Death was the one certain reality for the whole human race, because all but the few now alive were dead. All of the dead knew death's secret, but none came back to tell what it was. Millions of people had been born, grew, laughed, loved, wrote grand ideas and beautiful music, procreated, painted, grew crops and flowers, hunted, built buildings, and they all died, entering the cold blackness. Death was the end. Life was meaningless, and useless . . . Beth closed her eyes and tried to empty her thoughts. She felt her heart slow down until her body became the universal sum of everything—nothing existed outside of her, and then she fell asleep.

But she came alive again, and it was a rude surprise. Someone was gently shaking her in the dark. It was Theodore.

"It's 2:00 a.m. Your watch. Are you awake?"

"Yes."

"OK. You better get up before you fall back asleep."

"Where's Emily? She has the shift before mine."

"She doesn't feel well. Wake me at 3. You better get up."

Beth sat up on the edge of the bunk. For a long while she struggled against unconsciousness. At last she switched on her will and stood up despite all contrary feelings. The night was cool. She tiptoed across the dewy grass to the guest bathroom near the office, because she did not like the one in the cabin; afterwards she got a flashlight and began the patrol through the rooms. There was an eccentric medley of sounds: deep breathing, sighs, the squeak of old springs, and snoring as if it were a contest of who could be loudest, and weirdest—a fairy competition of the ids that no one would remember in the morning. Beth walked softly, heel-toe, all the way to the end of Cabin One and turned around. When she returned through Cabin Five, she saw Michael sitting upright and cross-legged in his bed, in the dark, his unseeing eyes wide-open and his ears unhearing. But Beth knew he knew. Did someone tell him his sister was dead?

She sat on the bed and he scooted beside her, took her hands, and began spelling. Would this be Spanish? After a short while, Michael gave up. There was nothing to do and nothing she could say, and so they just sat together. Beth listened to the crickets outside and the snoring all around. Time passed. She turned of the flashlight and closed her eyes tightly so that even the dim light coming in from the windows vanished. She plugged her ears with her fingers. Michael felt the movement through the bed and reached out with his hands. He gently placed them over and around her head and felt her clamped eyes and sealed ears. Then he withdrew his hands and they sat for a few minutes more. Again Michael reached up and took Beth's hands and spelled for her; she guessed and hoped it might be, "Thank you."

She stood up, stroked his hair, and continued her rounds. On her last pass, she saw Michael sitting up on his bed, rocking back and forth. Her nightwatch was over at last, and she went to wake Theodore in his tent—he seemed to have been awake already. She fell into a temporary oblivion on her bunk.

The next morning when they awoke to find the sky foggy, everyone seemed somber. There came a steady rain, but by early afternoon, the sun broke through thinning clouds, and the memories of most campers had been washed clean, and the fun mood returned, even if the counselors and staff did not feel it. This was a mitigating blessing of many campers' disabilities: to live in the moment.

Michael's parents arrived to take him home.

Beth called Tommy from the camp office phone, but there was no answer. She left a message saying she would contact him by Saturday.

+ + +

All week Gene lobbied hard to go fishing, and on Thursday it seemed that Theodore partially relented, agreeing to let him ride in the camp's extended-cab truck. Theodore and Beth loaded Gene's wheelchair in the back with the fishing gear, and Theodore scooted Gene into the middle place on the front seat and buckled him in. Beth was to drive the pickup, while another camper propped Gene from the other side. Two campers climbed into the back seats. Theodore drove a van containing the remainder of the fishermen.

The place was only a mile from camp at a different creek from where they had fished before. They drove a half-mile upstream on the main river and crossed a concrete bridge where dozens of naked people swam in the natural pools. The road forked on the other side and they turned downstream onto a dusty side road and drove another half-mile to a tributary that was crossed by another bridge, a very wide one. They parked the vehicles on the bridge, on the side, where it was shady.

"I wanna go fithing," Gene said urgently from the cab of the pickup. The other campers, along with Theodore and Emily, unloaded themselves, picked up gear, and began walking down a trail to the creek.

Beth held back one able-bodied camper to help unload Gene. But before she started to remove him, she first checked out the trail and was dismayed with how narrow and rocky it was, and how thick the brush was at its sides. When she returned to the truck, Gene again said, "I wanna go fithing."

Beth stuck her head inside the window. "We promised you could come, but we can't get your wheelchair down the trail."

"I wanna go fithing!" he persisted.

"I'm sorry, Gene. You'll have to stay in the pickup. I'll come up and check on you."

"I wanna go fithing!"

"Maybe, Gene. Maybe we'll think of a solution." Beth was only putting him off and giving him enough hope to keep him happy for awhile. She thought it was a mistake to bring him. It wasn't fair—Gene vegetating in the pickup with everyone scrambling along the rocks and having fun.

He's used to doing nothing anyway, so it won't be so bad, she thought, as she and the other camper worked down the trail to the creek flowing in the bridge's shadow. It appeared that everyone had gone downstream. Beth walked along, until she came upon a fisherman, and she hunkered down and observed him for a few minutes. Then, to avoid spooking the trout, she clambered up the bank into the brush to circle around. She did this several times, watching but not fishing. An hour and a quarter passed. They could not risk being late for supper again. She shouted downstream to Theodore, and he began the trek back with campers in tow.

Up on the bridge, Gene had persuaded somebody to get him out of the cab and into his wheelchair. He had been sitting in the chair looking over the concrete balustrade when she saw him and she felt a tug of guilt.

"I'm so sorry, Gene, for forgetting to check on you!"

"Thath alright," Gene said, happily. "A nith man lifted me out. He had a red truck."

Beth was amazed and did not know what to think. "We have to go now. I'll fetch Theodore to help you back in the cab."

"No, I want to go fithing. Pleath!"

Beth sighed and walked to meet Theodore who had emerged from the trail. "Gene still wants to go fishing," she said. "We don't have time. If we're late again, we might be fired."

Theodore went grim as he stomped along. "I can't believe you left him alone. You should have told me you needed help. Let's take the man fishing. This is why we're here, isn't it?"

Beth was angry at the rebuke from Theodore, and said, "You should have waited for me."

Gene struggled to straighten himself up in his chair when Beth and Theodore neared. "Pleath take me fithing! Pleath!"

"OK, OK, Gene," Beth said.

Theodore asked Emily to drive everyone else back to camp in the van, and he wheeled Gene in his chair to the trailhead. He and Beth tried lugging him down, but brush on the sides was indeed too thick and stiff. Beth was about to quit, but Theodore said, "I have an idea." He unbuckled Gene, leaned forward, lifted him out of the chair, and set him laying face down on his shoulder. Gene was flat and stiff, like a board.

"How are you doing, Gene?" Theodore said as he steadied himself.

"I'm good. I'm good. Leth go!"

Theodore picked his way down the trail carrying the uncomplaining burden, while Beth followed with a fishing pole in one hand and a bait jar in the other. They left the chair behind. When they reached the stream, Theodore began wending upstream where no one had gone today. Here, above a rocky fall pouring into the shadow of the bridge, were two pools, one higher than the other, and between them a flat, wide rock. He rotated Gene, set him gently down on the rock where he lay looking at the blue sky and grinning, his head pointing downstream. Theodore stared at Gene for a moment, thinking, and Beth stood nearby, astonished by Theodore's boldness and the spectacle of the crippled man sprawled on his back.

Theodore pulled his wallet from his pocket, knelt down and put it under Gene's head. "Here's a pillow, old man. We only have time for one cast." He stood back and nodded to Beth.

Beth baited the hook with a salmon egg and cast the line into the upper pool. She put the pole in Gene's useful hand and reeled in the slack. She kept her hands on the reel's handle. She then heard Theodore's voice faintly above the clatter of the stream: "Oh, Lord, give Gene a fish."

The line swirled in the upper pool and then whipped down the narrow channel beside the rock where Gene lay. From his position, he could not see the water. Beth watched the orange egg bobbing to the surface and diving into the white bubbles. Suddenly, the egg vanished into the dark green depths, and Beth felt a tremble through the line. Gene had a fish on! She heard Theodore beside her saying, "Hallelujah," and Gene bleated hoarsely, "Hallelujah, Hallelujah! I caught a fith!"

Beth played the fish for a few moments so Gene could feel its energy, and then she brought it up to the water's edge. Theodore leaped over to Gene, and bending down, lifted his upper body and turned him around so he could see. The fish was a rainbow trout. Beth took the line in her hands, removed the barbless hook, and cupped the fish between her hands in the water.

"What do you want, Gene?" Theodore asked. "Keep it or let it go?"

"Keep it!"

"Oh, but Gene, it's so beautiful," Beth pleaded. "Let it go!"

"I don't know." Gene was struggling.

"It loves being alive in his pool. If we keep it, are you going to eat it? How can we cook it?"

"I might eat it."

"Oh, let it go," she said. "You know, the best fishermen practice catch and release."

"OK. I'll let it go. But only becauthe I love you."

Beth did not know what to say to this. She slowly took her hands from the water, and the trout hung there motionless. It fluttered its tail, drifted forward, and then darted into the deeper water where it disappeared.

There was nothing to do but reverse the portage, bundling Gene up to the truck, and this they did without so much as a reproachful grunt from him. Camp was bustling and they managed to slip into the dining hall as the cooks were putting away leftover food. There were raised eyebrows at their tardiness, but the cooks served the three latecomers anyway.

Somehow Gene had gotten hold of someone else's trout, and in the evening, he paraded the dusty, glazed corpse all over camp, telling everyone it was his. Hearing about his joy, Beth was almost sorry she had persuaded him to let his fish go, but thought, *His beautiful trout is alive and will be a trophy I'll cherish forever.*

Minutes before campfire was to begin, Theodore rushed up to Beth, who was hanging her washed socks on a clothesline outside the cabin. "I nearly forgot," he said. "We need a Sasquatch squall. Jona will say it's Big Bertha."

She and Theodore hurried outside. They walked through the woods at the edge of the central lawn area and could hear a rousing song coming from the campfire area on the other side of the lawn. It became quiet, and Theodore said excitedly, "OK.

When I say three, we'll scream. You pitch it high. Make it a blood-scurdling cream. Hah! I mean blood-curdling scream. OK. Ready? One, two, three."

Beth could not believe what came from Theodore's throat. He shook his head violently, and his cheeks flapped like water-filled balloons. She might have laughed, but for the chills running down her spine, because he sounded like nothing human, but rather a lost creature, a species dying away, a primate of a deserted evolutionary tree, canny enough to conceal its existence from its God-like, yet corrupted cousins, smart enough to survive in the vanishing wilderness.

They repeated the call. A few voices around the campfire replied in kind. Beth heard Jona exclaim, "Big Bertha, Sasquatch of the mountains!" There was an "oooOOOOOOoooooo." Theodore and Beth slipped up to the fire to join the singing, skits, and story-telling.

At lights-out, Theodore and Beth settled the boys down for the night. Theodore sat at Gene's bedside for a while and they whispered. Beth went around the room and patted the boys on their legs or heads. Though Gene said nothing to Beth, other than "Good night," he watched her with radiant eyes as she left the cabin.

Later, after the counselors' meeting around the campfire, Theodore asked Beth to stay.

"It's about Gene," he said.

He poked the fire with a stick and put a piece of fir on the coals. The other counselors said their goodnights and left.

Theodore began, "I don't know what you should make of this, but you ought to know."

He paused, and then continued, "Every night before lights-out, I and another male counselor strip Gene and set him on the pot. We have to hold him because he can't support himself. Tonight he talked a lot because he knows camp is almost over. He said— he wants to marry you. I was flabbergasted that he's in earnest, and I would have dismissed it, but he asked me if I thought he could ever get married. I didn't want to lie, and I didn't want to say the blunt truth, so I said . . . something like, 'You realize, Gene, it would be hard for you to be married, because the girl would have to care for you the rest of your life. It would have to

154

be someone very loving and special. Not many girls are like this, Gene.'"

Theodore continued, "I'm not sure he understood because he asked me the same question again, and so I said, 'With God all things are possible, Gene. All things are possible.' Afterwards, we showered him in his chair and got him dressed and into bed."

Beth had listened without any expression. Her heart had grown cold. "Why are you telling me this?"

"Tomorrow is Gene's last day of camp. Whatever happens, I ask you to be kind to him. I know you have been, outwardly, but think from his perspective. You are a beautiful girl, but there's something hidden. You've been hurt by someone. You carry a pain, and you give signals of vulnerability. Some men will take advantage of you, and you'll respond to their attentions, even those who don't deserve anything at all from you. You can be cruel because you have learned cruelty, and I just ask you to be kinder than you know how to be. Think about Gene—beyond his deformity and naiveté, I mean—because . . . he's an honorable man."

Beth was intimidated by Theodore's insight, and felt defensive, but she was moved to compassion, too. Emotions conflicted in her and her words came out tense. "What are you saying? Is he going to propose? You're not serious."

Theodore did not answer, but stood to his feet. He took a step closer to Beth and rubbed her on the top of her head—the first time he had touched her intentionally. "Good night, Beth. See you in the morning. Oh, I'm really sorry I didn't stay to help you with Gene—on the bridge. You were right."

Beth was alone. She left the fire, showered, and went to bed in her cabin inhabited by the slumbering campers. For a long while, she studied Gene's unmoving angular form under his blanket in the shadows across the floor, until sleep crept up and lightly puffed away her sentience, a fragile candle flame. Early in the morning while it was dark, she dreamed about Tommy. They were building a wall or tower. She was working above him and by accident let a large stone slip. It knocked him off the wall. Stone and body fell together and the stone landed on his head. He writhed on the ground, his limbs flopping hopelessly.

She woke up with a start to find Emily shaking her, gently telling her that it was again time for her nightwatch shift.

The first Friday of summer camp was always Press Day, and reporters and photographers spent morning to mid-afternoon talking with people and taking pictures. After breakfast, they and the whole camp walked the mile to the fish hatchery, and it was a staggeringly slow, jubilant parade of limping, marching, trooping, and wheelchair-riding. Theodore cruised up and down in an ultra-light, pedal/solar powered car that he had towed to camp on a trailer—he was an Engineering graduate student. Beth pushed Gene in his chair halfway, passed him off, and carried a blind girl piggyback. She hoped to avoid Gene, except at meals when it was obligatory.

At the hatchery, Theodore led the crowd around to the stages of salmon reproduction. He expertly explained the tubs, tanks, and technology, and how they dovetailed with natural processes. The most popular part of the tour was feeding the fish, and each camper was given a take-out carton containing smelly pellets. It raised a laugh when Theodore asked everyone to not eat the fish food, and this admonishment may have saved the appetite of the less discriminating campers from being spoiled.

After being with people who were different from normal, Beth found it amusing to be mistaken for one of them. Prompted by the relaxed atmosphere, she accepted a dare from Deirdre, an impish junior counselor. Her victim was a TV cameraman—beefy and cute—and Beth had caught him ogling her several times. After lunch, while she and Deirdre sat on the wall outside the cafeteria, the cameraman was catching a few color shots. The timing was perfect: Beth waited until he stared at her again, admiringly. She smiled back and began—watching him the while—to pick her nose industriously. His eyes shot away as a spasm of disgust seized his face. But Beth was not finished; she jumped up with a screech, put one index finger on her nostril and the other in her ear and began twirling in a circle on the sidewalk, letting out a high-pitched, buzzing wail, like a personal watercraft machine. The cameraman gaped at the exhibition. Deirdre stood next to him and deadpanned, "Don't be alarmed, sir. She's only showing her excitement about you. Since she axed a fellow last year, they've gotten her medication correct and she hasn't had any more violent episodes. Isn't it phenomenal how society has become more humane? We don't isolate the schizophrenic anymore."

The poor man decamped inelegantly, meaning he tripped and almost dropped his equipment in his haste to escape, and Deirdre and Beth cackled with glee.

For the final afternoon, after spending nearly an hour putting on life vests, those campers who could, ran the river in rafts, floating a rapidless section. Beth guided a raft and enjoyed the voyage immensely. More than once, when she glanced behind, she noticed Theodore, who was guiding another raft. He was looking in her direction, his face calm and half smiling.

The last campfire was the climax of the week, with a fireworks show and the appearance of Big Bertha. Bertha had figured as a camp tradition for twenty years. Each year her look changed, depending on available costuming, but whatever her physical appearance, the campers always feared and loved her. This year Theodore brought a styrofoam mannequin's head and a bushy brown wig to help make the body puppet.

Campfire rolled along. Outside the far wall of Cabin One, Theodore assembled the puppet by sticking a rake handle into the mannequin head. Beth got under a large red bedcover and centered the head under the cover, while Theodore stretched the wig over the head outside the cover. He tucked a water bottle into his pocket and stepped under beside Beth. It was cozy. Beth could barely see through the fabric; they rounded the corner of the building and let out a blood-curdling scream.

The campers laughed and howled as Big Bertha lumbered across the play field in huge steps. Jona cried out, "Quiet down, please! Quiet down. We are honored that Big Bertha has come to our camp. It's rare for a Sasquatch to show herself before a large gathering. The scientific world would be fascinated to observe this creature most people believe is only a legend. But there's more. I have been able to teach Big Bertha a few tricks. Would you like to see one of her tricks?" There were loud affirmations. "First we need 10 volunteers. Nearly everyone raised his or her hand, and Jona picked a handful of campers and new counselors.

"Now, I want you all to lie down on the stage right here in a row."

The volunteers obliged, as Jona continued. "You may not know, but Sasquatches grow to huge sizes and Big Bertha herself weighs around 400 pounds . . . Make it 500 pounds . . . and this on a vegetarian diet of nuts and berries and hotdog buns." (This was a jab to Beth.) "But they are amazingly coordinated and delicate, and we are going to prove it tonight. Big Bertha will walk over all 10 people and not step on anyone. Don't worry this is perfectly safe. Maestro, drum roll, please."

A counselor beat on a cooking pot. Inside the costume, Beth was laughing and stifling it so hard that she thought she would pee. Under Jona's exaggerated commands, they moved over the volunteers and stomped their feet whenever there was a clear space, and as Beth held up the mannequin head—her arms nearly falling off—Theodore dribbled water from the plastic bottle over the volunteers. They squealed, and at the end of the line Big Bertha jumped from the stage while the crowd caterwauled in laughter.

On the stage, Jona held up his arms and said, "Quiet down, please. Quiet down! I'm very sorry, ladies and gentlemen. I forgot to tell you. Big Bertha gets nervous, you know, in front of a crowd, and . . . and . . . BIG BERTHA IS NOT POTTY TRAINED!"

The crowd laughed; some groaned.

Jona tried to calm them down again. Beth and Theodore began a rollicking, careening retreat, but several campers wanted to touch Big Bertha, and they collected around her, blocking her path. Jesse, who was one of the wetted volunteers, took a boxer's stance and threw a punch that hit the cloth.

Beth began to be afraid. Theodore called for help.

Other counselors saw that it was getting out of control, and formed an inner circle to escort Big Bertha away. Jesse attacked again, and when Jona pushed him off, he tottered backwards and fell. The campers laughed, and Jona yelled to Beth and Theodore to run. Bertha flew across the field and around the corner of the building. The puppeteers threw off the bed cover. Theodore quickly sat against the wall and stuffed the cloth behind his back. Beth sat on the wig and put the head behind her back. They suppressed their hard breathing when a second later a troupe rounded the corner in pursuit.

Between gulps of air Theodore said, "She bolted into the woods."

The campers ran to the tree line and listened. They were disappointed to not see or hear anything, and Beth and Theodore waited to move until the campers left.

Theodore went to hide the costume, and the fireworks began. For some reason, Beth felt sad, and sat on a bench near the cabins well away from the campfire. It was not a huge display— Mr. Amundsen shot a dozen rockets from the riverbank. When the fireworks were burned up and the last echo died away, the camp grew quiet and Beth thought they were praying. In a short while, from the near darkness, forms began approaching. Her campers passed by without speaking. Beth thought she had better get into the cabin. Another form neared, and it was a camper pushing Gene in his chair. The camper left Gene next to Beth and went along to his own cabin.

"Hi, Gene. Did you enjoy yourself tonight?" she forced with false naturalness.

"It wath nith," Gene answered.

"Do you want to go inside now? I don't know where Theodore is." She hoped to move conversation along and avoid further love declarations from Gene.

"I'm not in a hurry."

There was a horrible silence. To Beth it felt like the eternal moments before an execution; she did not know how to stop this.

"Beth, will you . . . " He had spoken, "will you marry me?" but Beth ignored the last two words, because a sudden commotion breaking out near the camp entrance mercifully delivered her. She stood up. There were articulate male voices arguing. They were not shouting, but in the quiet evening, the sound carried a long way, and it was angry.

Beth took the wheelchair handles and pushed Gene up into the cabin. The other campers were quiet and nearly asleep. Beth could still hear the angry voices. She lifted Gene over into his bed and could not believe how light he was. His body was rigid. Beth felt a pang of remorse for this poor man and wondered if he got enough to eat this week, having to feed himself.

"Will you help me put on my pajamath?" Gene asked. "They are in my thecond drawer down." Beth took out the flannel pajamas. They looked homemade. Gene had begun to unbutton his shirt with one hand. Beth did not want to wait for him and unbuttoned the shirt from the bottom. She had to hold him up with her arm and work the shirt off with her other hand. She saw his ribs. There was no fat on him, and little muscle. She fumbled him into his pajama top, laid him back and buttoned him up. He turned his head toward the wall and Beth took a deep breath and unsnapped his pants. She carefully pulled the pants down so as to keep his underwear in place, and he lifted his hips so she would work the pants under them. The pants came off easily then, and the pajama bottoms went on. She folded his clothes into a neat pile on the chest of drawers. Next, she pulled up a sheet and a blanket and tucked him in.

"I need to see what the fuss was," she said.

Gene burrowed into the bed and smiled a plain smile, with gums and no teeth. Everyone else in the cabin was asleep now, except—and Beth felt a twang of alarm—Jesse's bed was empty.

"Thank you, Beth. There'th one thing."

"What is it? Please hurry."

Hurt flickered on Gene's face, but it faded in an instant. "Ith your real name Elithabeth?"

"Yes. Elisabeth Kamaria Telford."

"Thath a nith name. My name ith Eugene Amoth Thatterfield."

Beth cringed when she asked, "Is there anything else?"

"There ith. Will you vithit me at the nurthing home?"

She was relieved he had not asked The Question again, but she seethed inside. She had done her job, which was far above what any regular job required, and here he was asking her to give up hours of her personal life. She had assumed that with the week's completion, no more involvement in any other's life would be demanded. She could give, but Gene had crossed a line. She wanted to escape, even by telling him a lie. But she felt sorry for Gene, so sorry that she felt paralyzed, because there was nothing she could do to ease his suffering. In this there was anger at the universe that had allowed such pain, that had allowed a human being to be born into such a pitiful family, and survive and suffer. Her rebellion against whatever was ultimately responsible affected the words she uttered next.

"Yes, Gene, I will come to see you."

"Thoon?"

"Yes, soon."

Gene told Beth the name of the nursing home in Northeast Portland, which would be on her way home. She took Gene's crippled hand, squeezed it, said, "Good night," and left. She arrived at the campfire the same moment as Theodore, who came from the camp entrance. Most of the counselors were sitting in a circle. It was hushed.

Theodore whispered, "He's coming. No one speak. Don't look at him."

Beth caught a movement and restrained herself from turning toward it. *What's the mystery?* she thought. Jesse slowly shambled by, heading in the direction of the cabin. After he passed out of hearing, there was a communal sigh. People began moving and talking.

"What was the shouting about?" Beth asked. She was the only person who did not know.

"Uhh . . . we had an argument with Dr. Maynard, the Assistant Director," said Theodore quietly. "Jesse was humiliated when he got worked up about Big Bertha and he said he was walking home. Maynard tried to physically subdue him, but Jesse ran. He walked down the road as far as he could and still see us standing by the entrance. I told everyone to leave, and Maynard disagreed. He wanted to knock Jesse out with an injection. Well, I got intense and said if we treated him like an animal, he'd never forgive us, and it might not work anyway. He's tremendously strong. Maynard said it was my call, but he left to get the injection in case my approach failed. I hid in the brush beside the road and watched Jesse. If he kept walking away, I would have sent for help and followed him. As soon as Jesse couldn't see pursuit, he returned. You saw the rest."

Jona stood up and yawned, after which he said, "Nice work, Theodore. I, for one, am going to bed. See you in the morning, folks. It's been a hard week, and summer's only just beginning."

Theodore walked back to the cabin with Beth, and they found Jesse asleep on his bed and the overhead light blazing. Beth pulled off his tennis shoes and put a blanket over him. Theodore disappeared outside, but Beth needed to speak to him and followed. He had unzipped his tent and was about to climb inside.

"You forgot," she said.

"What is it?"

"Gene."

"Oh, my goodness!" Theodore stood up and shuddered with his head, imprecating himself.

"I changed him into pajamas."

"Really?" Theodore seemed impressed. "But . . . you didn't take him to the bathroom?"

"No. He might wet the bed, right?"

"He usually doesn't drink enough water. But I'll wake him at the end of my watch. If he needs to go, I'll get the next person—Brandon—to help me. Sorry, I forgot about Gene. Thanks for getting him to bed. A formidable task."

Beth was relieved that the solution to the bathroom was uncomplicated.

They stood unspeaking for a few heartbeats in the starlight-tempered darkness. Beth felt attracted to this young man, who seemed purer than any she had known. He could be brusque and impervious; he was always on guard against her, but he had a kindhearted side. Though it was not that cold, Theodore shivered and turned away. He knelt down, sat inside the tent with his feet sticking out, and began undoing his sandals. Beth had not moved until then, but she sat on the ground close by and leaned back against a tree.

"It could wait until morning, but I'm wondering what Gene said to you tonight," Theodore asked. "I had an idea he might—poor fellow . . . " He blew out a small breath.

"He asked me to marry him. I think he did. But I didn't listen because I heard yelling."

"He did ask you? What did you say?"

"Nothing. What *could* I say?"

Theodore spoke quietly, "Hmmm. It's difficult."

Beth felt that he was hinting about her personality—her character. She wanted Theodore to think well of her, and so she said, "He wants me to come visit him where he lives."

"Will you?"

"Uh . . . Maybe. Depends. Why does it matter to you?"

There was silence. Beth rose, brushed away the leaves from her clothing and legs, and took a step nearer to the tent.

Theodore said, "Well, I'm going to sleep. We can talk later," and he flipped his feet inside the tent and disappeared from view. She heard the silky sound of sleeping bag adjustment.

It was a dismissal. Beth returned to the cabin to sleep.

A few hours later—when her nightwatch shift was just over— carrying a flashlight, Theodore appeared in their cabin before Beth could leave it to wake him.

"Oh," she said.

"I set my alarm. How is everything?"

"All quiet. No problems." She yawned hugely and closed her eyes where she stood.

"Good," he gently said.

With her eyes closed, Beth lost balance and began to topple. She put out a foot to catch herself, and at the same time Theodore dropped the flashlight and put his hands on her upper arms, and Beth relaxed and let him support her weight.

A camper stirred and murmured because of the noise of the flashlight hitting the floor.

"Are you awake?" Theodore whispered to Beth.

"Yeah."

"Are you sure?"

"I'm sure."

Theodore let go of her and picked up the still shining flashlight. "Goodnight, Beth. Sleep well. See you in the morning." He turned and walked slowly away, down through the row of cabins.

Beth smothered a giggle and got into her bed.

+   +   +

Departure from camp on Saturday morning was much the same as the arrival. Cars and vans picked up their precious cargo and drove away. Then almost everyone was gone. Earlier in the morning, Jesse had asked Theodore to drive him home, and he agreed and received permission. While Jesse waited in Theodore's small car, Theodore loaded Gene and his chair into the front seat of the nursing home's van. Beth stood by and handed in his luggage. Theodore rolled down Gene's window. Because of his knarled frame, his chin only came to the bottom of the window.

"Goodbye, Beth. Remember your promith," he said eagerly.

"Goodbye."

The bus rolled away and Beth could still hear him saying, "Come thoon and God bleth you!"

Theodore was now standing by his car, writing on a card. Beth ambled over to him. She was relaxed and in a funny mood. Theodore held out the card and Beth took it, swaying her body, half dancing. Theodore looked to the right and left of her as he explained: "Here's the address and phone number of the nursing home where Gene stays. It's in a business section with busy streets, but it's not a bad place. Has fish tanks and a garden courtyard. I went to see him last year. On the bottom is my number. Call if you ever need anything. Anytime. If you want, I'll go with you to visit Gene. I'd like— We can have lunch."

She put the card in her wallet. "Do you want my phone number?" Beth asked, and swayed.

Theodore smiled with exaggerated embarrassment. "I have it already. But I have all the staff phone numbers. Well, I have to get Jesse home. Have a good weekend, Beth, and see you on Monday, early."

Theodore started the engine. He waved, Jesse waved, and they drove away.

Beth waved weakly and said, "Bye." They could not hear her. She jogged to her car—maybe she could drive fast, catch up with Theodore, and follow him as long as they had a common journey, but she never saw him ahead. He apparently was a good driver and knew the curvy river road. She rolled down her windows and the wind blew in. Thoughts of Tommy came crowding. Perhaps she should have told Theodore about him.

She had not been honest with Theodore. He liked her; she liked him—he was different. But what was her relationship with Tommy? They had no commitment, did they? No understanding of their future? It was better that she didn't say anything to Theodore—didn't tell him that she had a boyfriend. But then, didn't Theodore already guess something about the quality of her relationships with men? Well, she would go home, wash her clothes, and take a nap. Afterwards, she would call Tommy. He surely would want to get together, maybe tonight or Sunday. He might drive into town from the farm. Because she lost her phone, they had not been able to make plans. She probably should have borrowed a phone from someone. She put some rock music on the radio and opened a bottle of soda; the caffeine and the sounds kept her from drowsiness. It had been a long week—a lifetime. The day promised to be hot. Here was a nice swimming hole with cars lined up along the road for a hundred yards. She stopped to dive in, wearing her shorts and blouse. They would dry out on the drive home and keep her cool. She could sit on a towel.

UNIVERSAL MAN/Graceful Runner

*In the dream, I am visiting my old junior high. Someone
approaches me wearing medical scrubs and says, "Is it true you
can gossamer?" I say* yes. *He asks if I will teach him. We walk
behind the school to a field with a sloping hill. The wind picks
up and I stretch out my arms. We are caught into the air like
kites and rise several thousand feet. But the fellow begins
sailing too close. I try to push him away, but he keeps coming
on. He turns somersaults. His antics are dangerous because we
can lose our ability to hold up in the air. Then I notice him
leering, his tongue hanging out. I tell him, "Get away!" and
pull a silver cross—a foot long cross—from my pocket. I hold
the cross to fend him off. He crashes into me and the cross
pierces his heart. He falls dead against the earth. My mind is
frozen. I drop to where the body landed. Already people gather.
When the police arrive, they arrest me. Since the police station
is nearby, we walk towards it. My hands are bound in front, but
I can carry the cross over my chest as during a liturgical
procession. Fog rolls by. We walk down the middle of the road.
People stand along the street to look. Music surrounds us. As
we walk, I look up at a hillside. This scene refreshes me, and
I speak to the police saying, "I think it will snow soon."*
-from the dream journal of Stan Timmons

Chapter Nine
Birth Begun

When Beth arrived home after noon on Saturday, she found the household in upheaval. The effect on her after her first fulsome week in forested land with "special" people was akin to culture shock. Her brother planned to visit overnight and her mother had arranged a dinner party for Sunday and was panicked over making everything perfect—her bridge partners had been invited and Beth was expected to be present. Her father lurked through the rooms and kept popping prying questions about her week. Beth tried to stay out of the way. She rummaged around the house and found her telephone on the floor in her bedroom, which had fallen into disorder during the school year. As soon as she could, she escaped to the back garden to call Tommy.

She loved the garden, especially at night. The garden was encircled by a high wall, which made it feel exclusive and secure. When their family moved into this expensive neighborhood, her father began jamming every space—other than the lawn near the patio—with trees, shrubs, vines, and perennial flowers, many of them native. Telford swung between depression and mania: He would stick a bush in the ground and do nothing for a month. Then, without any observable reason, he would buy a truckload of plants, have them delivered, and slave feverishly around the clock only to fall exhausted into bed and remain there for days.

Beth sat in a chair at the lawn's back edge, near the door in the wall that passed into the neighbor's yard. It was late in the evening when she reached Tommy. He was understanding about the telephone mix-up, but had hoped she would have spent the weekend at the farm.

"I really need to see you," he said, cooingly.

"I'll bet," she answered in a teasing tone.

"Oh, but there's more. You'll like it here. I've been working in the fields and fixing things. I'm getting in good shape, too.

It's peaceful and cool and quiet. There are woods, a creek, and a pleasant pond."

"Sounds delightful." She laughed at their quaint expressions.

"How about if I came over tomorrow night?"

"I just don't see how. I have to get up early Monday morning to drive to camp."

"What if I showed up for your Sunday dinner?"

"We agreed to keep our relationship a secret, remember?"

"Yes, right. Then tonight? It's been a long day, but I'll drink coffee to drive home."

"Are you sure?" she asked, her voice carrying doubt.

"Yes. I'll leave right away!"

Beth was inexplicably frightened and said, "No, Tommy, not tonight. It's a long drive for such a short time."

Tommy said nothing, and Beth felt uncomfortable knowing he was unhappy with her sensibleness. Beth stammered, "Buh, but Tommy, I can come next weekend. I'll tell my parents I'm staying with a girlfriend. Pop asks nosy questions, but he never interferes. This will be perfect. I'd love to see your farm. Sound alright?"

Tommy truly loved Beth, as much as he was capable, and quickly adjusted, saying, "I'm sorry I was pressuring you. It'll be wonderful next weekend."

They talked about his week on the farm and hers at camp, but Beth found it difficult to convey the meaning of her experience, and she was afraid Tommy would resent Theodore. While they were talking, Beth was startled by her father standing in the shadows, demanding, "Who is it?"

"Hey, you scared me. Just a friend, Pop. Don't worry."

"What *friends* do you have, anyway?" he asked.

"Let's talk about it later, Pop. Please? Can I finish in private now?"

"I suppose so," he grumbled and limped back to the house. Beth noticed that he was barefooted and his feet were very pale.

"Still there?" she said into the phone. "I have to go. I love you, Tommy."

"I love you, Beth. Call this week on Wednesday night, OK? Don't forget your phone!"

"OK."

"Grand."

"Yeah. Talk to you later and see you next weekend."

They exchanged "I love you" again, and hung up.

Beth slept in the next morning and skipped church. Her father went to Mass with her mom and brother, and Beth had the house to herself. She cleaned her room.

Dinner was a heartbreaking affair when nothing consequential was discussed, and Beth went hungry, the meal centering on meat. Beth said almost nothing. Her brother said absolutely nothing. She really did not know him. The vacant place between them would never be filled with laughter, comradeship, and the kind of unburdening a sibling can offer, one who has so much in common with the other. After dinner, her brother gave Beth a shoulder-hug, shook hands with everyone else, and left. Her mother moved to the sitting room with her friends, her father crept to the billiard room, and Beth stared at the dining room table. She cleared away the plates, put the decimated turkey carcass away, loaded the dishwasher, hand-washed the wine glasses, ate another helping of salad, grabbed pepper spray, a set of house keys, a light jacket, and went for an exercise walk. Traffic was light, but there was the noise and smell of city that a perfect sunset and golden rays pouring down the street could not mend. She stayed out until it began to grow dark and ominous.

She was a block away from home when she began to feel that a man she had passed in the park was following her. She turned behind to stare at him fiercely and made her eyes bug, hoping to veer him away, but his eyes locked onto hers and he smiled, bobbed his head and kept coming. He was short, chunky, and dressed in a ragged black T-shirt, and had a red bandana tied on his head. Beth crossed the street to the opposite side of her home, and he followed. She ran. Once past her house, she crossed the street again, made a left turn at the corner, then sprinted the block's length and turned left again. The blind running had made her more afraid. In the middle of the next block she checked to see if the man had kept up. He had not, so she lefted through a lawn, skirted close to the house and came to her parents' back wall. She hurriedly found the key on the ring of house keys, unlocked the door, and entered the back yard. Next, she rushed through her house, ran upstairs, and, breathing hard, peeked from her bedroom window. The man who had followed her was under the street light and strutting back to the park. She heard a sound behind her; she turned in fear, and saw her father standing in the doorway. He looked normal, for once. Beth wondered if a week with the developmentally and physically challenged had altered her perception.

"See what I mean?" he said, calmly. "But they're not all such obvious bastards as that one . . . You shouldn't walk in this neighborhood alone." Her father turned and trudged away, saying in a low voice, "Maybe we should move away from here."

When Beth arrived back at camp early on Monday morning, she jumped into the bustle of accommodating the new klatch of campers. She discovered, to her amazement, that Theodore had changed her to a different cabin. He explained only, "I like you, Beth, but working closely with you—an attractive young woman—makes me uneasy. I need more space." Through the week he was as sociable—maybe more so—and as standoffish as ever. He spoke with her often at meals and after campfire. He talked and she listened, but she did not ask him questions, and the conversations dead-ended. In any case, Beth did not give much heed; the planned weekend with Tommy had driven away her attraction to Theodore. And the campers demanded total attention, although none became as endearing to Beth as those of her first week.

On Friday night, Theodore unexpectedly asked her if she would visit Gene with him on Saturday after work, and without hesitation she said, "No, thank you—I'm busy, and I'm not going home anyway, so I won't be near the nursing home."

Saturday morning, after many farewells at the camp, she followed the map she had drawn from Tommy's description. As before, Beth drove west, away from the mountains, but when she came to Interstate 205, she headed north, crossing the river. After some miles, she exited the freeway to go east again. Soon the road turned right angles to work around square-shaped farms.

170

Hay fields had ripened and stood ready for cutting. Away from the road, low ridges ran dark with evergreen trees.

The pebble driveway to the heart of the farm was long. It passed beside the two-story farmhouse into a shady courtyard framed by several buildings. Beth got out of the car and looked around. Everything was tidy. An old collie walked up and nuzzled her hand. Beth climbed the steps to the back porch and yoo-hooed. There was no answer. An iron triangle and a ringer hung beside her. She peered through the screen door onto the covered porch and saw the kitchen door ajar. By the porch window there was an antique wringer washer. A delicious soup smell and a hint of wood smoke flowed out from the next door, and Beth ventured inside onto the kitchen's linoleum floor. On the right of the high-ceilinged room was a wood cooking stove that radiated a soft heat. On the left was a table covered with a red checkered cloth, set for two. A small vase of fresh flowers adorned the setting and below the vase was tucked a note, which Beth read aloud, "I'm in the SE field. Find me. –T."

Beth sighed in joy and spun around to take it all in, and then ran outside. She now could hear machinery sounding like a snare and a bass drum following each other in a steady two note rhythm. She walked past the buildings and across a lawn to a line of poplar trees and behind them to a barbed wire fence. On the far side of the hayfield, a tractor crawled, pulling a baler, laying out rectangular prisms in rows. The driver wore a wide straw hat and a white shirt. He was turned sideways in his seat, watching behind him. Beth did not see Tommy anywhere. A breeze filled Beth's head with the honeyed perfume of freshly cut hay. The figure in the tractor seat waved his hat to her, and Beth realized that the farmer was Tommy.

Beth was not sure how to cross the fence and she glanced around for a gate. Tommy had switched off the machinery and came jogging over. The wire fence was between them.

"Hi," he said, and she said "Hi" back.

Both seemed shy. Though they had been intimate, two weeks of separation left them uncertain as to the status of their relationship. But Tommy leaned over the fence and kissed Beth, and she, accepting the kiss, told him that nothing had changed. He stepped back, put a foot on the bottom wire near a post and vaulted the fence. They embraced for a few moments and walked—holding on to one another—to the house. He smelled like clean sweat and sunshine, and looked strong and healthy.

+   +   +

During a lunch of Tommy's soup, and a salad that Beth tossed, neither of them said much. Afterwards they moved to the front porch swing to talk.

"So, how was your week at the camp?" Tommy asked dreamily. He was sleepy.

"Amazing. I see people who have major challenges as being persons, not just annoyances. But I'm glad it's only a job. What about you? What was your week like?"

Tommy grunted long and contentedly, and flexed his body. "I went to a grocery store yesterday."

"Aren't you getting bored?"

"I have you to think about," Tommy tickled Beth in the ribs.

"Stop!" she squealed.

Tommy let off and said, "I've been watching TV in the evenings. There've been some first-class dramas and classic movies."

"Oh, this reminds me, you should visit the camp. There are some marvelous characters in the campers. You could collect dynamite character sketches."

"I've been thinking about my acting career. It's not seemed very important this summer."

Not ascribing meaning to what Tommy said, Beth began to describe the people from camp, including Jesse, Gene, and Theodore. Tommy felt a stirring of jealousy toward the men; they had possessed too much of Beth. He even wondered if Theodore might rob Beth from him.

He drew away. "This Theodore. He's not chasing you, is he?"

Beth turned her face toward him and opened her mouth. "What? Are you worrying? He's harmless."

"What about Gene? You undressed him?"

"Crud, Tommy, Gene's a cripple!" She took a breath to calm herself. "Besides, his stupid infatuation was repugnant."

"Alright, alright."

Beth rested her head on his shoulder and said sleepily, "He wants me to visit him at his nursing home."

"Will you?"

Yawning, Beth said, "I . . . Maybe next weekend."

"Why don't you go upstairs and take a nap . . . ?"

Beth sang out another yawn.

" . . . and I'll finish the hay baling."

The weekend was like a honeymoon for Tommy and Beth. It was the first time they ever were together this long with complete privacy. On Sunday they took a leisurely breakfast, relaxed until noon watching a movie, then they ate lunch, napped, and by afternoon when the dew had dried, they went to the field to bring the hay into the barn. Beth drove the truck and Tommy tossed the bales up. Every so often, she stopped so he could stack them, crossed back and forth to lock them into place. Once, Tommy drew her out of the cab and took about a hundred photos of her in a hundred poses. They worked at the hay until dark. Crickets singing slowly told of the dropping outdoor temperatures, but the barn sweltered inside. They showered, drank a cool beer each, then turned in early, and in the morning Beth got up and left without eating breakfast while Tommy slept.

The next weekend was like the previous one. Beth called her mother and said she would be staying with "friends" again. Each week at camp became a universe to itself with its own languages and customs, and little room for anything outside of its demands—though Beth did find space to ride horseback, run, and exercise for the upcoming soccer season. Theodore dropped into the background, and the summer camp became one dream, and the farm with Tommy another dream of a restful island and strenuous physical labor, and a similitude of joy; and thus the summer fell into a rhythm with Beth occasionally appearing at home. But the vacation from school finally drew toward a close, and just past mid-August, as she returned to the house with her obsessive parents and prepared to jump back into her other world of college, Beth began to feel ill.

During pre-season soccer practices, she could not compel her body to respond, and because Beth was not performing as well as expected, the coach worried that he erred in giving her a scholarship. She set up plays and scored goals, but she fatigued early and had to be removed from scrimmages to recover. She was not eating well.

At first, Beth denied her sickness, and later she couldn't pinpoint what it might be—maybe the result of camp food and her uneven diet, or stress from her hectic summer and the depression afterwards. She said nothing to her parents and she did not want to go to the doctor. Not feeling tip-top slowed her down enough to consider matters that she had pushed aside, and she remembered her promise to visit Gene. She found Theodore's note and the name of the nursing home in her wallet. Though she felt terrible in the mornings, she thought she might visit him on an afternoon before her classes began. On the evening before she planned to move into the dorm, while her parents were out, she called the nursing home, asked for Gene, and was put on hold.

A sad, mellow female voice came on the line and said, "I'm sorry, Miss, but Gene Satterfield passed away."

"No. What did you say?"

The voice put it bluntly. "Gene died."

"But, when?" she asked, dismayed.

"It was . . . several weeks ago."

"But I met him at summer camp. He was alive. I was his counselor."

"Oh, you were? Summer camp. I remember, he died two weeks after camp. It was on a Sunday. He had a visitor on Saturday afternoon—a tall young man with dark braids. His name was . . . It wasn't Teddy. Late that night, Gene became ill suddenly, and we took him to the hospital. He died on Sunday."

Beth paused in shock, and then, "What happened to him? He was young. How could he have died so young? Polio isn't fatal."

"He never was well, health-wise. People in his condition age early, and there are certain internal problems. To tell you the truth, he needed physical therapy. He also was malnourished, in my opinion. I don't know any more than this." The voice ceased speaking.

Beth softly said, "Thank you. Goodbye."

174

"I'm sorry, Miss. Goodbye," the voice said and hung up.

Beth slowly tucked the phone away. She helplessly wandered the first floor of the house for awhile, and then went outside to sit on the front steps.

Thoughts ran through her mind. *This human creature is gone. This keen, loving, brave personality has vanished into nothingness. And his deformed body is now, what? A handful of ashes?*

Beth then remembered that she had had a chance to keep her promise to visit Gene. Theodore had asked her and she turned him down. *I should have visited Gene with Theodore,* she thought. *What did I do that weekend? Oh . . . I spent it with Tommy . . .* Abrupt remorse surged through her.

Forced into recalling, Beth wrapped herself around certain details of that weekend—what happened with Tommy and . . . how she had missed her period afterwards, and how ill she was feeling now, and then all at once everything fell into place. The birth control pills had failed, or maybe she used them wrong.

She spoke the devastating fact outloud. "I'm pregnant. Oh, God, I'm pregnant—again," and fear and anger overran her regretful feelings.

Evening drew on. She rose from the steps and entered the house. In the front hall was a telephone cabinet that held a lamp. She opened the cabinet to find the yellow pages and on top of the book sat a folded newspaper from mid-June. In the upper corner of the paper was a Portland police-blotter article and a photograph. The top story told about a murder in the very park near her home. Jerome "Rusty" Ingersol, 21, had been found dead with multiple stab wounds. With her pulse quickening, Beth looked at the date; the man had been killed on the night she had been chased. She looked closely at the photo—the man probably was the same one who had followed her.

Strange, she thought, and was filled with sudden dread. Beth noticed the tremor in the newspaper that she held; she drew a sharp breath and instantly built a mental wall. She refused to allow herself to ask the question, "Would her father kill somebody who threatened her?"

"I'll think about it later," she said. The pages she sought at the front of the "A" section had been torn from the telephone book.

175

She was really tired. *I'll look on the internet.* In the kitchen she poured a glass of wine and went to her room to play a favorite comic movie—one she often watched when distressed. Before she went to sleep, she recalled the business card Talus Schenk had given her at the beginning of summer—an eternity ago—the card from the reproductive health clinic where he worked as a guard. She found the card in a basket on her dresser. She dared not tell Tommy who had supplied the birth control pills.

+   +   +

It was now three-quarters into September, the beginning of a weekend—Friday noon. The day was cool, with a ceiling of thick clouds gathering off the coast and moving inland. After the dryness of late summer, the air carried a refreshing relief—a vanguard of the coming fall season.

Tommy parked his truck two blocks away from his destination. With a dark coat hanging over his arm and wearing black gloves, he walked straight into the women's clinic parking lot. He smiled charmingly, and acknowledged, but did not stop at the beckoning of a woman who stood on the sidewalk and offered him a brochure packet. Beth had told Tommy that the appointment scheduler said, "The protestors are innocuous, but don't provoke a conversation with them. They'll only harass you with fake offers of help and misleading information."

Tommy came up beside Beth's car. He paused to glance down through the chain link fence to where the protestors stood. Some held posters. A female figure—a clinic escort—in a blazing orange vest hovered near Tommy, and he waved her away. He heard an amplified voice saying, "Good morning, sir. I don't know why you are here today, but . . . " He heard enough; he saluted in their direction, climbed into the car beside Beth and closed the door.

"What do you think?" Beth asked in a low voice. "Nothing has changed since we talked last?"

Tommy looked out of the window toward the protestors. Six or seven stood with their heads bowed. "Look at them," Tommy said. "They're praying for us."

"We've got to figure this out."

They both hushed, and silence threatened to grow into fear. Fear of the unknown. Fear of disruption.

Beth broke the silence. "I didn't see you drive in. Where did you park?"

"Not far away."

"Why?"

"I like to be anonymous . . . my license plate? Listen," Tommy took Beth's hand, "will you *marry* me?"

Beth did not answer.

There was silence again until Tommy said abruptly, "Three!"

"Three what?" Beth said with impatience.

"This is the third time I've asked you to marry me."

"OK. I have a counter proposal. I'll go through with this today, and we will get married soon with my parents' compliance. We'll have a big wedding—whatever they want. If they're against us, we'll marry next Wednesday afternoon, because I only have morning classes. If we go ahead with, you know, this choice, we can have children later, if we want. Let's get married and I can play soccer, keep my scholarship, and finish school."

Tommy felt despondent. He had tried to woo Beth into the dream he had composed, with them living forever on his grandparents' farm and writing plays for two, and performing up and down the West Coast, or teaming up with people to make independent films, or finding an agent and breaking into mainstream cinema—he had the money. The head of the theatre department had told him that he would introduce Tommy to people. There were so many possibilities, and as Tommy imagined it, children fit into his dream.

"I don't know," he said. "I want to climb out from this deranged hole of a world. I've been thinking. My grandparents lived in another totality, and it was a good place. They've given their place to me, and I'm trying to fit into it, and I would like to share this life with you. To be truthful, I want a change. I think we've been given a blessed opportunity. I have a farm, and money—you know, I found a large amount of cash in a drawer in my grandparent's house—and you have a baby."

"Don't say that word!" Beth shivered.

"What? Blessed?"

"It's not 'baby.' It's 'pregnancy'—a potential."

Tommy scooted closer to Beth and put his arm around her. "We've been given so much potential. But I'll learn to make it real. We should flow with the current."

"The current has brought us here. I'm not ready to be tied to a baby. Being sick, getting fat, the risks, childbirth pain, big boobs, sleepless nights, messy diapers, and staying home with the kid until he's old enough for daycare. And when my mother finds out about it, she will detonate. There's no telling what Pop will do. He might kill you."

Tommy was not daunted. "I'll stay home—at the farm—with the baby, and you finish school."

Beth was impressed by this offer, though she didn't know if his promise would stick.

They fell into silence again. Tommy could hear the protestor's voice on the public address system from the sidewalk. He opened the window a crack to let in air. The voice was gentle, but the volume loud enough to hear words, if he listened. Two people wearing orange vests patrolled the parking lot and Tommy turned around to glimpse them behind him.

"They're to make us feel comfortable," Beth said.

"They make me nervous."

"OK," Beth said softly. "I see your perspective and you understand mine. I'll let you make the choice. Whatever you say, we'll do. I feel strongly a certain way, but I don't want my complexes to interfere with our relationship. But we have to decide now."

Tommy said nothing, and reviewed all they had talked about before, since the time Beth knew she was pregnant. He felt an edge of panic. If he could have persuaded Beth to understand his dream, then they would have come to shared terms, but this way, the responsibility weighed on his shoulders, and it scared him. He doubted she could be content having a baby. She might end up hating him someday.

"Are you sure you'll go along with whatever I say?" he asked.

"Absolutely. My mother makes our family decisions and I disrespect a man who has no strength. That's what I admire in you—your confidence."

Tommy felt validated, but he was saddened. "It's not confidence, it's . . . that I don't take anything too seriously, but this is serious. I don't know what's best. If you were making the decision by yourself, alone?"

"I would end the pregnancy; but I'll do whatever you say." Beth sounded hard; her voice sounded hard, but she hoped for Tommy to be strong.

He, on the other hand, wanted to please her. He was sad, but he forced himself to say, "OK. End the pregnancy." He dug into his pocket and jerked out a wad of bills.

Now it was Beth's turn to feel weakness. "Are *you* sure?"

"No. If you felt differently, it would be easier for me."

Beth was sad, too, but would not admit it. "You're right. I'm not ready to give up my freedom. We can have both worlds—yours and mine, when the time's right."

They exited Beth's car, and immediately she felt assaulted by the protestor's noise from the sidewalk. The voice and words were not themselves offensive, but they stood in such violent contradiction to Tommy and Beth's plans that the dissonance compelled them to hurry.

Tommy put his arm around Beth's waist and ushered her toward the door. The air was cold on her legs. She had worn loose fitting shorts for the occasion. There was another couple ahead of them waiting for the door to open, which it did, and that couple slipped inside. Tommy and Beth stared at the door. On the glass window strip next to the door was a handgun decal with a red stop symbol superimposed over it. Inside through this window, they could see the couple before them being gone over with a metal detector wand, and Tommy thought of the gun in a holster tucked inside his shirt.

He whispered into Beth's ear. "Are you OK with me leaving?"

"No!" she said, shocked. "No! You won't come inside?" She had thought all along that he would stay with her. She desperately wanted him to be with her until she had to go back to the surgery rooms.

"I can't sit that long," he said. "But I'll return in what, four hours, and see if you can drive. Have you got your phone?"

Beth was crushed, and angry, but she steeled herself and lied, "I'll be alright. Yes, the phone's here, I think, but there's no need to come back. I'll drive myself home. I'm staying at my parents' for a few days, and we'll break the news to them about getting married."

"Your dad?"

"Pop will probably like you, if you'll marry me. And if I stay in school."

"You sure you don't want me go inside with you? I'll have to get back to my truck first—for a book."

"Don't. I just want to get this over."

Tommy and Beth kissed briefly, told each other, "I love you," and kissed again lazily. Beth pulled away and walked through the door, which opened to her before she touched it. Tommy bounded down the steps, put his hands in his pockets, and headed for his truck.

Wearing a black golf shirt with an official emblem, Talus Schenk hastily stepped out of the building and scanned the parking lot. Schenk spotted Tommy moving toward the gate.

"Hello, you!" Schenk called out.

Startled motionless, Tommy looked back and stared at Schenk. When he figured out who it was, he swore. Of all people, Tommy least wanted to see Talus Schenk.

"Hey," Schenk blustered as he drew nearer to Tommy. "What are you doing here?"

"None of your damned business." Tommy drew his hands from his pockets. Though he was infuriated at the personal intrusion, Tommy was also staggered that Schenk seemed to have no bitterness at the rough handling he had received from Tommy backstage at the theater.

"Oh, I see," Schenk said. "You brought someone. Telford. She's waiting for me to check her in. Damn it all, she looks nice today. Are you together? Well, I hope you don't mind my asking. It's my job to inquire. Dr. Ponder is a good choice. Whoops, I'm not supposed . . . If you have a chance, mention to the receptionist, Laurie . . . that I made the referral and I'll get a commission."

"Mark Ponder? Dr. Mark Ponder?"

"That's . . . that's not what I said."

"What do you mean by 'referral,' possum-brain?"

"Oh, I gave Telford a business card last spring. You should thank me. The doctor is good. Did you come to Vancouver for privacy? Your birth control pills didn't work, huh? You should use condoms for backup. I have some here I'll give you."

"How do you know about any pills?"

"Oh, uhh. Ponder gives away samples."

"You're lying."

"No, really. She probably picked some up here."

"You're a bad liar, Schenk. She's never been here before. You gave them to her."

"No, really, I didn't. She refused them."

"You're a fart-sniffing clotpoll, Schenk. You're worse."

Schenk laughed to break the tension. "I didn't bring my Shakespearean dictionary, Duckwitz. But if you're going to insult me, the conversation's over. Be sure you avoid the protestors. They might be more than even you can handle."

Tommy put his coat on, snapping his arms through the sleeves one at a time. Schenk flinched both times and stepped backwards. Because it was his nature to be curious, and to needle Schenk, Tommy walked out to meet the protestors.

The clouds had darkened during the previous half-hour, and Tommy sensed increased apprehension among these people. One, a young man a little older than Tommy moved to intercept him. The others edged away and avoided eye contact. Schenk stood in the parking lot with his hands on his hips and yelled, "I eat babies for breakfast!" None of the protestors reacted. Schenk shook his head and climbed the steps to the porch to watch from there.

The protestor waited for Tommy to speak first. Tommy said, "The clinic people say you lie. What's your version of the story?"

The protestor stopped smiling, bit his lip and looked away.

Tommy became impatient. "Well, you're out here blabbing. Can't you speak now?"

The protestor cleared his throat and said something Tommy could not hear.

Tommy moved a step closer. "Would you mind repeating that? I thought you people were bold."

"Umm, ah, I'm just being deferential. Would it be convincing if I said we tell the truth and our help is real?"

"Probably not."

The protestor met Tommy's eye and asked, "What would be convincing?"

"I don't know. Nothing."

Tommy glanced up toward the building and saw that Schenk had gone inside. Tommy turned back to the protestor. "Tell me what you've got. What can you do?"

"It depends on your need. We have financial assistance. We have an OB-GYN doctor."

"We don't need anything."

"But what's compelling you to bring your child here. Something missing in your life?"

What's missing? Tommy thought as he brought down his defenses a little. "What's missing? I don't know."

"Umm. Maybe she needs you to be the protective man that God made you to be."

A black Corvette—windows darkened—cruised by.

There was a quality about this protestor that freed Tommy into confiding in him. "I don't know what to do. She told me it was my decision. I didn't want her to abort, but her heart wasn't with me. There's hardness in her I can't reach."

"There's a hardness in you, too."

"Yep." Tommy resented this probing statement and wanted to end the conversation. He had not slept much the night before and barely stifled a yawn. He turned and began walking away.

The protestor followed. "Wait; please wait one more minute."

Tommy stopped.

"I shouldn't have said those words about hardness. Forgive me," the protestor said, pleading, the words pouring forth now. "Your wife or girlfriend has been hurt by someone close to her. She might have been abused or disappointed. But she needs you to be strong. Your child needs you to be strong. If they were going to kill your two-year-old in there right now, you would be charging in like a bull to save him, and no one could stop you."

"But it's not a child. It's a fetus."

"Not a child? Then, look at this." The protestor took a folder from under his arm. He removed a thick sheet of paper and handed it to Tommy. It was a large glossy color photograph. Tommy's stomach knotted as his eyes absorbed the hideous bloody form, its mouth open and entrails splayed out. The little feet and hands.

"This is an image of an actual aborted baby at about 10 weeks gestation," the protestor said.

"This is sick."

"You're right."

"Where did you get this?"

"Well, we bought it from a group in Texas. They paid an abortionist to take pictures."

Tommy kept staring at the picture and making faces. "I've never seen anything like this before . . . grotesque . . . sickening. I suppose this is what the clinic people call a lie."

"They have to say that, don't they?"

"I suppose. They have to believe it too, or go insane."

"How far along is your friend?" the protestor asked.

Tommy glared for a second before answering, "Maybe . . . 10-11 weeks."

The protestor said carefully, "Your baby will look like this unless you do something. If you love your friend, go inside and bring her out."

Tommy considered this idea. His mind spun around as he allowed this knowledge about abortion to rearrange his worldview. He stood still, not moving, and then said, "I'm telling Beth I've changed my mind, and taking her from here. This alters the balance of our decision." Waving the picture he said, "Why didn't anybody show me this damn thing before? Can I keep it?"

"Sure, it's yours."

Tommy tucked the photograph away, jogged up to the clinic door, and pulled the handle. The door refused to open. He beat on it with his fist and turned to face the parking lot, wondering what to do next.

The door opened and Schenk slid out, blocking the door before Tommy could react. The door closed. "You can't go in now," Schenk said. "It's too late."

"What?" Tommy blurted.

"Clinic policy. If you don't go in with the patient, or if you go in and then leave, you can't go back inside. It's for security. The doctor receives death threats, and we have to limit traffic in and out of the building."

"That's ridiculous. She's my girlfriend and I need to talk with her."

"Sorry. If I let you in now, I'll lose my job."

"If I can't go in, ask her to come out so we can talk a minute."

"Nope. Can't do that, either. We can't pass messages. In fact, I'm not supposed to acknowledge when someone's inside. It's a security and privacy issue."

Tommy paced back and forth. He whipped off his coat, warming up in his emotion. "You're insane!" His voice rose in anger. "This whole place is insane. I want to talk with my girlfriend! Let me in!" he roared.

He tried the door again, and it did not budge. He took his phone and pushed the speed dial for Beth's number. It rang 15 times and cut off. He tried it again with the same result. "Oh, shit." He moaned. "She forgot her phone again." He walked up to Schenk, who was trying to back away, and glared at him inches from his face so that he smelt the coffee on Schenk's breath. Lowering his voice, he hissed, "Listen, Talus, you goddamned, mothering son-of-a-bitch. It's not too late to bring rape charges. Let me in, now!"

Schenk always feared this possibility, but Tommy might be bluffing—he couldn't force anyone to file charges. Schenk hated Tommy, but he had to treat him with professional courtesy. The protestors on the sidewalk were watching too, now, and one wore a camera. With all of the politeness Schenk could muster, he said, "I'm afraid I have to ask you to leave, or I'll call the police."

"You? Call the police?" In fevered desperation Tommy ran down the front steps and stalked out to the protestors.

The protestor with whom he had spoken waited for him at the property line.

"What can I do?" Tommy said, gushing out his words. "They won't let me inside and they won't give my girlfriend a message. I have to speak with her! Don't I have any rights?"

184

"The law doesn't recognize father's rights with abortion. You lose them once you submit to these killers."

"God!" Tommy paced up and down, running his hands through his hair. He accidentally kicked a soft object on the ground; the object was leaning against a light pole. "What in hell is this?"

The protestor's voice trembled. "It's a baby gift bag. We present it to a mother who changes her mind about abortion. Listen, if you want, I'll walk up with you to ask them to let you in. It might work. Or, they'll call the police and have me arrested, which would make a disturbance, and your girlfriend might come out to see what's happening."

Tommy reached out and squeezed the protestor's arm. "No. I don't want your help that way."

There was a dangerous light in Tommy's face and his hand moved to rest flat upon an object under his clothing. A girl wearing a wool stocking hat stood close behind the male protestor and said, "Let's call the police. Please. We can tell them there's a potentially violent situation, and they can diffuse it by negotiating with the abortion people. They might let a female police officer inside to talk with your girlfriend."

Tommy looked up from his anxious musing and muttered, "If I don't talk with her, someone in that building will hurt. I swear."

The protestor nodded to the girl who dialed 911.

A car slowed down and stopped, and the driver, a woman, stuck her head out the window. "Don't you people have jobs? Why don't you help someone who's alive and already in the world? You're just making it harder on the girls." She drove off without waiting for a reply.

An abrupt idea flashed into Tommy's head. "A bull, you said. A china shop. This bull's goin' to kick glass." He searched the nearby ground. Not seeing what he wanted, he sped across the street. In front of a neighboring business was an old, dry-laid brick pavement. Tommy pried up a loose brick from the edge. He put on his coat once again and glided up to the clinic door, with his hand pulled up into his coat sleeve and holding the brick through the fabric.

Schenk was still outside watching Tommy but did not see the brick until Tommy pulled the coat over his head to protect

185

himself. Tommy swung his arm back and smashed the window beside the door. Schenk ducked and tottered backward as shards of glass sprayed. Tommy reached through the hole and felt around on the door's inside for a way to release the lock.

"What are you doing!" Schenk lunged to try to pull Tommy away, and Tommy withdrew his hand, took two steps backward, and kicked Schenk with a heart-stopping blow to the midriff.

Schenk fell back and hunched over, the breath knocked from him. His lungs vainly sucked for air. By then, orange-vested escorts had arrived from patrolling the back perimeter looking for anything suspicious, such as trash that could contain a bomb; one of the escorts, a balding male with thick glasses, tried to grab Tommy, and he received a kick similar to Schenk's. He fell to the ground writhing. His glasses had fallen off and were lying on the pavement. The other escort hung back, gaping, then ran away and fumbled for her telephone. Tommy thrust his hand back inside the broken window and the next instant yelled in pain. Someone inside had smashed his hand.

By now Schenk had risen to his feet, wobbling, and saw a police car drive up. The car stopped along the sidewalk outside the fence. "Thank God," Schenk cried in a weak voice. "Ducky, it's over. Get away."

Pumped on adrenaline though he was, Tommy evaluated his predicament. He would be arrested, searched—his gun discovered—and he would not be able to speak with Beth. For an instant, he considered pulling the gun. He could keep the police at bay long enough to tell them he wanted to talk with Beth. The brick wall would shield him for awhile. But he knew that police shot people like this before asking questions. He could take Schenk as a hostage . . . All this flashed through his mind. Kneeling on the concrete ramp, Schenk stared at him.

All of a sudden Tommy quit, feeling it all futile.

Schenk had gathered enough composure to bleat, "Go now! Don't get caught." He noticed Tommy's hesitation and said, "Go! Go!"

Tommy understood Schenk's purpose and said, "You should be afraid of me, bastard." He pulled his collar up and limped across the parking lot and out of the gate. He continued with a painfully slow gait and rounded a corner down the street. Seeing no observers anywhere, he whipped off the coat and dashed away.

The police officer was waiting in his car for backup, his windows up. Had he been responding to the demolished window, he would have gotten out to assess the situation, but he had answered the earlier call from the protestor and did not realize immediate action was required. From his position inside the patrol car he could not see up to the building's porch.

A protestor was trying to get the officer's attention, but at that moment the officer's radio went wild. He wondered, "What in Hades? There's a riot somewhere!" The next instant, he realized that the "riot" was happening before his eyes. Still in his patrol car, he peered all around. All he could see were the usual protestors praying or visiting in small circles, plus a few children. The protestor flapped her hand back and forth at him. He exited his vehicle. All was calm and quiet.

He approached the protest leader—the girl with the wool hat. Before he could speak, other police cruisers began speeding in and parking all over the place—up on the curbs, sideways in the streets, in neighboring lots. The protestors did not react beyond moving closer to one another.

A SWAT commander came up to the patrol officer. "My team's a minute away. What's happening?"

"Uh . . . excuse me a second."

The patrolman, who knew most of the protestors by name, motioned for the leader to come aside to talk with him. "What's happening here?" he asked quietly.

"Well, the young man I called about," she said. "He went up and argued more with the abortion people. I heard a noise like a window breaking, there was some scuffling, and then he left."

"Oh. Which way did he go?"

She nodded in the direction. "On foot."

"Did he go straight or turn?"

"I didn't notice. Some of the others here may have seen more than I did."

"Oh. OK." The officer rolled his head around to loosen stiffness in his neck. The SWAT team's van came into view. "Don't worry," the patrol officer said to the girl wearing the hat, "This has nothing to do with you."

187

"That's fine."

About then, a man in his 60's passed by on foot along the opposite side of the street. He wore long grey hair and beard, and a tie-dyed shirt. His feet did not falter as his eyes alternated between watching the pavement and his hands, which were fervently crocheting a rainbow-colored material.

By now, the police had ascertained that there was no immediate threat. A captain made his way to the front porch with several officers. Some stood around and talked, and a few began driving away. Ponder's people frequently cried "wolf" when there were only sheep. A broken window and bruises, however, were unusual, and the police immediately initiated an investigation, conducted in a manner to disrupt the abortion business as little as possible. The patrols in the neighborhood picked up no suspects.

The police watched the security film of a man in a dark coat and a stubbly beard breaking the window, attacking the clinic people, and leaving; they questioned the protestors, who did not know Tommy's name, nor had they taken pictures of him. The police listened to Schenk describe the interchange with Tommy. Schenk said the perpetrator was a homeless person who made drunken threats about burning the place down before he exploded the window with a brick. Schenk's version did not match the protestors' story, and the police investigator initially concluded that the protestors were lying to protect the homeless person. They interviewed the office manager who monitored the security cameras. She had only seen a hand reaching into the window and had hit it with the metal detector. The two escorts witnessed little of the initial conflict because they were behind the building, but they were certain they could identify the attacker. They thought that he had arrived with a patient, and so the police went over the films again from an earlier time frame, and the escorts' story seemed confirmed, except the cameras had not been zoomed in during crucial points. There was no clear image of the attacker's face.

The police ran the plate of the car that the suspect had been shown leaving, and they found it was registered to Valerie Telford, of Portland, Oregon. But Elisabeth Telford inside a clinic recovery room was not feeling well by then, and could not answer questions. She was, in fact, quite ill. Later in the day, an officer called Schenk and asked if he knew the younger Telford, and he admitted he had dated her once and had performed in a play with her. He couldn't say who her current boyfriend might be. The police searched the neighborhood for the man who had been knitting, but they discovered nothing about him.

After breaking the window and escaping, Tommy had entered the garden of a nearby church.

The garden was enclosed by a solid rock wall, except for a massive, locked gate. Strangely, there was a gap between the gatepost and the wall, and Tommy easily slipped inside to the garden. The door to the church there was locked also, and he threw himself onto the ground. He sat a long time, brooding, and tormented. What if Beth came out of the clinic and found him gone? How could she have allowed Schenk to go over her body with a metal detector? How could she let Ponder touch her? Why did she forget her phone again? Or did she turn it off? Was their baby dying?

When everything had quieted down and the protestors had departed, and while a few police officers went about their investigative business at the clinic, and while Beth was still inside, Tommy returned to his pickup and drove by the front of the clinic, with an immense sorrow crushing him. A few hours later, thinking he might drive her home, he returned, hoping to find Beth waiting for him. The parking lot was empty by then but for a few fallen leaves; the gates were shut, and Beth's car was nowhere to be seen.

Tommy did not notice the unusual light in the sky.

A large airliner floats in the sky not far overhead. The jet carries two hundred people or more. As I watch, the plane begins to dive. To my horror, it picks up speed and then cartwheels into the ground. The ground trembles and I fall to my knees.

-from the dream journal of Stan Timmons

Chapter Ten
Stanley's Hopes

That same Friday evening, not long after Tommy drove past the abortion clinic entrance for the second time, Stan backed out of his driveway and headed toward Mindy Sterne's Vancouver home. Tonight was the book discussion group. His late forties Chevrolet Woody hummed along, and Stan put on a classical music radio station. All day the sky had been overcast, but the sun in setting dropped below the cloud bank and turned everything amber, even the maple trees, which carried their own golden autumn leaves. Stan breathed deeply and reviewed the day—a day in the first month of his second year teaching high school English. A student in his fourth period class walked out because Stan had asked him to stop talking to his neighbor. But today had been easy because there were no pranks, threats, vandalized cars, or petty violence. The month had been challenging. The college work, student teaching, and a year of experience had not prepared him for the problems he had encountered this term.

Stan tried to imagine why this year was so bad. Perhaps the peace and order of society deteriorated at an increasing rate.

Children in schools needed literature, Stan preached quietly to himself. Classic literature was among the few resources allowed in schools where values could be taught. When morality became scrubbed out of the public sphere, those old stories were the only chance these children had to be exposed to the heritage of civilization. In this regard, Stan thought of himself as a subversive to contemporary culture. He recalled a speech he heard while in college; an aged former Soviet Union dissident said, surprisingly, that the moralist Leo Tolstoy had been read in the government schools during the communist régime. Most of Stan's incoming students did not understand history or language, other than what was the current fashion.

Stan had discovered his life's mission by simply reading novels. Never having traveled far from home, he lived life and explored the world through books and other media, and now he wished to share the stories that he loved with the next generation.

His idea might have seemed outdated, except that he had fewer discipline problems than other teachers in his school. Stan attributed this to his teaching method—he had taken film courses in college and now he incorporated movies into the study of literature. His class would read a book and watch a movie interpretation. Often he took a group of students to the theater at his expense, or rented a film to show at the pizza joint near his house. Because of this, Stan was among the few teachers at his school who were popular with students.

Today after school, Stan had walked an hour through the streets and parks in his section of Vancouver. Often he rode his bicycle and went farther. No matter how hard Stan exercised, he remained overweight. He had a body type made for surviving rough winters. After his walk, he prepared a casserole for the oven, showered, took a short nap, and ate his meal alone, facing the television news. Then he dressed for the evening.

Tonight, driving along, he carried his life purpose to real adults at the monthly book discussion group. There, he could relax and let the conversation flow. He was a young man, not widely experienced, chaste and unmarried, with no specific marriage prospects. The best reason for going to the discussion group tonight was to see Mindy, if he could.

Stan always enjoyed the Sterne home overlooking the Columbia River. This river was a compass in his life. Like explorers and sailors who once were guided by the stars, Stan relied upon the river for directions; west and east were not as important as downriver and upriver. Stan's favorite novel was *The Adventures of Huckleberry Finn*. Instead of steamboats, in the air above sailed the airliners, circling, landing, and departing the Portland International airport.

As he neared the Sternes' place, the underside of the clouds glowed rosy. Stan parked and climbed the long steps to the back deck of the house. He paused a minute to contemplate the tint that was radiating from Mt. Hood upriver. Angels lived in the everlasting snow up there, he had thought as a child.

An angel lives in this house, as well. Mindy might be home—after all, she had invited him. Without knocking, Stan stepped inside the glass door. Dark-haired Mrs. Sterne rose elegantly from a carved chair near the door and greeted Stan, whispering in his ear, "Nice to see you, Mr. Timmons. Your sister and Guthrie are away, visiting with college friends this weekend."

"Thank you; it's a good indication," he whispered back. She took his jacket and Stan helped himself to a cup of decaf coffee in the hallway and entered the large front room. Talk was underway already, as Stan was late. He scanned the circle and estimated two dozen people. Alone, none of them would be noticed in an ordinary crowd, but as a group, with their informal dress and intelligent faces, they could have been mistaken for college faculty, or attendees at a political function. Stan lifted his hand slightly as a greeting for Dr. Sterne. To Stan's disappointment, Mindy was not present. He settled into a spot on a couch made free by someone shifting over, and tuned his attention to the discussion.

The book for the evening was a Pulitzer Prize winning account of an Eastern European military conflict, featuring leader and prisoner of war, Major Karađorđević. The writer of the book, Saul Bonesteel, was an American Civil War historian. This book had not been Stan's choice because he had already read several similar prisoner accounts, but it had been selected last month by consensus of the group.

Every so often, movement at the room's entrances caught Stan's eye, and he glanced to see if it might be Mindy, but it always was, as he supposed, one of Mindy's brothers or sisters.

The discussion flowed forward. Stan contributed a reflection upon how human beings endure traumatic circumstances, and he compared the main character's experience with other political prisoners. "Primo Levi wrote about survivors at Auschwitz. They created schemes to buy extra food from workers from the neighboring villages. Some prisoners stole such things as brooms, some mended clothes. They had to appear healthy to avoid the extermination selections. Extra food meant life. But no one starved in the camps; they would have been gassed first."

A young wide-shouldered fellow with pleasant features expressed how he admired a prisoner mentioned in the Bonesteel book, a celebrated violinist named Sebastian Tocsila. Tocsila, he said, had been imprisoned by Karađorđević's faction and had been in the group of prisoners exchanged for the Major near the end of the conflict. Tocsila's crime was political in that he dared to play folk music of the side opposing Karađorđević in the war. His captors refused him his violin, but he practiced for a year with a carved board, and for a bow, he used a stick. Not only this, but he composed music and, because they did not give him pencil and paper, committed it to memory. A month after his release from incarceration, he performed a solo concert to a gigantic audience. The young fellow said, "The concert stunned the world with its depth and beauty. Tocsila's political enemies—those following Karađorđević—had made a mistake from their perspective by arresting him in the first place, because he became a focal point for resistance."

After a moment's pause, the fellow then compared this to Solzhenitsyn's writing and memorizing poetry during his years in the Soviet Gulag. The young man's throat constricted with emotion and he almost could not speak, but at last he said, "Great suffering often breeds great art and the character qualities needed for leadership."

Stan realized this must be a Sterne child. He once heard Mindy sound the same when she was talking about a school assignment—an interview with parents whose children had committed suicide. Stan did not know this young man's name. He ventured to ask if the fellow had recordings of Tocsila that he might loan him, and he enthusiastically said, "Yes."

Discussion surged along about art and suffering. The subjects diverted, branched, circled around areas the group wished to avoid, came back to a previous stream of thought, and then disappeared into a confused sea of current politics. The talk encompassed rescuing Jews, famous prison escapes, the psychology of genocide, and slipped into an argument about which side in this small-scale war in Eastern Europe owned the moral high ground. The majority of the group agreed: Major Karađorđević was a noble, sensitive character, even if sometimes forceful and violent.

Dr. Sterne had remained silent throughout the evening, and occasionally nodded to himself in a way no one noticed. For awhile, a child of about seven came and sat in his lap. During the discussion he jotted quick notes on a yellow pad, and at last as the hour grew late, and the participants spread an infectious yawn around the room, he spoke.

"We must keep in mind, Karađorđević is a war criminal—not an honorable combatant in a just war. No matter what his motives were, he killed thousands of innocent civilians. His perspective is warped, and therefore we must question the values he purports, no matter how winsome he is. This, however, isn't what Professor Bonesteel's general reading public thinks. Because his victims were of a certain class and an unpopular political stripe, Karađorđević is a hero to many people in our culture, Mr. Tocsila's fame not-with-standing—recall how he was maligned in the book."

From the corner behind Stan, someone Stan had not seen before jerked his body upright saying, "Karađorđević should never have been released! They should have executed him!" He was a short fellow wearing bushy hair and a trimmed beard, and the man bore a daunting arrogance.

Stan cringed and thought, *This guy is taking the discussion too seriously.* Stan felt jittery at the change of direction introduced by Dr. Sterne, and even more jittery at the outburst.

A tortuous silence followed until Dr. Sterne responded quietly, contradicting the offended and offending speaker. "I agree, Karađorđević deserved to die, and he never should have been released, but his enemies treated him humanely in hope that he would understand and renounce his cruelty."

After the disturbance, the thought-currents began meandering again, and people who had not spoken before offered opinions. Sterne scribbled notes. The meeting ended at 11:00 p.m. Stan made an unhurried circuit through the room and spoke to everyone he knew. He noticed the fellow who had burst out with the unpleasant remark speaking with Mrs. Sterne, and overheard him apologize. She said, "Don't worry, Doctor; it's an emotional subject." The meeting thinned and there was no hint that Mindy was home. When Stan asked Dr. Sterne about her, someone immediately took Sterne's arm, pulled him away, and began talking about golf.

Stan thought angrily, *People are so rude.*

He collected his jacket and stepped onto the deck. The air was chilly. The Portland lights across the river illuminated a broad band of horizon before him. The lights near the darkness of the river were blue. He trotted down the long steps to his car and stopped, feeling for his keys. From the direction of the ground level of the Sterne house came the sound of a small gate closing, and Stan turned to see Mindy walking toward him. His heart lurched. She carried herself with a gentle, lilting gait. Stan did not mind that she was taller than him, and he admired her slender figure, framed by long, rich blonde hair that she alternately wore down, or braided, or folded up under itself in her own creative style. Tonight she had double braids like an Amish girl. She was wearing an ample woolen skirt, and a blouse under an oversized sweater. What Stan had always found appealing was her immense calm, and she never seemed embarrassed by his discomfort in being near her. She usually smiled when she spoke, but tonight there was something different.

She walked around to the curbside. "Did you enjoy the discussion tonight?" she said as she leaned against his car, facing the river.

"Yes," Stan said, leaning next to her, "but why didn't you come?"

"I sat in, at first, but I left before you arrived. Someone . . . came to the meeting."

"Who?"

"Mark Ponder," she said, shuddering and looking toward the lights on the horizon. "He's someone my dad knows from the hospital, from his medical work."

"Why avoid him?"

Mindy hesitated and wrapped her arms around herself. "Well, please don't misunderstand me, but he's a woman's doctor."

"Oh, and?"

Here Mindy stopped for many seconds. Her voice quavered when she finally said, "He's an abortionist here in Vancouver."

"Ohhh, I see." Stan said tenuously. He had not thought much about this distasteful subject except once in college. Speakers from both sides had been invited to address his rhetoric class. Afterwards, his professor had pressed him to articulate his

196

position and all Stan could say, was "I don't know what to say."
Now, he thought with trepidation, *a girl I like is involved.*

"But it isn't me," Mindy said, seeming to know his mind. "It's
Beth Telford. Anyway, she got pregnant by your friend Tommy,
and, well, I think she has an appointment tomorrow at Ponder's
clinic. I tried to talk her out of it. Beth's boyfriend tried to talk
her out of it, too. He was angry at first, she said."

In speaking those words, Mindy's voice had begun tight and
higher in pitch and ended quiet, and Stan knew that, behind the
calm exterior, she was extremely upset.

"Oh, no," Stan said. "I haven't seen Tommy for awhile. I
knew . . . I knew their relationship wasn't what it ought to be."

"I called her earlier this week, and she told me her situation. I
pleaded with her not to do it, but it wasn't any use and I've been
heartbroken ever since." Mindy wiped her eyes with the sleeves
of her sweater and took a slow, deep breath. She resumed
speaking, now in her normal voice. "Beth won't answer her
phone. She's been feeling rotten, I guess, and missed her classes
today. No one answered their family phone. I thought I'd go to
the clinic tomorrow as . . . a last attempt, and see if she'll talk. I
don't know what else to do."

"Why do you think it's . . . who? Ponder's clinic?"

"She . . . I don't think she meant to tell me."

"Aren't there protests? Aren't you afraid of being arrested?"

"No, not really, but I came to ask if you'll go with me."

"Oh. Yes, but . . . I plan to hike with the Snowbird Club
tomorrow. They're covering a section of the Pacific Crest Trail.
We leave Vancouver at 6:00 a.m."

"I really need someone to go with me," she said, moving closer
to Stan. "I don't know the protestors. None of my brothers are
available. Won't you come? If you do, we may have time
afterwards to drive up the Gorge highway and hike somewhere,
like climb Beacon Rock."

Stan was amazed she had made this suggestion, but his voice
did not reflect his inner feeling. Instead, he sounded like an
older brother. "OK, I'll go with you. But there's one condition."

"What condition?"

"You come with me on the next Snowbird hike."

"Well, I won't promise, but I'll think about it." Noticing his frown, she said, "Possibly, if I don't have too much schoolwork. Back to tomorrow—I'll drive. My car will be better in the Gorge than yours, lovely as it is. I'll pick you up at 7:30."

Affected by her feminine power of persuasion, Stan was agreeable. He opened the passenger side door and searched for paper to write his address for Mindy, but she said, smiling with her eyes, "I remember how to get there."

His thrill in the arranged adventure with her, and his nervousness, made him forget she was still nearby. He hurriedly scooted over to the driver's seat, as if that would make tomorrow come quicker, then he realized how silly he was acting.

Mindy walked around to his window. It was rolled down and she said, "Goodnight."

She turned away and stepped toward the house, but Stan called out, "Oh, what does Ponder look like? Funny hair?"

"Yes. Why?"

"That's crazy, him being here tonight. Oh, do you have any recordings of the violinist Sebastian somebody? Your brother said he would loan some to me."

"That would be Anselm. If we do, I'll bring them tomorrow."

Stan said goodnight and drove away. Mindy waved and then danced her lilting step into the house. Stan, watching in the side mirror, thought she couldn't help walking that way even when sad. Things had turned out well for him—he had a date for tomorrow with Mindy! It was delightful to drive this old luxurious car, especially this evening. He tuned into a favorite jazz station of his, an AM station broadcasting all the way from Arizona that he was able to pick up only at night.

When Dr. Mark Ponder drove away from the book discussion, he was angry with himself for acting like a fool. He sometimes had a temper like that—explosive and forceful. With age, he had learned to make a plan for controlling his temper in situations when he anticipated trouble, but for tonight he had not made such a plan.

Well, he did not have to go back to that book club. He had no need to repair his credibility within the Sterne circle. Because of the rumors he had heard, he had been chary about these meetings ever since Sterne invited him, and he came this night partly to see if his guesses—that he was being set up for harassment or a conversion attempt—had been true. He had, in fact, been mistaken—people were courteous and respectful, and the conversation stimulating and balanced.

He hated the merciless questions that often arose during new social situations: "You're a doctor? Where do you practice? What's your specialty?" Usually those questions stopped after he told them, "I'm a gynecologist." But Ponder could read the thoughts behind the smothered interaction: *Ponder's an abortionist? Ugh.*

There had been confrontations, especially from his zealous anti-abortion niece. Or, protestors used to recognize him at the grocery store and announce, "A baby killer is in the building!" and so he hired a valet to do his personal shopping. He knew also that even those who celebrated him as a champion of women's rights did not really like him. He was their patron saint, but not their friend. Both society and the law protected him, but it should suffice to say, Dr. Ponder did not have many genuinely warm acquaintances.

He had Barbara, twenty years his junior and his third wife; and he had one child by his first marriage—that brat despised him and he seldom got to see his grandchildren, not even at holidays. But with Barbara he had produced two children, Tyler and Alyssa, and those cherubs adored him. Barbara had an active social life in the community and drank too much. She held positions on a handful of non-profit boards, including the symphony guild. She was a trustee at her church as well. Busy as she was, and having all the money she could wish for, she seldom interfered with his mistresses, some of whom had been patients. He and Barbara were comfortable; it was convenience and friendship—and the children—that kept them together. They seldom fought. From the bitter experience of his first two marriages, Ponder had learned to avoid fighting.

He sped along in the new Porsche toward his gated community. (He had sold the Jaguar.) Tomorrow was another procedure day, so it was best to go to bed early.

When Dr. Ponder arrived home, he switched off the security system and opened the garage door from his car by remote. Barbara was still away at a party. He glanced in at the sleeping children and paid the frumpy, nervous babysitter, scarcely listening to her summary of the evening. He entered his bedroom and looked at the logbook on the computer. Out of habit, he scanned the photo gallery of the heat and motion activated surveillance. Two deer and a family of raccoons had passed near the house. The deer must have jumped the fence, which brought in a deputy sheriff to check the cause of the alarm. Ponder presently recalled why he had been edgy tonight. It had been a trying day. A procedure went badly and they had to transport a patient to a hospital; fortunately the hospital released her to go home. Worse than the procedure going awry, some kook broke his window and mauled Talus Schenk, and the police came and nosed around.

He scratched a note to remember to call the feds on Monday. "They've got to become involved now," he said to himself. He must not let these occurrences bother him.

Ponder's electronic-mail brought him the invoice for the evening's silent alarm call. It was worth a good night's rest, knowing that no assassin lurked outside his windows. He earned the amount of the bill in five minute's work—the thought of which reminded him about something important.

He donned his pajamas, poured a glass of red wine, set it on the bedside table, and read the newspaper for a few minutes while sipping the wine. Now he was getting sleepy. What was it he wanted to think of? Yes. It was the right time to open another clinic. One at the coast, so he could buy a villa there and stay a few days a week. He had researched and found he could profit especially during summer months. He also wanted to sell the therapeutic value of the ocean—to help in emotional recovery—and he considered buying a motel. He might invite girlfriends to join him, or maybe he would meet someone local. Under his current business strategy, he would retire 10 years earlier than other doctors in this region . . . He could change his name, settle in another part of the world, and be safe. With this enchanting reverie, Ponder drifted into sleep and did not wake when his wife returned much later. She took a medication to make her drowsy, and she too slept the sleep of the dead.

+   +   +

Southeast of Ponder's gated community, soon after the abortion doctor's wife fell asleep, Stan's phone rang, and he awakened instantly. It was dark in his bedroom. His eyes were not yet focused and his mind was half-numb, so he could not see the clock, but he lifted the receiver.

"What time is it?" he said.

After a slight pause, the man's voice on the other end was businesslike, as if the call was normal, "1:28 a.m. Don't go to the abortion site tomorrow."

"What?"

"Don't go to the abortion site."

"Why? Who is this?"

"A friend, and I'm asking you a favor. Please don't go to the abortion site. Just wait and I'll contact you again soon."

Then, whoever it was hung up. Stan was befuddled and his heart slammed inside his chest. He sat on the bed and turned on the light. He looked at his phone's display; the number from which the call came was untraceable. He sat awhile and let himself awaken more fully until the call's import began to clarify. Should he give credence to this call? What did it mean? Could he break a commitment to Mindy because of some creepy crank? He couldn't possibly sleep now.

The house was chilly, and he put on a sweatshirt. He grabbed a sleeping bag from a closet and lay down on the couch in his front room. He reached to the lamp table for a relaxing novel—a cozy murder mystery—and eventually he dozed off with the book open in his hand and the light burning. Nevertheless, at 7:00 a.m. he woke refreshed. There was no time for considering the strange telephone call now. He dressed for hiking and ate a quick breakfast. It was not long before he heard a "beep, beep." Mindy had arrived in her blue VW bug.

Stan dashed out the door, coffee mug in one hand. Mindy wore a floral perfume, a colorful blouse, and khaki pants. She never wore makeup and didn't need any. The car heater was on. The morning was dark with fog drifting in from the ocean 100 miles away, and they drove slowly with the headlights shining. It was twelve minutes to the women's clinic. Mindy did not speak and Stan watched the dreariness out of the side window and wondered if he should tell her about the phone call. They both were tense and gloomy.

The women's clinic was a Mansard-roofed building in a neighborhood populated by business offices and a few homes. There were two churches nearby within visible range. Mindy and Stan drove up a narrow street leading to the clinic. When they were three blocks away, they saw a mystifying sight ahead in the heavy fog—cold blue lights fiercely glittering, suspended in the air. As the Volkswagen drew nearer, police cruisers emerged below the lights. The cruisers were parked at odd angles at the intersection. The VW drove closer. The road was barricaded. A handful of officers stood on the far right corner.

"Pull over to the side," Stan said with suppressed anxiety.

Mindy stopped and they looked at the situation. A woman materialized from the corner opposite from the police officers. Mindy was startled. The woman was wearing a knitted wool cap and an overcoat. On her face she wore a kindly smile.

Mindy rolled down the window. "What's happening?"

"Good morning," the woman said bending down and looking into the window. "My name is Maria. There's been a bomb scare. No one's hurt, but the place is closed. Here, please take this." She held a packet of brochures. Mindy noticed the image of a red rose on the top brochure.

"Oh, we're not here for abortion," Mindy said. "We just came to find someone."

"I know. But you might find this information helpful."

Mindy took the literature and handed it to Stan. He folded it in half before stuffing it into his coat pocket.

The woman leaned in further. "Would you like to meet somewhere more relaxed to talk? A restaurant? I'll buy you breakfast, if you like."

A truck came up behind the Volkswagen and honked. A policeman stepped from the barricade and motioned for Mindy and Stan to move.

"No, thank you," Mindy said. "I mean really, thank you. Bye."

"Back into that driveway and turn around." Stan said.

"Why?" Mindy asked mystified.

"Please, let's get away from here first and I'll tell you."

Mindy said, "OK."

The woman returned to the sidewalk, her attention now focused on the impatient truck. Stan noticed another person standing back holding a sign that said, "Let Your Baby Live!"

As they drove down the street, Stan watched out the rear window, and then turned frontward. "They thought we were coming for an abortion," he muttered.

"They have to treat everyone as potential abortion seekers so they don't miss one."

"I need to tell you," he said. "This is really weird, I received an anonymous phone call last night—early morning. The caller told me to avoid the abortion place today."

"Really? That is strange." Mindy paused a moment and said, "I wonder if your call was connected with the bomb scare?"

"How could it be? I have nothing to do with abortion or the right-to-life movement." Stan glanced at Mindy. If she gave this unusual situation much consideration at all, Stan could not tell. He did not know her very well, but it seemed she either did not think deeply about things, or else she had a strength that abnormalities could not disturb. She appeared to be concentrating on driving.

"Did you tell anyone about coming here this morning?" he asked.

"No. No one outside the family."

"Maybe it was a wrong number," Stan said. "Coincidence."

Stan did not think it had been a wrong number, but instinct warned him to cease discussing this subject. He had distaste about abortion, not because he was squeamish, but because he felt awkward. But this new feeling was far from vague. He was afraid. What if the call was not some perverted prank? What if the call *was* related to the bomb scare? What if abortion killed babies, as the sign implied? The best response would be silence. Telling the police about the call did not cross Stan's mind.

"Well, I don't believe in coincidence," Mindy said. "We should park and wait to see if Beth comes."

"No," Stan said firmly, "there's no way we can find her. There are several streets to the clinic and we can't watch them all. Do you know what kind of car she drives?"

Mindy shook her head. "It's grey, like fog."

"We might as well go on to Beacon Rock," Stan said. "If she comes for the abortion today, she'll have to postpone it. You should have a chance to talk with her later."

"Probably you're right," Mindy said with a deep sigh. "Besides, it will be nice to forget about this for awhile. I'll try again to catch her at her house, or her dormitory."

They drove along, not speaking. Fog closed in. They joined the highway traveling east.

Mindy broke the lull. "Did Ponder say anything last night?"

"Did he? Oh yeah." Stan rubbed his itchy nose with his fingers. "He sort of yelled that a war criminal deserved the death penalty."

"Really? Funny coming from someone who deserves the death penalty himself."

In a few minutes Mindy turned from the highway onto the exit to her house. "I have to pick up something," she said.

She drove up to the house and turned off the engine. "I'll be back in a second." She stretched up the stairs, stepping two at a time, and it was more than five minutes before she returned. Someone wearing solid boots followed her. Stan was frustrated when the someone squeezed into the back of the VW.

"Stan, this is my brother Anselm, but we all call him 'Ants.' Ants, this is Stan. He graduated last year and he's teaching at William Strong High School. Ants is going to the community college and taking history and pre-law."

"Yes, Stan," Anselm said, "you spoke well last night."

The men shook hands between the front two seats. Anselm was about Stan's height, but trim, and broader in the shoulders. His handshake was not painful, but his hand was hard like iron, and yet not rough, as a manual laborer's would be.

"Actually, I'm bypassing law school and taking the bar exam," Anselm said. "This fall I began working part time as a researcher in a law practice."

The VW turned right and pressed the three comfortably back against their seats as Mindy accelerated onto the road running behind their house. This, the old Evergreen Highway, followed along closer to the river than the four-lane.

"You must be a weight lifter," Stan guessed.

"Not really. I worked during the past few summers in a lumbermill. Lumber paid for my first two years of college. I tried the Camas papermill, but even though it paid more, I didn't like the changing rhythm of shift work. At the lumbermill, I started on the green chain and moved around to different jobs and then was promoted to lumber grader. Every once in awhile I sharpen the saw blades."

"Amazing," Stan said, impressed with Anselm's skills. This was definitely an unconventional family. "So, doesn't the bar association require a law degree to take the exam?"

"Yes. Now. But it wasn't too long ago when you could clerk for four years and take the bar."

"How do you plan to get your license?"

Anselm grinned. "How else? Sue the state bar association, and win."

"That's audacious. Why don't you just go to law school? Don't you think you'll be better prepared for the future if you have your degree? What kind of law do you want to practice?"

Anselm did not answer right away. He watched out of the window, and his teeth tapped together inside his pursed lips. "The future?" he asked. "First, I don't have time for law school. Second, I don't want to move away from home to go to school at a state university. Third, Dad is already putting out big bucks for Mindy to attend school in Portland. And fourth, I want to move forward with getting married and supporting the family. As for my specialty, I'd prefer to study Constitutional law, but I'm afraid that with the way things are, I'll probably prosecute criminals."

Though Stan did not agree with this approach, he was somewhat awed. Listening, Mindy did not understand her brother as much as she loved him, and she was surprised at his talkativeness.

"How do you keep fit between summer weightlifting marathons?" Stan asked.

Mindy had a ready answer. "He's a mountain climber and loves the outdoors and physical challenges. He won't tell you, but he climbed the major glaciated peaks in the Northwest; and during high school he summited Denali—the south peak—in the winter."

Stan was struck silent. The praise was a conversation killer because of Stan's sudden envy of this younger man who had done what he only daydreamed about. Mindy began telling a story about one of Anselm's early climbs up Mt. Hood, but Stan barely listened, at first. Anselm had led a rope for the Snowbird club in the early spring. He knew that bad weather was coming, but the climb leader insisted on not canceling. On the descent they got hit by a blizzard.

"Anselm," she was saying, "felt that they should not bivouac. They had food, but no survival bags, and only one shovel. He said he would continue down the mountain and begged them all to go, but they wanted to dig a snow cave. It almost broke into a fist fight, and in the end Anselm and two other climbers went down to safety and initiated rescue efforts. The leaders and the other six climbers perished from hypothermia in their cave. Anselm struggled with survivor syndrome afterwards and questioned his courage. If he had stayed, he kept thinking, with his training and experience, might he have kept them alive? He really struggled with this."

Stan's thoughts froze onto his boring life, and this interfered with his appreciation of the tale. His adventures occurred only through books and movies, and he could see the admiration that Mindy had for her brother. The story heightened his feeling of inadequacy. Mindy was not bragging—she had related the incident with sincerity and horror. Why had Anselm come, anyway? His presence was a boorish imposition. Stan had hoped to spend time with Mindy alone.

Here he is, Mr. Universe, he thought. *Adventurer, survivor, good looking, intelligent, powerful, son of a wealthy doctor, a warrior ready to take on the world.*

Since Stan's day was not turning out so well, he consciously lowered his expectations—he would just try to enjoy the outing. The road up the gorge was fast and curvy, and Mindy handled it expertly in the fog. As the road mounted to higher elevations, the atmosphere grew bright, but the sun never cut through. At last the VW came to a sharp left bend. At Anselm's urging,

Mindy pulled off right where there was room to park. They all got out and stood at the edge of a cliff.

Mindy described what they all knew. "If we could see through the fog, there would be Beacon Rock. Behind it, Bonneville Dam. River and farmland far below."

Stan noticed Anselm creeping away, looking pale, and taking deep breaths of the bracing air. Stan turned away and smiled. Ants felt carsick! *Nobody's perfect,* Stan thought with satisfaction.

Mindy asked Stan to ride in the back and Anselm got in front. Stan did not like the arrangement, but he felt further smugness over his ironclad stomach.

It did not take long to reach Beacon Rock, a great basalt monolith rising nearly a thousand vertical feet in the middle of the Columbia River Gorge. In 1909, a team blasted and carved a zigzag trail to the top. Mindy's was the only car in the small parking areas along the road.

The threesome began walking up. Condensed moisture dripped from the tall evergreen trees at the base of the rock. For Anselm, this hike was nothing but a favor to his sister and a dab of his minimum daily exercise, squeezed into a busy weekend. For Stan it was diversion from sitting in a coffee shop writing lesson plans and grading papers. Despite having lived in the Northwest his whole life, he never had climbed Beacon Rock. Plus, he had the pleasure of being near this certain fascinating female. For Mindy, she was entirely occupied with the fate of her friend, Beth. None of them held hope that they would get a view through the fog, which stuck to them like a raincoat wet on the inside. Still, it was pleasant walking in the cool air.

The trail began on the rock's north side, wrapped around to the west, and ascended back and forth on the south side, at last coming out for a final push on the east side of the rock. As they climbed, Mindy paused at each overlook, holding on to the handrail, and told Stan what they might see if the view had not been obscured: Cape Horn, where they had stopped on the way; Crown Point on the Oregon side; boats moored in an inlet below; high ridges south; the dam to the east. The sky grew radiant overhead. Anselm had slipped away early and found death-defying routes on the nether sides of the handrails. Every so often he rejoined them for a short section before he would fade again into the vertical lines of the landscape. They entered a grove of trees near the top and at last neared the summit where the fog took on structure. The light grew blinding. As they completed the steps to the bare summit, their heads broke above the cloud layer and they found themselves floating on a sea of white vapor under a pure steel-blue sky. Nearly circling around, north and south, 3,000 feet above them, were ridges and peaks like foam-streaked waves, as shreds of clouds ascended and hung over them.

The hikers stood on top a short while and pulled out wind breakers. The fog was burning off, and their rock island grew in size moment by moment.

Anselm said, "I'm glad I came." He jumped down from the summit to the trail a few feet below. "Let me show you something fun. Follow me!"

He dashed down the trail and just before it curved left, he placed both hands on the iron railing, swung over, and landed on the other side. He waited for Mindy and Stan to catch up. Then he ducked through a short tunnel of tree limbs. "Careful!" he said. "The rocks are slippery. Mind the poison oak."

Mindy pursued and Stan followed more sedately. As he clambered over the railing, he nearly slipped off—there was no danger here, but he felt clumsy. Emerging from the tree limbs, he climbed a piece of rock and peered ahead at the narrow-edged ridge. It looked OK to the left because the trail was twenty feet below, but on the right, the bottom was straight down 1000 feet. In front, Anselm was walking upright, leaning into the rocks on his left. Mindy had sat down and was crabwalking on all fours. Stan decided he would do likewise. They proceeded like this until the rocks formed a bench with a back. Anselm sat down, casually dangling his feet over the edge. He removed his pack and felt around inside for his lunch. Stan gingerly crept up and snuggled into a rocky seat away from the edge.

Mindy smiled and said, "Isn't this gorgeous!"

Anselm muttered, half-ashamed at the pun, "That's why they call it a gorge. But listen! What do you hear?"

If someone a day later had asked Stan what he had heard on Beacon Rock, he would have said, "Our voices. The wind." But

208

as he listened, a sound grew as if the volume had just been turned up. From below them to the south, there arose a low roar.

"It's traffic on the interstate across the river!" Mindy exclaimed. "And a train!"

"We are so accustomed to noise we don't notice its compromises to wilderness," Anselm interpreted. "And there's light pollution, too . . . "

Conversation ceased as they took in the view. Stan appreciated the natural beauty and environmental concerns, but he was occupied just then with vividly imagining what it would be like to fall. It did not take him long to relax, however, and he began enjoying his lunch.

Munching on a sandwich, Anselm asked Stan, "What will you do with the rest of your life?"

"I guess I'm open. I mean, I'd like adventures, but safe ones. Dangerous adventures always seem so far away from here. I'd have to leave home, and I'm comfortable now. What about you, Ants? You've had lots of adventures already."

"We were climbing mountains before we were born, right, my dear sister?"

Mindy mumbled, "Literally," her mouth full of carrot.

Stan remarked to himself that she could be unrefined elegantly.

"It's practice and preparation," Anselm continued. "When we were children, we never gave adventure much thought, because it was all unalloyed fun. But now, I can see that Dad had plans. He wanted us to be strong and to know how to survive in the wilderness, and how to take risks. It's still fun, but I appreciate the serious side now, too."

"What about the military?" Stan asked. "Did you ever think about seeking a commission?"

Anselm glanced sharply at Stan.

"Oh, look," Mindy said and pointed. An eagle soared upriver at eye level in the distance.

Anselm smiled when he found the eagle and then answered slowly, carefully, "No, I never considered the military."

Stan leaned back against the rock and watched the bird until it passed out of view and then he sat up and looked at Anselm. Anselm's reaction to his question interested him. "What's the preparation for? You're planning to be a lawyer."

Anselm paused a long time. It was like when the police, or parents, ask you a surprise question and you can't think of a lie fast enough. The lengthening silence only confirms suspicion.

Stan thought he would alleviate the discomfort with humor. "I suppose your family is a secret militia plotting to overthrow the government."

"Well, what if we were?" Mindy unexpectedly answered.

"Uh, it would be interesting."

"No, seriously, what if we were part of a secret militia?" Mindy asked again.

The conversation was becoming strange, but Stan decided he would treat it seriously. He ran through his mind the problems and evils in society. He considered the growing antagonism in the country and the divisiveness, which threatened to break into widespread violence. He considered how neighborhoods and communities had deteriorated, and how the press pretended to be somber and alarmed, but really regarded news as propaganda or entertainment just to sell commercials. Over the past few years, areas of the United States had grown to resemble the historic trouble spots in the world. The government appeared inadequate to keep the peace; moreover, it exacerbated hostilities. Stan ruminated this way, and then answered, "It depends on your purpose. Could you bring change without hurting anyone?"

No one spoke for several seconds. Anselm tossed a fir cone over the side. It dropped away into the silence. Then he said, "Good question."

"Well, the question is hypothetical," Mindy said with force.

Anselm said quietly, almost sadly, "There could be people below, on the trail."

Stan thought it would be better to drop the subject. This family was eccentric, to be sure, but he could see that their eccentricity was wholesome in some ways, and it stood against the insanity in the world. The militia bit had been a joke, but on the other hand it seemed consistent with things related to this family. The unusual phone call in the night, for example. In the few months of his acquaintance with the Sternes, they had introduced him to new thoughts and ideas. These seemed a little odd at first, and as Stan got over his initial shock, he became unperturbed by them because they made sense. But if he pressed the subject now, he might cause offense.

Stan thought these things, and Anselm guessed he was thinking them, and approved. Mindy could only tell that Stan was being courteous, or that he thought the matter to be insignificant.

They finished their lunches, worked their way off the exposed ridge, and headed down the trail. Anselm suggested that they drive further upriver—to the Bridge of the Gods—because he wanted to buy honey from a beekeeper at a roadside stand there, and Mindy and Stan agreed, happy to extend the day. They reached the bottom of the rock, and 25 minutes later arrived at the two-lane bridge spanning the Columbia River. Anselm made the honey purchase and put the gallon in Mindy's car, while Stan and Mindy strolled to the bridge and waited. There was no sidewalk. The three of them walked onto the bridge at the edge of the car lane, and Stan felt dizzy when he looked through the steel grate under his feet and could see the river far below. It was like walking in air. They gazed downriver, watching a barge powered by a tugboat plowing upstream toward them, and then they crossed to look upriver at kite surfers skimming along the surface and leaping high into the air.

On their way back to Vancouver, Mindy recalled the violin recording she brought. They listened to it enraptured, as the car sped around the curves. Stan felt goosebumps at the hypnotic folk melodies and bittersweet chords penetrating his brain. Mindy dropped Anselm at their home, and by the time she left Stan at his house, it was early evening.

Though his mother might call him, he switched off his phone's ringer and took a nap rather longer than he wanted. When he awoke, he was disoriented; it took him a minute to figure out that it was still Saturday night. He wasn't particularly hungry, and because tomorrow after church he would feast at his parents' home, he prepared a plain meal of oriental noodle soup and cabbage. By the time he finished eating, it was late, but he couldn't sleep, so he put on a movie that he wanted to preview for his classes—a new version of *Tess of the D'Urbervilles*. When the movie ended, he completed some notes. It was now far past midnight. He remembered that he had turned the phone's ringer off, and put it back on. "Do it while I'm thinking of it because I might not think of it again," was one of his mottoes. He pushed open the window to let in the night air, climbed under the covers, and listened to grasshoppers sawing their final, bleak tunes. He still did not feel like sleeping, but he knew he would drift off soon. It had been a satisfactory day, "*a wonderful day,*" he thought, being with Mindy.

The phone rang. Startled, he snatched up the receiver from the bedside table before the ringing ceased. It was Mindy. She nearly strangled with sobbing.

Beth was dead.

The story of **UNIVERSAL MAN** continues with:

part two; *The Chinook Assembly*

and part three; *Then, A Soldier*

Contributions toward the publication
of these works may be made to:

**Life Advocates
P.O. Box 19205
Asheville, NC 28815**

lifeadvocates@earthlink.net